THE LAND OF
EMPTY HOUSES

D1166049

A NOVEL

THE LAND OF EMPTY HOUSES

JOHN L. MOORE

BROADMAN
&HOLMAN
PUBLISHERS

Nashville, Tennessee

© 1998
by John L. Moore
All rights reserved
Printed in the United States of America

0-8054-1648-X

Published by Broadman & Holman Publishers, Nashville, Tennessee
Page Design: Anderson Thomas Design
Acquisitions Editor: Vicki Crumpton
Page Composition: PerfecType, Nashville, Tennessee

Dewey Decimal Classification: 813
Subject Heading: FICTION
Library of Congress Card Catalog Number: 98-8383

Library of Congress Cataloging-in-Publication Data
Moore, John L., 1952–
    The land of empty houses / John L. Moore.
        p.   cm.
    ISBN 0-8054-1648-X (pbk.)
    I. Title.
PS3563.06214L36   1998
    813'.54—dc21

                                                    98-8383
                                                    CIP

1 2 3 4 5 02 01 00 99 98

DEDICATION

To Debra.
My "Deborah."
My wife.

PROLOGUE

My name is Jesse. This is my father's story.

My father passed away recently, leaving a wife, two daughters (my sisters), and me. In disposing of his personal effects we discovered a microdiskette with the following story. The information disclosed surprised all of us, even my mother. She, of course, knew the background information: the Plague, earthquakes, wars, and droughts that ravaged the world during this time period. But neither of my parents ever discussed this dark period in any detail. "Some things," my father once told me, "are better left untold."

At least untold until the proper time.

In the months leading up to the publication of my father's book I have tried on my own to confirm many of the details he recorded.

The effects of the Plague are well known even though the origin and identity of the virus remain a mystery. It struck quickly, spread like fire, and left millions dead across the entire world, particularly in North America and Europe. No one who contracted the disease survived. Those who lived apparently had some mysterious sort of immunity.

The worldwide earthquakes occurred at the peak of the Plague, striking first near Yellowstone National Park. The wholesale destruction throughout the heartland of the nation and the virtual disappearance of vast areas of the West Coast—from Baja, California to Alaska—brought a total collapse of the country's infrastructure. Similar quakes occurred throughout the world.

The impact of the two disasters sent the nation into madness. Rumors circulated that the lost civilization of Lemuria had risen from the ocean, complete with cities hosted by angelic beings. Thousands of wayfarers, "Pilgrims," trekked toward this "New Mu," while food riots and crime sprees ignited the cities into burning infernos, forcing the government to impose martial law.

My father, Daniel, was home on leave from the U.S. Army when the quakes hit. By the time he buried his parents, he learned the U.S. military had been placed under United Nations control. Refusing to submit to this ominous new order, he became a wanderer in the vast land known as the Interior.

This is his story of those wanderings and the amazing events and people he encountered before the settling of the New West.

Through research I have determined the existence of many of the people mentioned in his story:

The leader of the Patriots was General Jerry VanderVoosen, a paramilitary leader from Michigan who moved his militia to the Missouri Breaks region of eastern Montana prior to 1999.

The Irreverend Flowers was Frank Thompson Flowers, a popular televangelist of the late twentieth century. Flowers rose to celebrity status through a flamboyant preaching style, rugged good looks, and sensational prophecies. His decline began when the date he predicted for the Messiah's return came and left with not so much as a change in the weather. Flowers slowly faded from view, taking his remaining ardent followers to his religious enclave in southcentral Montana.

Lady LeClair was Lucia Ellen LeClair, a wealthy New Age speaker, author, and channeler from Topanga Canyon, California. Ms. LeClair predicted the widespread earthquake destruction and moved her cult to the mountains of southern Montana in 1999. Hers was once the largest New Age movement in the world, but it began to disintegrate as she enforced increasingly violent rituals, including self-mutilation and cannibalism.

The men identified by my father as Stinson, Jones, Quito, Quarro, Mr. Simon, and Malachi Watts must have existed, but evidence is scarce and fragmentary. In my own travels I did find a grave by the Yellowstone River with a plain wooden headstone marked *Catfish*. This, I believe, is the older friend of my father's who is mentioned in the story.

As to the two other characters, Robert and Deborah, there is no official documentation available from the U.S. Army about a project or a person code-named *Robert*.

And Deborah? It is best if I let my father himself tell you about her. For in a very real sense this is not my father's story at all. It is hers.

Deborah's.

CHAPTER 1

I am the man whose nights were dreamless and whose days were a flight from memories. My name is Daniel, and I am a survivor of The Land of Empty Houses. The Interior. My story begins and ends with a woman. I first heard about her from the lips of a dying man, a man pulled down by predators on the plains of eastern Montana during The Season of the Burning Sun.

I had chanced upon tire tracks—the first I'd seen in years—and followed until I found an abandoned truck laden with empty gas cans. A set of footprints trailed northwesterly, and miles later, those prints met the smaller tracks of another person. The two had stood and probably talked, then went their separate ways. I chose to follow the man from the vehicle, not knowing that my life would be changed forever by the person who left the other prints.

The man's trail soon intersected the pugmarks of wolves, and I ceased believing I would find him alive. Why I wanted to find him at all, I don't know. Curiosity, maybe.

I found him near death, sprawled face up on the dry prairie, partially eaten by the predators that had fled seconds before I arrived. His pale blue eyes flickered like a dimming pilot light. "God of the heavens," he rasped. "God of Isaac, Jacob, and Benjamin. All of Abraham's sons." His parched lips clicked like a firing pin falling on a spent shell. "I'm dying."

I reached down and cradled his head. I usually avoided victims, particularly those drenched in blood. But he seemed sane and harmless, and an inexplicable compassion rose in me. "Yes," I agreed. "You are dying."

"Who are you?" he asked.

"Daniel."

"You the Lieutenant?"

"Used to be."

"Army Ranger?"

"Yes."

"Heard of you," he said.

"You've heard of me?"

"Yes." He shivered with a sudden chill. "Met someone . . . she was looking for you."

I thought of the tracks. He'd met someone, probably a Pilgrim, but I doubted it was a woman seeking me. Only a creature named Robert looked for me. Robert was an agent of death.

"She's looking for you," he repeated. "Blonde. Hair almost white as snow."

I decided he was delusional. He had reason to be. His soiled clothes were stripped to ribbons, and his left hip was a bloody mess of exposed flesh.

"Before you came," he said, "all I could see was dirt and sky. The sky was like a big blue bowl."

"There is little else here," I said. "It's a land of dry prairie and big sky. A land of empty houses."

"This certainly could be hell, Daniel," he continued, his breaths deep and painful. "They were eating me alive until you came. Thank you. It's no way for a man to die."

"I understand," I told him. "Death should allow for some dignity." But I knew it seldom did. Instead, death in the Interior made a spectacle of itself with humiliation and degradation.

"I'm thirsty, Daniel. Have you any water?"

I unclasped a small canteen from my belt and brought it to his lips. "Little sips," I said.

The dry burn in the man's throat seemed to slacken. "My name's Storch," he said. "In case you want to know."

"Where were you going, Mr. Storch?"

"Alberta, Canada. Going fishing." His face stitched with pain as the mercy of shock receded. "Got a cabin up there." He coughed the words through clenched teeth.

"You did well to get this far. No one's brought a vehicle this deep into the Interior in a long time."

"How far did I get? Where am I?"

"Eastern Montana. Couple hundred miles below the border."

"And here I die. Do you know . . . what the worst part of being eaten by wolves is? The sound and the smell. They snarl and bite at one another while ripping your flesh. And their breath . . . it's enough . . . to kill a man . . . all by itself."

"I've heard that said of bears too. The smell, that is."

"The sounds . . . low, gurgling growls. Like they're gargling with your blood."

"You probably shouldn't talk."

"I probably should," Storch argued. "You will be the last one to hear me. Eaten by wolves. I suppose there are . . . worse ways to die."

I thought of the Cannibals. "Yes," I agreed. "There are many worse ways." Worse ways to be eaten.

"I'm weak and cold. Think I'm bleeding . . . to death."

"You are." I watched the dry soil darken with his life's fluid and carefully avoided making contact with it. The Plague had made cowards of all men.

He tried to grip my hand. "You don't want . . . to shoot me, do you? To end it."

"I'd just as soon not," I told him. "But I will if you ask me."

"I won't ask," the man said. The pale blue light in his eyes dimmed more. "This is . . . a violent land. You must be . . . a violent man . . . to live here."

"I can be."

"Will you . . . bury me?"

"The best I can."

"I don't want . . . to feed . . . anything . . . else." He shivered.

I didn't respond. I knew nothing died in the Interior without being picked clean by the scavengers. Wolves. Coyotes. Mice. Rats. Man.

He exhaled his words in short strangles of breath. "Bet you see . . . plenty like me . . . don't you?"

"Hundreds," I admitted. "Maybe thousands. But at least you were going to your cabin. That's not as crazy as those who chase The Myth."

"West . . . to The Myth," he said. "New Seattle . . . New Mu?"

"Yes. That's The Myth."

The man smiled peacefully. "No myths . . . for me. I'm going . . . to die now," he said.

We both paused, waiting for something to happen. Finally Storch said, "Never could fish worth a lick anyway." His eyes slowly rolled backward into his head.

I thought he'd died then, but he hadn't. Instead he raised his head, and his eyes flared brightly for an instant. "The woman will find you," he said. His head lowered. "I'm glad she found me." The phrase came in one short and shallow gasp, taking his life with it. The blue light evaporated, and his vacant eyes stared at a sky torched by a rising, fully lit, vengeful sun.

I smoothed the eyelids closed. The pooled and drying blood drew a whirring of flies. "I have nothing to bury you with, Mr. Storch," I said. I sat quietly for a moment, then I slung my assault rifle over my shoulder and dragged the corpse to a cove of sculptured sandstone that rose from the dry prairie like a windswept mausoleum.

I laid the body in a shaded cairn and covered it with handfuls of sand. It wouldn't keep the wolves away, or the buzzards, or the mice for that matter, but I had given my word to bury the man. I placed an empty cartridge shell on an outcropping of rock. It glistened in the sun like a tiny brass rocket minus the nose cone. The scent of powder would temporarily fend off the animals.

"You talked like a religious man," I told the sand-coated mound. "I should say a prayer for you." I lowered my head, but a queer embarrassment unnerved me, as if an audience awaited my words. "God," I said finally. "Take this man to a better place than this."

That shouldn't be hard, I thought. *Any place should be better than the deep recesses of the Interior.*

If you think I have opened my story with a particularly gruesome scene, please understand that the Interior was haunted by the most debasing evils. I tell the events not to shock the reader or to exult myself, but to illustrate the courage necessary for one woman to invade this prevailing darkness. For this really isn't my story. It's hers.

I traveled all morning then denned during high sun in a cool, deep fissure littered with wolf droppings. I dozed lightly because sleep was never a blanket for me, just a thin sheet that could be tossed back in a second. Alertness was a costly ally.

At dusk as I resumed my travels, I saw a Babbler on the edge of an expansive prairie dog town. I studied the man through my rifle scope to determine whether he was timid or vicious. I knew this one. He was safe. Babblers all look and smell similar—as dirty and foul as the rodents they prey upon. Most are harmless except in the winter when the prairie dogs hibernate and the Babblers go mad with hunger.

"Babbler," I called out as I approached.

The wrinkled, filthy man swiveled and beamed a clownish smile. His rags were more dirt than cloth, and his gray hair and beard matted into a single carpet pricked with grass needles. "Daniel, Daniel, the man-wolf of the prairies," the Babbler shouted. "The fortune of the gods, the luck of the ages, the spinning of the wheel. Buy me a vowel, Vanna. How goes it? How goes it?"

"It goes well," I answered, maneuvering upwind from the Babbler's stench.

"Buy me a fowl, Vanna," the Babbler cackled through yellowed teeth. He clapped his hands. "A chicken, a bird. It is a fowl wind that blows no good. Spin the wheel of fortune, for this is how the world turns for all my children all the days of our lives. Daniel, Daniel. My guiding light. My guiding light."

Small leg-hold traps hung around his neck like an oversized necklace, and he held a burlap bag like a purse. The sack undoubtedly contained two dead rodents.

"Your trapping goes well," I noted.

"Providence provides for he who provides for himself. Pray for what you want. Work for what you need. All of your deposits are federally insured, and the blood of Jesus flows from a living stream."

"Babbler, you've learned new phrases. You've had contact with someone lately." I thought of Storch. "Was it the man that drove a motor vehicle?"

"Toyota saves and sets you free," Babbler sang. The traps clanged as he danced heavily in his soleless shoes. "Toy-yo-ta. Like a rock. I was strong as I could be. Toy-yo-ta sets you free, and he who is free is free indeed. I never saw a motor car, did thee?"

"Who have you seen, Babbler? Patriots?"

"No, no. Bang-bang, boom-boom, bad mans."

"'Postates?"

"Never saw 'em, never saw 'em, never saw 'em."

"Lady LeClair's Cannibals?"

The man's eyes bugged with fear. "No eat me, no eat me," he whined.

"You know they won't eat you," I soothed him. "They're afraid to eat Babblers. They think they become what they eat. Only the Babblers are safe from Lady LeClair."

The man ceased trembling and began humming softly to himself, reassured.

"Pilgrims?" I asked. "You met Pilgrims going west, chasing The Myth?"

"Pilgrims no like me." He seesawed to a cold rationality. "I scare Pilgrims. They say I smell bad. They should smell themselves."

I wanted to ask about the federal assassin, Robert, but knew even the mention of my pursuer made Babblers lie down for days, curled up like weathered fetuses in filthy swaddling clothes, crying, and sucking their thumbs. "Babbler must be playing games with me," I chided. "Perhaps the Babbler has seen no one at all."

"Yes, I have," the man snapped. "I saw she and she asked for thee. 'Where is Daniel?' she said. Daniel, Daniel, Daniel. That is all she could say. No talk of weather or wars or wolves but only of Daniel, Daniel, Daniel."

"*She* asked for me? Who seeks Daniel?"

"Person of the Word seeks Daniel. Pretty eyes. Hair like snow. I woulda made 'er an appointment. 'Step into my office,' I say. 'Have a seat. Coffee? Tea?'"

"You saw a woman?"

"Must I draw it for you?" he asked sarcastically. His bushy gray eyebrows jumped and retreated into a mat of crusted hair.

"A Mono?"

"A what?"

"Mono. A Monotheist." I knew it would be hard to explain it to him.

"Person of the Word," he said.

"Yes, that. Which way, Babbler? Which way did she go?"

"You wanna find? I take you."

Babbler was not my idea of a traveling companion. "No, just tell me which dogtown you were working when you saw her."

"Saks."

"Saks on Fifth Avenue?"

"Only one. Only one Saks."

"Which way did she go from there?"

"Go where people are. 'Postates, Cannibals, Patriots with their bang-bangs." He collapsed loosely to the ground, opened the grimy sack and pulled a rodent out by its neck. "Eat?" he offered. "Eat with me? I say grace."

"No, Babbler. I've told you before, I only eat prairie dogs when there is nothing else."

"Babbler only eats prairie dog. Babbler can only catch prairie dog. Prairie dog dumb. Babbler dumb. Daniel hunts buffalo, wild cow, big elk. But Babbler and prairie dog dumb. And the mounds of the ground are supermarkets. Mounds on the ground, Piggly-Wiggly, Safeway store, aisle three and aisle four, express lane, twelve items, no more. No more! No more! No more!" A long line of white spittle hung from his cracked lips and slid off his stubbled chin. He suddenly dropped to a squat and began eviscerating his catch with a dull pocketknife.

"Babbler," I asked, "why is the Mono looking for me?"

"You the great guide," he mocked, sawing at his meal's entrails.

"Jim Bridger of the Interior. Hugh Glass. Coulter, Cody, Clark and Lewis. Daniel been to the New Coast. Daniel seen the great cracks in the earth. Only Daniel goes where the cold wind blows. You like Buffalo Bill. You like Clark and Lewis. She go to all the peoples. Spread the word, preach to the masses, share the light, salt the earth."

I sighed. "If that's what she wants, then she doesn't need me. If she stays alive long enough, the tribes will find her."

Babbler's face drained to the color of cold, gray steel. A spastic tremble shook the knife from his hands, and he gazed with a slack jaw at the darkening sky.

"You are remembering something," I coaxed. "What is it?"

Babbler rolled over into a fetus-like ball and stuck a filthy thumb in his mouth. I reached over and pulled the thumb out. "Babbler, what do you remember?"

The word rattled in his mouth like a marble before he spit it out. "Robert." He said the name like a child saying *bogeyman.*

"You saw him? No one sees Robert and lives."

"Babbler no see. Babbler keep eyes closed. Babbler asleep. Robert lay knife on Babbler's throat and ask if Babbler seen woman. Babbler lie and say no then Babbler pee his pants and Robert go away disgusted. Call Babbler bad names. Say he kill Babbler next time just for practice."

"It was a dream, Babbler. Robert spares no one."

"This no dream." He pulled back his filthy collar and showed a long red scratch on his neck.

"A prairie dog could have done that."

"Prairie dogs no tell Babbler they seek the pretty-eyed one. Hair like snow."

The woman again. I released him and settled onto my haunches with my rifle across my lap. Darkness fell on the prairie like a crisp black sheet as I waited for the rodent-man to relax and unwind from his frozen position.

"Daniel do Babbler favor?" he pleaded in a small, childlike voice.

"Maybe."

His voice was weak and terrified. "Daniel kill Robert," he begged. "Only Daniel can do. No one else Clark and Lewis."

Before I could answer, the winds came up, escalating from a breeze to a gale in seconds. Dust and grit stung our faces and hands like birdshot. The freshly-skinned pelt of the prairie dog began rolling across the dogtown over mounds shining fluorescent in the moonlight. The pelt whirled and bounced as if it were alive and seeking a hole.

I rose and pushed into the wind.

"We need shelter," I yelled. The Babbler followed me to a dry creek bed where we curled in a small washout. The wind howled with such force that even the Babbler's stench was sucked away as if he'd been dry-cleaned. Babbler began sobbing again.

"What's wrong now?" I asked.

"Wanna go with you," Babbler cried. "Robert kill Babbler."

"No. It was only a dream. Robert is not concerned with you. Robert is after me. Why don't you join other Babblers?"

"They all gone. Robert kill."

I doubted that. Robert was a government agent who killed only those he was assigned to eliminate. If he had killed Babblers, he was beginning to kill for sport, not solely for duty. "Well, you can't go with me," I said.

He continued to whimper like a kicked pup. "Daniel," he blubbered. "Why we here?"

"In this hole? To escape the wind."

"No, no. Here. Why we here? What happened? Babbler forget."

"You mean the Interior? Why are we in the Interior?"

"Yes, yes. Why we here? Babbler forget."

"Good. Keep it that way. You don't need to remember."

"Babbler wanna remember. Babbler see bits and pieces." His cries bubbled up like tiny geysers that choked in his throat, and his face tightened like a cork to repress formless memories. "Can't find my mind," he cried. "Can't find it. Where Babbler put it?"

"Forget the past," I told him. "Think about something else. Think about trapping many prairie dogs."

The wind's roar abated, but mournful howls and a chorus of snarls replaced it. Babbler looked up wide-eyed. "Wolves." He gripped my faded army shirt. "Babbler go with Daniel," he insisted. "Babbler keep up."

"OK," I relented. "But only as far as the dogtown where you saw the Mono."

"Saks," Babbler said. "Saks of Fifth Avenue. Aisle four. Pretty-eyed one."

"Saks," I agreed. "Aisle four. And maybe we will see this pretty-eyed one." I said it to humor him. I was not convinced this "pretty-eyed one" even existed. The Interior was a land where dead dreams fluttered like ghosts, and memories were as uncertain as delusions. Nothing was as it seemed to be.

CHAPTER 2

The night cleared and stars jeweled a black velvet backdrop. The moon arced slowly westward, and the wolves circled the washout where the Babbler and I huddled. Red fire burned in the wolves' glistening eyes. Their guard hairs glowed as if lit by mercury. And they floated noiselessly, almost bodiless, like dark mists on padded paws, emitting deep, primordial growls. Bored, I impulsively stood and snarled back at them, terrifying Babbler. He burrowed deep into the hole, shivering and crying softly for a mother he could not remember.

At daylight the pack retreated, so we moved westward through sagebrush bottoms, across abandoned wheat fields infested with noxious weeds, and off graveled slopes dotted with greasewood and sharp, spiny yucca. I ate as we traveled, plucking fingerfuls of rubbery leaves off the woody stems of greasewood and handfuls of the creamy white flower blossoms from the yucca. Babbler winced and cried as he brushed against the hard, spear-like leaves of the yucca plants. "Babbler hurt, Babbler hungry," he whined.

"Babbler a big baby," I scolded, and he became downcast and cloudy. "Sorry," I said softly, and he brightened immediately.

"I forgive you seventy-times-seven," he said.

Forgiveness, I thought. *More evidence that 'the pretty-eyed one' possibly existed.*

We pressed on, crossing a hardpan flat spotted with volcanic rock, where I dug wild onion roots while Babbler picked shiny objects from the ground. He displayed a cupped handful. "Babbler find diamonds," he said.

"Babbler find mica," I corrected, crumbling the flaky mineral in my hands.

"Not diamonds?"

"Not diamonds."

"But pretty," Babbler said, clutching his other pieces protectively to his chest. "Shine like eyes of pretty-eyed one."

"She was a dream," I said.

"No dream," he argued. "She is hope. Hope in clothes."

I stifled further cynicism. Who was I to dispel hope from the mind of the feeble?

We passed through the southern edge of a small dogtown where Babbler checked his trap sets. The traps were empty and sprung, and Babbler circled them for minutes, trying to understand how the prairie dogs had escaped.

"Your traps have been raided," I explained. "You caught two—" I pointed to the scratch marks where the rodents had tried to dig themselves free, then to the splatters of blood on the mound—"but someone came by, clubbed the dogs, and stole them."

"Ray-did? Someone take Babbler's dogs?"

"Three men." I gestured to tracks that pointed westward through the grassless streets of the dogtown. "Patriots. The tracks were made by military boots."

"Bang-bang, boom-boom take Babbler's dogs?"

"Yes. Probably a scouting party that ran out of food."

Babbler shook his head in disgust, knelt to the ground, and began resetting his traps. "Bang-bangs bad mans," he mumbled. "Bad to steal. Thou shalt not. Thou shalt not. Pretty-eyed one speak truth."

I shook my head. He almost had me believing she existed.

We left the dogtown and crossed a high, treeless flat fruited with prickly-pear and sage. Rattlesnakes buzzed electrically from the dense cover of black brush.

"Rattle . . . snakes! Babbler scared!"

"Babbler stand still," I ordered. "This is my supermarket." I moved through the brush slowly, forcing the reptiles into the open with my gun barrel then stepping on their heads before they coiled to strike. I soon returned to Babbler with five snakes dangling from my hand like scaly, skinny ropes.

"Ugh." Babbler shuddered and looked away.

I put the snakes in my canvas fanny pack. A mile later we stopped beneath the white skeleton of a cottonwood tree, and I had Babbler gather firewood while I skinned the snakes and threaded their tubular carcasses onto sharp branches. Then I lit a fire and began roasting my meal. "I have one ready for you," I said moments later, nodding to the white rope of meat.

"Babbler no eat snake," he insisted.

"You better try it," I told him. "Might be the only food you get today. The Patriots are on their way to Saks. They'll probably find and raid your traps there too."

Babbler bent down and cautiously poked the stick toward the fire like a small child roasting marshmallows. When the meat browned, he copied my way of eating it off the stick with his fingers.

"What does Babbler think of snake now?" I asked.

Babbler was eating hungrily. "Not bad. Not bad. Not good as prairie dog, though." Suddenly he dropped his stick, leaped over the fire, and hid behind the white trunk of the dead tree.

I grabbed my rifle and scanned the skyline for trouble. "What's wrong?" I whispered.

"Snakes come alive."

I looked to where the remaining snake bodies lay on a wide shedding of tree bark—two were coiling on their branch as if preparing to strike. "It's OK, Babbler." I laughed. "Snakes do this. They're dead but the muscles still move."

"Pretty-eyed one say devil that way. He defeated. He dead but don't know it. He just twitchin'."

I suddenly heard a dry, raspy sound, like a greasewood branch rubbing against stiff material. "Shush," I said. I didn't need to hear about Satan when real devils were coming. I slid a round into the rifle chamber and locked the safety. "We have guests," I told Babbler. "Come here and sit by the fire."

"No wanna sit by snake."

"Do it." I crawled off into the brush. Babbler slunk dejected-
ly from behind the tree and sat in pouting obedience next to the
dying fire.

Moments later, three men in faded camouflage fatigues approached,
coming out of the greasewoods from the north. A short corporal
walked point, a stalk of grass protruding from his stained teeth. He was
followed by a heavyset sergeant and a tall, spindly private with thick
glasses and a depressed glaze to his magnified eyes.

The corporal approached the fire with his Chinese rifle at the
ready. "I toldchya I could smell smoke. And lookee what we have here."
He laughed. "A rodent-man has made us lunch. A rattlesnake sheesh-
ka-bob. I didn't know a dog-eater could catch snakes."

Babbler rolled onto his side and curled into a ball. The short man
kicked him heavily in the ribs. "Whatdya think, Sarge? You think this
idiot killed these snakes his ownself?"

"I don't know," the sergeant answered. His eyes darted about, trying to penetrate the tall, silver sage and greasewood. "I don't think so.
They ain't that smart. Or brave." The tall private's head swiveled on his
skinny head. He couldn't see anything. He didn't want to see anything.

The short one kicked Babbler again. "What about it, idiot?" he
demanded. "Didcha kill the snakes?"

They never saw me coming. My rifle stock striking the corporal's
head sounded like a bat hitting a watermelon. He crumpled to his
knees, then collapsed face first into the dust. I turned my Ruger Mini
14 on the others. "Lay your weapons down," I said.

As they dropped their AK-47s, they stared wide-eyed, their slow
minds wondering who I was and where I'd come from. The pupils of
the myopic private seemed to leap through his glasses, but the

sergeant's eyes finally dilated with recognition. "Shoulda known it," he said. "You're the AWOL army officer. No way a Babbler caught those snakes."

The short corporal moaned and rose to his hands and knees. The Babbler scurried away into the brush to hide.

"What are you doing here?" I demanded.

The sergeant puffed himself up. "That's privileged information, Lieutenant. Information for true patriots and soldiers, not for runaways from the Zionist Occupied Government."

I hated propagandists. I lowered the rifle, pulled my titanium combat knife from its leather sheath, and in an instant, reached over, pinched the earlobe of the sergeant's left ear, sliced it off, and tossed it into the fire.

The man screamed. His pudgy hand grabbed the side of his head, and blood trickled through his fingers. The tall private stared at the fire where the sergeant's earlobe sizzled and smoked like a glob of bacon grease.

"Again," I said, "what are you doing this far from your camp? Why are you raiding Babbler's traps?" Behind me the short corporal staggered to his feet.

"We intercepted a radio transmission a week ago," the private blurted, his eyes riveted on the fire. "It was an order from ZOG to the machine-man to search this area for a fugitive. A woman. General Jerry sent us out to find her before Robert gets her."

"Your general considers the three of you expendable," I said. "Robert would kill each of you slowly and with great satisfaction." I reached down, grasped the small corporal by the back of his shirt, pulled him to his feet, and shoved him into the sergeant. "What do you want this woman for?" I asked.

"I dunno," the sergeant said. "Guess we need women. Guess we could trade her or somethin'. Maybe sell 'er to Robert."

"Leave," I commanded. "Take your weapons and get out of here."

"We'll settle this," the sergeant snarled. "Next time, we slice off your ears and give you to the clone-man. Everyone knows he's only here because of you."

That was an ugly truth. I glared at the sergeant with a ferocity that made him despair for his other ear. He reached up reflexively to protect it.

"Get going," I ordered.

The awkward private gathered the rifles, and the men backed away. The short corporal spit in my direction.

The sergeant cast his muddy brown eyes on me. His shirt was drenched with blood. "This changes things, Lieutenant," he warned. "The General has let you live up till now. He thought you might even come to your senses and join us. But you done crossed the line. You a dead man, Lieutenant."

They moved away. I watched until they were distant specks on the horizon, then I searched the greasewood and found Babbler rolled into a tight ball, humming to himself.

"Let's go," I said, lifting him to his feet. He glanced worriedly to the north. "The Patriots won't be back," I assured him.

"Daniel look for the Mono . . . Mono . . . you look for the pretty-eyed one?"

"I don't know."

"You must, you must," Babbler insisted. "It is destined in the playbook. The playbook of life."

"Life has no playbook," I argued. "Life is random. Chaotic."

"No," Babbler retorted. "Life a story." He walked off ahead of me. "A story God wrote," I heard him say.

Later I left the rodent eater in Saks, a dogtown that stretched for miles, and turned south, quickening my pace. I jogged down dry, narrow creeks and past abandoned farms and ranches where tractors rusted in weedy fields. Once I glimpsed a small pack of young wolves, but the predators caught my scent and faded like smoke into heat waves radiating off the baked plains. I searched for prey and checked water holes for fresh signs of wild cattle, elk, buffalo, or, most importantly, horses.

By midday the sky bleached to a pale white—a Clorox sky, I called it. And the sun's rays burned down as if only the faintest layer of atmosphere existed to filter the scorching radiation.

Late in the afternoon, as I came to a larger creek lined with cottonwoods and willows, my ears detected the splashing sounds of something moving heavily in the mud. I eased quietly through a thick stand of young trees until the scene opened to a large mud hole in the creek bend. There an old man with a long, gray beard and ponytail was sloshing through the slimy ooze, a three-pronged manure fork raised in his right hand, a sawed-off shotgun slung across his back, and a cartridge belt crisscrossing his scrawny chest. He was as tall as a hat rack, with knobby elbows and knees.

Bubbling trails moved ahead of the man's feet as an unidentifiable creature fled through water coated with stagnant slime, leaving a wake of mud that rose and rolled like molten plastic. Suddenly the man thrust the fork downward. The mud boiled for an instant, quieted, then the fork lifted with a heavy carp embedded in its sharp tines.

The man labored to the bank near me, plucked the fish off, and tossed it on the ground beside another gape-mouthed bottom feeder and a bearded bullhead.

"Catfish," I whispered.

The man jumped backward, the fork tines raised against the voice. His aged yellow eyes were intense and wary but showed no sign of fear.

"Relax, old-timer," I said, stepping from the willows.

"You," the old man said. "The Lieutenant."

"It's me, Catfish, but why are you spearing suckers this far from the river? You have setlines and gardens to tend."

Catfish lowered his fork, and his thin shoulders slumped. "I got ambushed," he said. "A war party of Cannibals came through. They never saw me, but they got my lines and took my tomatoes, potatoes, and melons. And they was green, too, the tomatoes and melons, especially. Not ready for eatin'."

"This is too far east for the Cannibals," I said. The Interior had its own social order, and the Cannibals' adventurism had upset it.

"Well, I thought I was safe there on the river," Catfish said. "That's why I made camp there. I see some 'Postates now and then, even trade with them a little. I've traded with Flowers himself. But the Cannibals this far east? They must be runnin' out of Pilgrims to eat, I suppose. I hope they didn't eat Flowers. I can't say I savvy his religion, but I sorta like the man. He ain't like the Cannibals. The Cannibals are, well, they're . . . cannibals."

"How many raided your camp?"

"Six, maybe seven. I was too scared to count. Eunuchs, the whole bunch of them. Naked except for loincloths and shoes. And covered with tattoos, even on their bald heads. The leader had a tattoo of a flyin' saucer comin' out of his belly button. Ain't that a fright? He came so close to where I was hidin' that I stared him straight in his nipple rings." Catfish shuddered. "I was nearly their main course."

I purposely changed the subject. "You haven't seen a lone woman?" I asked.

"A woman?" He laughed. "You been dreamin', Daniel, m'boy."

"A Babbler says he saw one. A Monotheist."

"Monothesist! You mean Pilgrim."

"No, a Mono. A missionary."

The old man cackled. "Babblers are all crazy. A woman all alone out here? Can't happen. A Monotheist at that. That's illegal. No way one could survive this far into the Interior. She'd get killed or captured. All the tribes need women. 'Specially the Patriots and the 'Postates. A young woman would be worth a lot, if one dealt in such commodities, that is."

"Babbler says the Mono is asking for me," I explained. "She wants me to guide her to the tribes."

Catfish spat again. "Dang preacher. If she exists at all, she'll get things all riled up. It's bad enough that Robert is lookin' for you and the Cannibals are eatin' everybody in sight. Now a Mono's on the loose. And a woman at that. We'll all be glancin' over our shoulder until our necks twist off."

"Perhaps the woman is only a rumor," I said. "Another myth, like New Seattle and New Mu."

"You better hope so," Catfish said. "A man shouldn't be so doubly cursed as to be chased by both Robert and some female zealot." He gestured at the fish. "Join me, Daniel. Another gun is a good thing if Robert is about. But we best find a hole to build our cook fire. Don't need the clone-man seein' our flame."

"You can't hide it," I said. "His helmet shield can detect heat."

Catfish gave me a suspicious look. "How do you know that?" he asked.

"He must have a shield," I said. "We all had them when I was on active duty."

The old man grunted and sludged through the mud, trailing his string of fish. "Helmet shields," he scoffed. "Ha. I worked with computers and gadgets a long time ago," he said. "A lifetime ago, it seems. Now I don't even have a calendar. You got a calendar, Daniel?"

"No, calendars are for walls. I have no walls."

"That's right," he agreed. "A calendar would do you about as much good as a laptop."

We took shelter in a hillside sinkhole, where I built a fire while Catfish cleaned and filleted the ugly fish. When the fire had burned down to glowing coals, the old man pulled a plastic pouch from a canvas bag. "My most precious possession," he said, unfolding a rectangle of crinkled and stained aluminum foil. "This stuff is as valuable as silver. No, far more valuable than that. Who cares about silver?" He wrapped the three fish in the foil, laid them on the coals, and covered the fire lightly with dirt. "You find me some more foil, Daniel, and we will do some serious tradin'."

I wiped my rifle with an oiled rag. "What do you have left to trade?" I asked. "The Cannibals raided your setlines and garden."

"Zucchini. Lots of zucchini. I plant it on the islands. And I got a few other small garden plots. Diversification, that's how you survive. I was an investment broker, you know."

I became silent. The past was a dead and distant land that I refused to visit.

He noticed my withdrawal. "Thinkin' 'bout that woman, ain'tchya?" he said with a cackle. "That's good. A young man like you should think about women. Means there's hope for this world yet. Find her and make her your wife. Multiply and fill the Interior with little Daniels."

"No," I said. "I don't need a wife."

Catfish shook his head sadly as if there were no hope for me after all.

An hour later we picked at hot bits of steaming fish, wiping our fingers on our shirts as we ate. Afterward Catfish took the first turn sleeping, and I pulled watch duty. Nights in the Interior could be so quiet and peaceful it was hard to believe any threats existed. The stars sparkled brightly, and the moon glowed like the face of an old friend. But one never knew who or what roamed the darkness, so vigilance was the first commandment for survivors. Only Robert could see in the dark. The rest of us strained our eyes and hoped for luck.

After Catfish relieved me, I fell asleep wondering if *she* were really out there. The Mono. Alone. Sleeping under the stars. Looking for me.

Pretty-eyed one, I thought. *Will you find me?*

CHAPTER 3

At dawn I told Catfish I'd escort him back to the river. He was afraid the Cannibals were still near, but I assured him it was safe.

"You know what, Daniel?" Catfish said, "You're the most respected person in the Interior."

"I doubt that," I said.

"No, it's true. Lady LeClair, General Jerry, Irreverend Flowers—they're feared, not respected. You're the marshal of the New West, Daniel. The Wyatt Earp of the twenty-first century. No one else carries your weight."

"You're forgetting Robert," I said.

"Robert! Oh, Robert is a different subject entirely. I suspect a person must be human to command respect, and who knows if Robert is human at all? I mean, does he have a soul? Does he feel? Exactly *what* is he? Does anyone know? Do you know?"

"I've never considered Robert's humanness."

"Well, you should. Another thing you should do is hunt him down yourself. Get him before he gets you. You'd be doin' us all a favor," Catfish said. "And heaven only knows we could use a favor or two."

"I think you are overestimating my abilities," I said. "No one's seen Robert and lived. I might be able to kill him when it comes down to it, but how am I supposed to find him?"

"Put an ad in the Personals." Catfish chuckled at his own humor.

"Do you spend your spare time becoming a comedian?" I asked.

"Actually, I was wondering about the O. J. trial the other day—"

"The what?"

"O. J. The O. J. Simpson trial. You remember."

"Not really. I was pretty young back then," I said.

"Well, the other day I was baitin' my setlines, and for some reason I got to thinkin' 'bout that trial and wonderin' if it's possible for a man to kill someone and not remember. I mean really not remember. And for some reason that got me to wonderin' about Robert. I wonder about a lot of things. And Robert is a good one because you never know when you might see him; so I wonder what he looks like, how he thinks."

"You don't want to know how Robert thinks," I said. "You just want to know how to avoid him."

Catfish saw the flint in my eyes and didn't push for more.

The sun was three hours above the hills when we arrived at Catfish's home, a simple hut woven from green willow saplings. The old man walked past it to a sandy bank where he'd rigged an irrigation system using pulleys, ropes, trees, poles, and buckets to bring water to his vegetables. He stared sadly at his ruined garden.

"At least you escaped with your life," I said. "All of this can be rebuilt."

"Yeah, I'll be fine. I still have caches. When the cities were looted I got my share. I have canned goods stashed everywhere—just like you, I suppose—and there are still fish in the river. The Cannibals didn't find half my setlines."

"You'll be OK now," I said. I was fidgeting and looking toward the distant hills.

"You gettin' restless, Daniel? You gonna hunt down Robert?"

"No."

"You gonna look for that woman?"

"No."

"You need a wife, Daniel. Go find your mystery woman."

"I'm not looking for a wife. I'm looking for a horse. That's why I travel. To find horses."

Catfish stroked his thin beard. "A horse. That makes sense. Progress. A horse would be a great advantage."

"Society must be rebuilt," I said. "Domestication of horses is the first step."

"We've fallen backward in time some three hundred years, haven't we? Savage tribes. Wild horses. Cannibals." He rummaged in the bushes and came out with a bag of weed and pages from an old book. He rolled himself a smoke. "Need a hit?" he asked.

"I don't partake," I said.

"Helps keep you from rememberin'."

"I don't need any help."

"Well, I smoke dope. I like it. Besides that, Flowers pays me for growin' it. He likes good dope." The old man inhaled deeply, held the smoke, then exhaled a gray cloud at a buzzing deerfly.

"You should grow more zucchini," I said. "There'll always be a market for muffins long after dope is gone."

He smiled. "What do you think I put in my muffins?" he said. "Flowers loves my muffins." He took another hit.

Voracious deerflies were biting my bare arms, and I slapped several dead. They did not appear to be bothering the old man. "I'll bring you aluminum foil," I told him, "in exchange for some zucchini muffins. Muffins without dope."

"I make the best zucchini muffins on the river," he said. "With or without dope." He slumped quietly to the sandy shore, mesmerized by the slow rolling of the muddy river. A thin smile creased his lips, and a numbed peace blossomed on his face, as if the water were his mother and he were a child in her rocking arms. He was still smiling moments later when I slipped quietly away through the willows.

I ventured upstream, hoping to strike a horse trail. I found no sign of horses, but I did find the prints of bison. The quakes had freed the buffalo from Yellowstone Park, and they returned to the prairie in small, paranoid bunches. The shortsighted beasts hated humans, and Pilgrims had been gored to death after approaching bison, thinking them a spiritual totem. Pilgrims were always looking for answers and only finding death.

I also saw the track of a lone elk. Had it been fresher, I would have followed it, hoping to add to my winter larder. In the Interior, winter

was called The Season of the Starving Moon, and anyone who hoped
to survive it spent the warm months laboring like an ant to store supplies. All summer I jerked elk and bison meat by cutting it in thin
strips, salting it, and hanging it in trees to dry.

I crossed the recent pugmark of a grizzly bear and the short hair
on my neck bristled. Grizzlies, too, had returned to their native plains.
Along with the smaller black bears, they rummaged in the rubble of
cities, denned in buildings, and scavenged human remains. Billings,
once the largest city in Montana, had been renamed Bear Town. Other
grizzlies took to the brushy draws and creeks of the prairies, and few
travelers were sufficiently armed to deter them. The Patriots had
wounded several bears, and these animals haunted the plains in mad
quests of vengeance.

There were no tracks of mule deer, antelope, or cattle. Deer were
all but extinct, killed by humans and wolves, and antelope and wild
cattle were equally rare.

I saw no signs of horses, though I knew several herds existed. I'd
spotted them from a distance before, but predators—animal and
human—kept them constantly moving.

By noon I was skirting the ruins of a small town, evading the
crumbling shells of brick and plastic and the burned-out homes and
businesses. I avoided all enclosures. No empty houses for me.

The sun sizzled in the bleached sky, and I decided to chance a dip in
the river. I stripped naked, stacked my rifle, fanny pack, and clothes in a
pile of driftwood, and eased into the cool, murky water, wearing only my
webbed belt and knife. The rocks beneath my feet felt smooth, round, and
slippery. I lowered my head into the water, scrubbed my hair and beard
with my fingernails, and, for lack of soap, rubbed my body vigorously

with leaves, bark, and small willow branches. I shaved by pulling my facial skin tight and running my razor-edged knife across my cheeks.

I shaved because facial hair was hot in the summer. It had nothing to do with the Babbler's mentioning of the pretty-eyed one. I did not need to be encumbered with a female. I wanted a horse.

Women? Why was I even thinking about them? I began wading back to my clothes. Then I glimpsed the canoes—two aluminum craft beached upriver, moored to an uprooted cottonwood tree. Their stainless steel hulls blended perfectly with the bleached-bone whiteness of the barkless tree trunk and branches. I quickly scooped up my clothes, scurried into the willows, and dressed. Then I crept quietly through tree cover to the canoes, inspected their loads of foodstuffs and weapons, and noted the six pairs of footprints leading up the sandy bank. Staying in the shelter of the thicket, I paralleled the trail.

It was a grisly scene I came upon, but I must tell you what I saw. It might better explain what I did. On a sandy shore six Cannibals lay around a smoldering fire, surrounded by shards of broken glass. They were ill and unconscious and naked except for loincloths and shoes. Hanging from a nearby tree were human remains I presumed to be an area moonshiner's. The eunuchs had gorged themselves on human flesh, Catfish's green tomatoes, melons, and the moonshiner's liquor before passing out in a tangled sprawl.

A sickening odor of burnt meat, vomit, and diarrhea hung like foul smoke in the air. I considered slipping away, setting the canoes adrift, and letting the Cannibals hike 150 miles home to Lady LeClair. But how many people would they kill on the way? And would one of their victims be the "pretty-eyed one"? Like it or not, the mysterious Monotheist was rooted in the recesses of my mind.

The Cannibals were an infestation, a cancer that required radical surgery. I could've shot them where they lay, but the sharp pops of my .223 might have attracted the wrong attention. Had there been a .22 available I could have put the muzzle to their sleeping heads and extinquished them one by one, but there were no small weapons in sight. Slitting their throats was bloody and blood was dangerous. Who knew what diseases flowed in the toxic veins of the eunuchs?

Use the river, I decided. Bad puppies could be drowned. I crept to the feet of the closest unconscious man, gripped him by the ankles, and pulled him slowly down the sandy bank to the water's edge. The man groaned but didn't awaken. I unloaded a canoe and laid the bloodied, vomit-covered eunuch in the craft. I did this five more times until they were all sprawled in one canoe, stacked like cordwood—Cannibal lying on Cannibal, their arms and legs, garish with tattoos, dangling over the sides.

I stripped again, clenched my knife between my teeth, and pushed the aluminum craft into the current, guiding it forward until the greenish-brown water lapped at my chin. Then I plunged the knife three times into the canoe's hull, twisting the stout blade as if opening a large can of tomatoes. Then I set the craft adrift. It began sinking slowly, tugged by eddies and whirlpools, claimed by the strong arm of the river until it finally listed from sight.

I knew a Cannibal or two might survive, but they would be weaponless, wet, sick, and afoot. And alone they were as cowardly as rats. Their courage came only in packs.

I did what I could for what was left of the moonshiner. I wrapped his remains in a tattered tarpaulin, laid him in the bottom of the other canoe—along with the Cannibals' weapons—punctured its bottom, and set that craft adrift as well.

Do not think about what you have done, I told myself. *You did what you had to do. Now move on. Put it behind you with the past. All is past.*

I left the river bottom, dressed quickly, and sought the solace of the open plains and the twisting haunts of the badlands. With my pace both urgent and controlled, I didn't seek shade during the heat of the day. Instead, I pushed on, stopping for water only twice, driving myself toward the sun as if its blinding rays could purge me of my sins and erase the memories of a canoe with human limbs sticking out like tree branches, sinking slowly into a dark and forceful stream.

I ran and ran, but the canoe remained fixed in my mind as I topped a hill and stumbled into the camp of two bedraggled travelers: a woman and a man. Immediately I thought of the Monotheist. Perhaps she had found company. But this woman had coal black hair. She did not match Babbler's description.

They were Pilgrims pursuing The Myth. Their clothes hung ragged and dirty, and their haunted, hungry eyes stared vacantly. They appeared more like apparitions than people, their forms so devoid of vitality and purpose that I looked through them as if they were ghosts.

The man approached pathetically, his cupped hands extended like a beggar. "Can you help us?" he pleaded. "We are lost. We have no food."

I pulled my last strands of elk jerky from my pack. It was leathery tough and salty, but they grabbed it ravenously, gnawing on the dried meat like puppies chewing on bones. I didn't ask where they were from. Asking for a Pilgrim's origin was like questioning the birthplace of clouds. Detroit. Cleveland. St. Louis. What did it matter?

Their cheap, homemade jewelry marked them as some form of cultists, and I smiled, realizing they had probably once been vegetarians.

"New Seattle," the woman said between bites, her eyes dull but hopeful. "The City of Light in New Lemuria? Do you know where it is? Is it far?"

I shook my head and lied. "I do not know."

"New Mu," the man said. "It is also called New Mu."

I shook my head again.

"The prophetess Lady LeClair?" asked the woman. "Can you lead us to her?"

A third time I denied them. What good was the truth? Did they really want to know their esteemed prophetess was a vampiress who bathed in the blood of women and turned men into sexless slaves? They would not have believed me. I wondered how they had made it this far. They carried only empty water containers and a few soiled blankets rolled together and fastened with leather belts.

The man approached me again. His face was a fragile canvas streaked with fear and fatigue. His weakness revolted me. "Water," he begged. "We're so thirsty."

I unhooked the canteen from my belt and handed it to him.

The man gulped desperately then passed the canteen to the woman. "When we left the cities we were warned about someone named Robert," the man said. "Are you him?"

"If I were Robert you would be dying a slow death," I said.

The woman looked at me in terror. "We were told we would be protected," she said.

"Protected by what?" I asked. "Your higher vibrations?"

They nodded dumbly.

I hoped they could answer questions better than they had asked them. "Have you seen a woman?" I said. "A lone woman with . . . pretty eyes."

They looked at me as if I was the insane one. "We have seen no one," the woman said. "No one. Not for days. Not for weeks."

"Can you help us?" the man asked. "Can you help us at all?"

"I can't help you," I said.

A woman took a tentative step forward. "Who?" she asked. "Who are you?"

"The last person to see you alive," I said softly. They looked startled, but I walked past them and broke into a paced, ground-consuming run. I had to leave the dead behind. All the dead. The man-monsters in the canoe, the walking dead, the talking dead, the memories of more dead.

I ran for miles and miles through sagebrush bottoms and abandoned wheatfields, down gravel creeks and up rocky slopes. I ran until my lungs burned and my arms ached. I did not stop until my legs failed me and I collapsed into a shallow, bowl-shaped depression in the earth. I huddled there with my rifle clutched to my chest. I was Daniel the warrior. The Lieutenant. But I was weary of the struggle for mere existence.

Later, sleep came in light and troubled steps that descended to the cellar of my subconscious, where bald, naked, and tattooed men—with ears, eyebrows, and nipples pierced with rings—rose white and bloated from a black river. Their red eyes stared toward the shore, seeking the trail of their murderer. Then they stepped from the water in single file. Their loincloths dropped from their wet, scrawny legs, exposing their mutilations.

I saw myself raising my rifle and heard myself screaming, "Fire!"

The men marched forward. Black water dripped from their sunburned bodies.

I froze to the weapon, unable to pull the trigger.

The first eunuch came near enough to touch me. He stretched out his arm.

Do not remember this dream! I demanded, and my eyes flashed open. Morning had come and a circle of sky filled the hole above my refuge. Or almost filled it—would have filled it, except for a smiling, sunlit face staring back at me and a hand with long, tapered fingers extended toward me. A person. A real person.

"Daniel."

I thought I heard my name but couldn't have. The lips had not parted. The person had said nothing at all.

Instinct and training demanded I raise my rifle, but I didn't. I blinked once, hoping to dispel the vision. It remained. I did the unimaginable and extended my hand to be assisted from the hole.

"Daniel," I thought I heard her say, not as a question, but as a confirmation.

"I am Daniel," I whispered.

CHAPTER 4

Her.

I stood and she released my hand. She smiled from a face of simple but flawless beauty—clean, clear skin tanned golden brown, wispy tufts of platinum hair sailing from beneath a red scarf and—as Babbler had insisted—bright, blue eyes sparkling like flares.

Her hands seemed large for a woman's, but slender and strong, their firm grip suggesting a trimmed, muscled athleticism. Her faded denim jeans hung loose and long from a narrow waist, and she appeared tall. But as I rose to my full height, I realized I was several inches taller than she was.

Behind her a large, white malamute lay as silently as a snowbank. The dog was fitted to a travois of wheeled aluminum poles (as if fashioned from an old shopping cart) extending from a harness about its chest. Lashed to the poles was a small bundle of belongings. I wondered why Babbler had never mentioned the dog. He'd been entranced by the woman's eyes and saw nothing else, I decided.

When she spoke I felt disarmed and captured. "Hi," she said. "My name is Deborah."

I stared dumbly, as awkward as a junior high geek at his first dance. Her teeth were white and clean, indicating a concern for hygiene not common to the Interior's natives.

"You have not told me your name," she said.

You know my name, I thought. *I heard you say it. I am the one you have been seeking.*

She waited quietly for my reply.

"I am Daniel," I said finally, and the white dog whined softly.

Her bright eyes flashed with satisfaction. "I have been looking for you," she said.

I felt like a trophy obtained after a long pursuit. She moved a step closer to inspect me more thoroughly, and I noticed her clean, pleasant scent. Most travelers reeked of body odor. I probably did too. In the Interior one grew familiar with his own smell.

"I need you to be my guide," she said. "You know this land. Will you help me?"

Everything in me screamed *No!* I had never escorted Pilgrims or anyone else. There was danger in numbers. I believed the only way I'd survive was singularly, like a vigilant, cautious, and deadly lone wolf.

She looked at me intently but peacefully, as someone who needed me yet had no need of me at all. Her air of independence angered me. Was she a fool? Robert was after her. And the Patriots. She needed me not as a guide but as a bodyguard. Didn't she know that?

"Where do you want to go?" I asked.

"To the Patriots first," she said, suggesting the Militia was simply one step in a series of successive movements.

"The Patriots are already looking for you," I said, hoping to dissuade her. "They are idiots, but it's still not safe for you to go to them. They need women, and if they don't keep you for themselves, they will trade you to someone worse."

She showed no reaction. "Will you take me?" she challenged.

I countered with another warning. "Do you know about Robert?" I asked.

"Yes."

"And you still want to travel the Interior?"

She sighed and crossed her arms. "I know I'm asking you to endanger your own life," she said. "I'll understand completely if you refuse."

She was worried for *me*. She wanted to protect *me*. She was challenging *me*. I felt the need to prove her wrong. "I will guide you," I said, motivated more by chauvinism than chivalry.

She tossed her head affirmatively. "Good. Then let's be on our way. You lead, and I'll follow."

As she moved I noticed she lightly favored one leg.

Her eyes caught my concern. "I have a slight limp," she said. "But don't worry. I can keep up. I've made it this far."

How far has she come? I wondered. For once I was interested in someone's past, but I didn't ask. I didn't have to.

"I'm from Chicago," she said. "Three of us departed months ago."

She nodded at the white dog. "It's just Dunamis and me now."

Dunamis? What type of name is that? I wondered.

"The name is Greek," she said. "Should we go now? Which way, Daniel?"

I didn't answer her question. Before we began I needed to lay some ground rules. "I hope you're not a talker," I said. "I don't talk much, and I will not talk about the past."

"OK," she said with the slightest reluctance in her voice. "Anything else?"

"I usually travel at night and rest during the day."

Her brow wrinkled into a thoughtful frown. "That won't do. I'm not a creature of the night. Besides, I have things to do then."

Things to do? "What kind of things?"

"You'll see," she said.

The ball landed in my court. The future pivoted on my decision, and she waited quietly. I relented. "All right. We travel during the day. But it gets terribly hot."

"Great. Now, which way to the Patriots?"

I looked toward the northern horizon as if it were the edge of a destiny larger than my own plans and disciplines. "This way." I began walking.

My course followed the dry, winding creeks that stretched and cut across the parched prairie like a webwork of capillaries. I moved robotically, numbed by the irrationality of my actions. The woman and the dog followed silently behind me. Her limp, though noticeable, did not affect her pace. The day dragged on until I finally halted beneath a lone, living cottonwood and told her we should rest until the day cooled.

I expected her to resist, but she nodded and unhitched the white dog while I eyed her supplies, wondering what she carried. Hunger gnawed on my backbone. "Do you have any food?" I asked.

"A little," she said. "Are you hungry?"

"That's OK," I replied. "I have a cache nearby. I'll be right back." I climbed briskly to the top of a nearby hill, pushed a heavy, flat rock from an old badger burrow, and pulled out a nylon bag containing four tin cans, a razor blade, hunting knife, bandages, and ammunition. I took the tins and put everything else back.

Looking around at the dry, lifeless hills, for a moment I was tempted to leave her. Take the food and run. It was a cowardly action. It made sense, but I couldn't do it. When I got back to the tree, she was reclining against the trunk with her shoes and socks off.

"Peaches," I said, holding up the four tins. Their paper labels had worn off long ago.

She thought for a moment then smiled. "No," she said. "Stewed tomatoes."

I shook my head. I hated stewed tomatoes. "No," I argued. "Peaches."

She reached for a multipurpose BuckTool sheathed on her belt. "I have a can opener," she said. "Let's see."

I crouched beside her and handed her a can. For an instant, as the tool's blade plunged into the tin, I remembered my knife stabbing into the side of an aluminum canoe.

She peeled the can's top back. "Tomatoes," she said.

Can't be, I thought. I knew the location and contents of a hundred caches and was certain this one had peaches. I thirsted for the sweet, fruity syrup. She opened the other cans. All contained tomatoes.

"We should thank the Lord for it anyway," she said softly, "even if it wasn't what you were expecting." She reached for my hand, held it lightly, and prayed a brief prayer of thanksgiving. Then she began eating quietly.

"How did you know?" I asked her. "How did you know they were tomatoes and not peaches?"

She stabbed a tomato with the knifeblade of her tool and looked at it. "Do you want an answer?" she asked. "Or are you just asking questions?" There was an authority in her voice that surprised me.

"I'm just asking questions," I confessed.

She fed the dog tomato slices. A vegetarian dog? I had no use for malamutes or most dogs for that matter.

Eventually she leaned against the tree and slept. I remained vigilant a few feet away, pretending to watch the hills but mostly sneaking glances at her—her poise and strength, straight shoulders, long neck, arched feet. All rightly fitted together. Though peaceful and beautiful in repose, at the same time something about her repelled me. Maybe even scared me. When she finally stirred, I rose, turned my back, pretended I hadn't been staring, and feigned sleep.

When we left the tree, we continued north. At dusk we topped a gumbo knoll and looked down on a ranch house on the bank of a dry creek. I was familiar with the place. A faded and peeling white sign near the county road still said Miller Ranch. It pointed like an arrow to the simple frame house, corrals and barn, metal shop building, and power poles that stood tall and useless like totems to a deceased god. An old car with four flat tires squatted on a concrete basketball court. The windows were broken out, and three of the four doors were sprung open. I stared at the car and could not remember the last time I had driven one.

"I need to go inside the house," she said.

"I never go inside empty houses," I told her.

"I do," she said. "It's one reason I'm here."

"Empty houses attract mice," I explained. "Mice attract badgers, raccoons, skunks, and snakes."

"So?"

"So they attract the next level on the food chain. Like lions, wolves, and bears."

"Yes?"

"And people. Sometimes crazy people hide in the houses. Sometimes they even think everything is normal and they talk to people who aren't there."

"Interesting." She started off the knoll without me, the white dog trailing behind her obediently.

For several minutes I maintained my resolve and let her go. I watched her through my rifle scope and scanned the old house for signs of movement near the windows or the glint of a rifle barrel. Finally, I could bear it no longer and trotted after her.

I caught her just as she reached the door. "Stop," I said. "Don't go in there."

Her blue eyes bleached to the color of a Clorox sky. "I must," she insisted.

"Then let me go in first," I said. I slipped past her and entered the house with my weapon pointed. The rooms were awash in a dim radiance, and shadows stretched and fled as the last evening light filtered in through the dirty west-side windows.

I strained to hear, ready to fire at the slightest noise, but the only sound was her steps coming up behind me.

She entered the house, holding a lighted candle. "It's OK," she said quietly. "You can put the gun down." Soft, golden candlelight bathed her face, and she spoke softly in some sort of prayer. The prayer seemed to lift and pull her slowly and lightly to the next room. I followed, my rifle a heavy distraction attached to my hands.

She went first to a child's bedroom. The bed was overturned, and the mattress was ripped apart. Mice manure was scattered everywhere, and the vermin's nests fouled a chest of drawers and the closet. The walls of the room were bare except for a single, brightly colored poster of Michael Jordan, in his red Bulls uniform, dunking a basketball. Jordan's shaved head gleamed, and a fierce intensity lit his eyes as he soared down on the basket like a demon. Suddenly I remembered where I was the day Michael Jordan retired, and the images of family swirled about me like smoke.

"What are you thinking?" she asked.

"Nothing, I—"

"You were remembering your family," she said. "The day Michael Jordan retired your father had promised to take you fishing, but he got called away on business."

"How did you know?"

"Are you ready for answers?"

I shook my head and we moved to the next room. Deborah continued praying under her breath. The master bedroom had been ransacked and vandalized as looters searched for something—anything—of value. She stood silently with the candle extended high.

Darkness had fallen and I worried about someone seeing the light. "I'd better watch the front door," I whispered.

"Dunamis will tell us if anyone comes," she said.

It wasn't that I didn't trust the dog. I simply had to get out of the house. "I gotta go," I said.

I stood outside, inhaling drafts of fresh air, my rifle cradled in my arms, my legs arguing with my mind whether I should stay or run away. Finally, when I heard Deborah complete her sweep of the building and return to the living room, I went back in.

"I have been in many empty houses," she said, "and they're all basically the same. There's clothing left behind. Furniture. Even toys. But there are seldom any photos or photo albums."

"I guess they took what they considered most valuable," I noted.

"Yes. And there's nothing more valuable than the memories of loved ones and happier times, is there, Daniel?"

"Why do you do this? What good does it do? Are you simply curious about who lived here?"

"Yes, I'm curious, but I'm more interested in who will live here in the future." She followed the candle to a bookshelf. The flickering light glistened on the spines of the few remaining books, as if breathing fire into forgotten stories. "Do you read, Daniel?" she asked.

"I seldom take the time," I said.

She ran a hand lightly over the dusty books. "You really should read. The lack of reading contributed greatly to our culture's downfall. Reading requires investment, not mere idleness. The people who lived here were readers, and they took their favorite books with them."

"I wish you would put the light out. Robert will be drawn to it like a moth."

"Let him come," she said simply. Then she placed the candle on the bookcase, went to a small hallway closet, found a tattered old broom, and began sweeping the filthy floors.

"What are you doing now?" I demanded.

"The second phase of the cleansing," she explained. "Because I'm sleeping here tonight."

"Here? It's not safe," I argued.

"It's quite safe," she said. "And you are welcome to one of the bedrooms."

Most men would have welcomed a night alone with a woman as beautiful as Deborah. I was not most men. "You know I won't sleep inside," I said.

"You will when it is time," she said.

Time? What time? "I'll be nearby." I turned for the door.

"Sleep well, Daniel," she said as I stepped over the white dog. "And do not stay up all night worrying about me."

I retreated to a cleft in the gumbo bank where I wrapped myself in a thin blanket and stared down at the little house with candlelight shining through broken windows. Soon the sound of singing came softly on the night breeze. Her voice was lovely but the words indistinguishable. As she sang, the light in the house strengthened, and I assumed she'd lit more candles. I watched until I fell asleep. Then I slept with my face turned toward the empty house.

That night I dreamed dreams I could not remember. I awakened anxious and troubled. When I came down from the hill, she was sitting on the front porch like a ranch wife waiting for a rural mailman. "Did you sleep well?" she asked.

"Fine. We should be moving on," I said. "There is a flowing spring west of here. We need to stock up on water."

We set out immediately. I kept looking back, not at Deborah, but in the distance. I was sure we were being followed, either by wolves or

Robert. Or both. Deborah saw my concern but said nothing.

Before noon we reached the spring marked by a vent pipe on the side of a hill. Lower, in a cove of sandstones, a single black pipe protruded four inches from an earthen bank. The clear, sweet water flowed at a gallon a minute before collecting in a small pool that grew reeds and slough grass. A red-winged blackbird and magpie flew away as we approached.

I checked the pool for tracks and saw signs of several buffalo and two elk. One of the buffalo had rubbed its thick hide against an outcropping of rock. I needed meat but wasn't about to fire my rifle if Robert were nearby. "You wash up," I told Deborah. "I'll stand guard on one of these hills."

I climbed the brittle gumbo of a southerly hill, watched for danger, and spied on her through my rifle scope. She unpacked a toothbrush and plastic container of baking soda, then undid her scarf. As she bent to put her head under the pipe, her platinum hair spilled in long white ribbons.

At that moment I knew I wanted her.

The passion of the moment suddenly chilled as I felt a presence far behind me. Scanning eastwardly, I glimpsed, for an instant, a single dark, distant form that radiated the purposefulness of death. Robert on a mission. I watched intently but the figure wouldn't reappear.

Logic told me to set an ambush. Kill him before he killed me. Kill him and be a hero in the Interior.

But an instinct stronger than logic moved me off the hill. I wanted to think I was protecting Deborah, but I knew that wasn't true. I was afraid. Living with the threat of Robert did not scare me, but planning his murder was different. My mind became hooded, my legs trembled, and a cold blade of terror stabbed my heart. To avoid him was one thing. To confront him was something altogether different.

Panic tempted me to flee. Leave the woman. Let her die a martyr for her strange cause. But my attraction to her overruled my fear. I wasn't being heroic. Death was so common to the Interior that one more corpse dotting the landscape meant nothing to anyone. I was being selfish. I had never met a woman like this one.

CHAPTER 5

I rushed back to the spring. "We must go," I warned. "I saw Robert."

"Don't you want to wash up?"

"I said I saw *Robert.*"

"Daniel, you needn't fear him."

"He is after both of us," I snapped. "And he doesn't take prisoners."

"How far away is he?"

"A couple miles. He has the capability to overtake us anytime."

"Then why doesn't he?" she asked.

"He's toying with us. It builds the suspense for him. Either that or he wants us to lead him to someone."

"You know him well," she said.

"I know nothing." I began walking quickly northward. She and the dog followed. I pushed through the day's heat, burning in my own frenzy. Several times I briefly left her and backtracked to see if Robert were gaining ground, but I never saw him again.

Late in the afternoon I circled our back trail again and spotted two elk bedded on a distant hillside. I cursed the circumstances. If Robert hadn't been near, I could've killed for food. The elk distracted me, and when I looked for Deborah she had disappeared out of sight. I panicked and ran to catch up.

As I topped the ridge that separated us, I looked down with horror upon a distant sagebrush flat. Deborah, with the white dog lying at her feet, stood talking with a tall figure dressed in a grimy black duster and floppy black hat typical of Slingers. Slingers were dangerous, but at least it wasn't Robert. Crawling, I stalked through the brush, stopped at two hundred yards, leveled the rifle against a rock, and trained the crosshairs on the gunman.

Whether Robert was nearby or not, I would have to shoot.

Slingers and Ma Men were once common in the Interior. They had been mostly Midwestern boys with romantic fantasies about living in the Wild West. The Slingers fashioned themselves as gunfighters, while the Ma Men pretended to be mountain men. Few Ma Men and Slingers remained. Those who did were dangerous, as rabid as foam-mouthed dogs, scratching and snarling at the bottom of a pit of delusions. They had to be avoided, and when that wasn't possible, they had to be killed.

I placed the crosshairs on the Slinger's ugly face. Scabs from sunburn crusted above his thin, blond beard, and his eyes glowed red as coals in the shadow cast by the brim of his dirty hat. He opened his mouth to speak. The words cracked from parched and bleeding lips.

My finger caressed the trigger but I hesitated. Deborah stood only a foot away. The bullet's impact would shower her with flesh, bone, and blood, leaving an indelible imprint on her memories. But what did memories mean to me? I crept yards closer—hoping for a better bullet angle—until their voices became distinct.

"What is your name?" Deborah asked.

The Slinger stepped back and pulled his long coat away from the revolver holstered on his hip. "I am Kid Curry," he proclaimed. "The greatest outlaw to terrorize Montana."

"What is your real name?" Deborah demanded.

"I'm Kid Curry," the Slinger shouted, his hand on the pistol butt. "And you're Charley Siringo, the famous Pinkerton detective. You've been huntin' me for years. Well, now you've found me, Siringo. Slap leather!"

"My name is Deborah."

"You're a master of disguises," the madman screamed. "Even make yourself look like a woman, but I know you, Siringo. Go for your gun."

Deborah extended her hand. "Tell me your name," she demanded.

"Kid Curry!" the Slinger yelled.

"You leave," Deborah shouted. "You leave him right now."

I understood Deborah's shout as a cry for help. In retrospect, I know that I understood nothing at all. The Slinger began shaking, his fists clenched into knots and his face contorted as if he were vomiting lava from his gut.

"Leave!" Deborah yelled again.

A high-pitched scream, like a mountain lion's, burst from his throat.

"Leave!"

He screamed three more times, took a deep breath, shuddered, and seemed to relax.

Deborah reached out, saying something I couldn't hear, and the Slinger's right hand slid toward his gun.

My instincts took over, the little rifle blasted, and the wanna-be outlaw flew backward, thudding on the hardpan like a sack of oats. Deborah screamed and rushed to him.

I approached cautiously, fully ready to put another round into the man if he so much as twitched. A frosting of pink bubbles lined his lips, and his breathing was low, raspy, and quickly failing. Lung shot, I figured. A red hole high in his chest confirmed it.

"Get back, get back," Deborah shouted at me.

"What?"

"Get back. And turn your back. You're not ready to see this."

Not ready to see what? I thought. I had seen more death than a hundred morticians, but there was such authority in her voice that I didn't question her command. I spun around on my heels and stood at attention, staring into the opposite sky, my rifle pointed at the ground. I strained to hear, wondering what strange workings were occurring behind my back. With sharp, strong pleas, Deborah called for help as she untangled death from the man's spine as if it were a snake wrapped around a tree limb.

"OK," she said finally. "You can turn around now."

I turned and was shocked to see the Slinger sitting up, supported by Deborah's embrace. The man was alive. His eyes were open, his head hatless. He breathed in evident pain, but he breathed. His bare chest showed no gaping wound where my hollow-point had entered, just a quarter-sized circle of fresh scar tissue inches above his heart.

"He's not dead!" I automatically raised my rifle.

"Daniel, put the gun down. Lay it on the ground." Her voice was so stern even the dog whined.

I did as she said.

"Now help me get him to his feet."

We each got under an arm and lifted. The man was skin and bones, as light and framy as a kite. Close up he looked boyish and innocent— I guessed him to be in his early twenties—and I felt a sharp pang of guilt for having shot him. We set him on his high-heeled boots, and he wobbled until his head cleared.

"Are you OK?" Deborah asked.

He grunted in the affirmative.

"What's your name? Tell me your name."

"Malachi," he said. "Malachi Watts."

"Good, good. And what century are we in, Malachi?"

"Twenty-first." His voice sounded young and responsive, as if answering questions in a college classroom.

"Good, excellent." She looked at me. "Give me your canteen, Daniel. He's thirsty." I handed it to her and she helped him sip.

"What's going on?" I asked.

"More than you're ready to know," she said.

"Where's the bullet hole?"

She laid her right index finger on the scar. "Here."

"But it's healed."

She slowly turned the Slinger, and he pivoted on the underslung heels like a sunburnt marionette. Below his left shoulder blade was a second circle of scar tissue, this one the size of a silver dollar. "That was the exit wound," she said.

"He's a dead man," I said.

"He was." She turned again so he was facing her and brushed back the long strands of filthy blond hair that hung in his eyes. "Malachi," she said. "Who is Kid Curry?"

His eyes looked confused but alert. "An outlaw back in the old days," he said. His awakening mind slowly focused, appraising the situation. "Where am I?" he asked.

"You are in eastern Montana," she said. "Where are you from?"

"Franklin, Tennessee."

"Daniel, do we have any food?"

"Two cans of tuna fish," I answered, feeling like a clerk at a convenience store.

"Would you please give them to Malachi? And bring me the canteen that's strapped to the travois. He will need it too."

While I was playing gofer she instructed the kid. "You can't come with us," she said. "You're too weak. Take the food and water. When you're stronger, begin walking east. Leave the Interior, do you understand?

"He'll never make it," I argued. "It's a thousand miles to anywhere, and you're sending him right toward Robert."

"Don't listen to him," she told the Slinger. "There are others coming. People like me. They will have food. Robert will not see you. He will pass by you while you're sleeping and never know you are there."

He lifted the pistol out of his holster. "What should I do with this?" he asked. "I ain't had bullets in a long time."

I took it from him and broke the cylinder open. The six chambers were hollow and rusty. It was an early model Smith & Wesson. At one time it had been worth a small fortune as an antique.

"Throw it away," Deborah told me. "He won't need it anymore." She went to the travois and returned with a plastic pouch. "There's a map in here and some energy bars, matches, and a card with a password. When you meet people who do the things I do, hand them the card. They will take care of you."

He stood wooden and confused as would any man raised from the dead and thrust into stark, sun-scorched reality. He held the pouch, tuna fish, and canteen in his cupped hands. "Thank you," he said.

She put the sweat-soaked hat back on his head. "You're welcome, Malachi." Her voice sweetened with a compassion that I hungered for. "Eat and rest tonight. You have a long journey ahead of you." Then she turned and walked away as if one order of business were taken care of and there were more to do. "Come on, Daniel," she called, and I had to jog to catch up with her and the white dog.

When I reached her side, she scolded me. "Daniel, I'd really rather you didn't shoot anyone unless I ask you to."

"Unless you ask me?"

"Exactly."

"Deborah. This is a dangerous place. Slingers are madmen. Not to mention Patriots, Cannibals, Robert, and other examples of insanity."

She stopped and faced me. "How many people have you killed?"

My mind quickly flashed to the six Cannibals drifting out of sight in a sabotaged canoe. "How many?" I asked.

"Yes. Can you count them?"

"Well, no, not that there are so many or anything, but in some cases you don't know."

"You don't know?"

"You don't know, Deborah. This is war out here. No one has food, but everyone has guns. You get shot at. You shoot back. Sometimes you hit. Sometimes you don't. Sometimes you don't know."

"But you have killed people?"

"Yes, I have killed people."

"Fine. I'm simply asking that you don't kill any more." She began walking briskly away.

"Or what?" I asked. "Are you going to fire me?"

She stopped and faced me again. "OK, OK. I can't fire you because I'm not paying you. I understand that. And I understand that you thought shooting that poor kid back there was necessary to protect me. But I don't need protection. I know you're doing me a favor by being my guide, and I can't impose my will on anything you do for your own sake. I'm simply saying, don't shoot anyone for *me*. OK?"

"Fine," I snapped. "I'm supposed to let Robert carve your heart out with his fingernails, and if the Patriots want to make you the General's concubine of the month, I'm just supposed to smile. But I draw the line at Cannibals. If Cannibals come anywhere near us, I kill them. Understand?"

"I understand," she said. "But you do it to protect yourself, not me. I don't need your blood on my hands."

We each walked in angry silence for a while until I broke it. Anger was an energy drain I couldn't afford. "You think that kid will be OK?" I asked. "You really think he will make it out of the Interior?"

Her attitude, too, had softened. "I think so," she said. "I don't know for sure. But he was too weak to go with us, and we're going in the other direction anyway."

"And there are more people coming?"

"Yes. Like little bunches of army ants. First a trickle, then a flow."

"But why? Why are they coming out here? Are they afraid of the cities? Is it that bad . . . back there?"

"They're afraid of nothing," she said. "They've done their work in the cities and left that work in the hands of others. They're coming to the Interior to do a work here."

"To this land of empty houses and warring tribes? And what are you, some sort of scout?"

"That's right. I am some sort of scout."

The conversation ended with a mutual, unspoken agreement that walking was work, and it took too much energy to form words. Before long the sun was glowing like an inflamed pumpkin, and dust layered the sky in pink and crimson sheets. We walked directly toward the sunset as if it were a portal to another world.

At dusk we came upon an isolated ranch house.

"You're going to want to sleep here, aren't you?" I asked.

"Yes. This one even looks cleaner than most."

"It's because it's so remote," I explained. "The Patriots have probably been through it a few times, but not many Pilgrims or scavengers get this far north. They stay south, closer to the Yellowstone River."

"Then it's probably safe for you to sleep inside this house," she said.

"I told you, I don't sleep in houses."

"Why?"

"I've told you that, too. They're filled with mice and snakes and skunks."

"That's the only reason?"

"The only one I'm going to talk about."

"OK. But are you going to go through it with me and make sure it's safe?"

"Do you want me to?"

"Yes."

I entered the house in front of her, this time holding a small flashlight I'd taken from a cache. The living room carpet was still relatively clean because the doors were closed and the windows hadn't been broken.

She lit a candle and began praying. I held the flashlight in my left fist with my arm perpendicular to my body, my rifle resting across my forearm. With the safety off and a shell in the chamber, the pad of my finger tickled the trigger.

"It was a family of five." Deborah held the candle beneath a wood plaque inscribed with their names: Dean, Heather, Shanna, Shonie, and Sharlie.

I cast my light into a corner where a disarrayed collection of trophy ribbons had fallen to the floor like a liquid rainbow spilled and dried. "The three girls were rodeo contestants," I said.

Each girl had had her own bedroom. The blankets and sheets were gone, but the bare mattresses and box springs waited untouched, like a motel room stripped for the next guest.

"I believe this family will be back," Deborah said.

"That's crazy," I whispered. "How can you know that? In the morning you might find three or four crosses in the backyard. People died so fast the morticians couldn't handle all the business. Families buried their own."

"No, I think these escaped the Plague."

"Escaped? And where would they have gone? The cities were worse than the country. The corpses rotted in the streets."

"There were safe havens," she said. "There are always cities of refuge."

I suppressed a contemptuous laugh and completed my inspection of the house. "Well, no lions or bears here," I said. "I guess you can do your thing now."

"You won't stay?"

"No."

"OK, then as you say, I will do my thing."

I turned for the door.

"Daniel—"

"Yes."

"I want to apologize," she said. "I was too rough on you for shooting the Slinger. This is your world, and you were only doing what you thought was necessary to protect me."

With my back to her, I grasped the doorknob. "That's OK," I said.

"Then you forgive me?"

"Of course." I didn't turn around. I walked out the door, stepped over the malamute, and found a sheltered place to curl up for the night.

Again I watched the house until my eyes grew heavy. I heard the singing, and I saw the light increase. And I know my eyes were playing tricks on me, but as I was fading to sleep, I imagined I saw several people in the house with her.

I shook the thought from my head. Imagination could be as bad as memories.

CHAPTER 6

For three more days we traveled northwest. I raided my winter caches for food. She spent her nights in empty houses while I camped nearby. We talked little. The silence finally became larger than the two of us. Not the silence between us, but the silence that surrounded us.

"Do you hear it?" I finally asked her.

"Hear what?" she said.

"The quietness. Sometimes the silence is like a roar."

"Like a roar?"

"That's right. We've traveled for several days without hearing a wolf howl. Wolves never howl when Robert is near. And owls don't screech and birds don't sing. There is only stillness. Only the sound of death walking."

"You are so sure that Robert is following us?"

"Yes," I said. "I can hear him in the silence. Can't you?"

"The only voice I hear in silence is God's," she said.

I stared at her without responding. I had no answer to such an odd statement.

That morning we entered a large burn. For miles in every direction the scorched prairie lay like a soot blanket, sprouting tortured, stubbed fingers of blackened brush stems.

"What caused this?" she asked.

"Lightning, maybe," I said. "But just as likely it was the Patriots. They found a herd of bison or elk and tried to use fire to drive them into an ambush. The fire got away from them. The bison or elk probably did too."

"You don't like the Patriots, do you?"

"They're fools," I said. "They bring disgrace to the uniform."

"Then you miss the military?"

"My military does not exist anymore, but that doesn't mean I don't respect the training and discipline."

"But there are wars and rumors of wars. . . . "

"It's not my battle," I said sharply.

With no alternative but to cross the burn, we soon were dusted and streaked with ash and soot. The white dog became charcoal-colored. There was no place to rest, no water, no trees, just rolling black prairie, dried, fried, and dead.

"Daniel," Deborah said. "What put the fire out? Did it rain?"

"Rain? No, it hardly ever rains here anymore. Most likely it burned until it ran out of grass. No fuel, no fire."

"It never rains?"

"Not very often."

"This land needs rain," she said. "Especially this burn. It's all so bleak, so dark."

Suddenly part of the darkness stood up. A dozen men, covered with soot, rose from the ashes with their Chinese rifles aimed at us. "Halt," a man ordered. "Put down your weapon."

I laid my Ruger on the ground, angry at myself for having walked into a trap. I aimed my frustration at Deborah. "Congratulations," I whispered. "You've found your Patriots."

The sergeant approached, his left ear swollen and scabbed from our last encounter. "Shut up," he snapped. The butt of his weapon caught me across the right temple. Lights flashed in my mind like tailing comets, and the ground rose up and struck me in the face. "We meet again, Lieutenant." His voice sounded far away. "And with luck, by morning I will wear both your ears on a necklace."

Rough hands forced me to my feet and secured my arms tightly behind my back.

The sergeant grabbed Deborah and pushed her forcefully ahead of him. "March," he ordered. "And don't talk. We don't want to hear anything you have to say until the General can hear it too." A man put a rope through the white dog's harness and jerked him forward. Dunamis followed obediently.

This was a moment I had been dreading. Poor Deborah. So simple, so naive. I was sure she had no idea of the degradation that awaited her.

We walked for several hours, our trek taking us deep into moon-scaped badlands. Narrow, single-file trails once used only by deer and bighorn sheep were now packed by the stompings of military boots and webbed with hair-triggered land mines. Clay cliffs rose like stark cathedrals from brittle avenues of hardpan sod. At dusk the ambling Missouri River appeared as a long, silver ribbon reflecting the glow of a muted, setting sun. Armed sentries, hunched and mean-eyed like gargoyles, peered from sandstone pinnacles as we descended to a bottomland of cottonwoods and willows. There half-hidden travel trailers littered the landscape like discarded beer cans. Lean, hard-faced women emerged from the aluminum shells, their eyes darkened by a savage curiosity. Slender, sallow children clung to their mothers' legs. The men had thin, hungry mouths and vicious, darting eyes.

We halted in front of a log cabin at the base of a cliff. A high wall of flat stones mortared with gumbo surrounded the cabin. One of the men tied the white dog to a post.

"Y'all keep your curs away from this animal," the sergeant ordered the onlookers. "Could be the General will want this animal's hide tanned for his wall." He dismissed the men but they lingered anyway, perhaps curious about the disposition of the captives.

A guard opened a thick wooden gate, and the sergeant paraded the two of us up a sandstone pathway to the cabin.

From a reclining chair on the cabin's porch, the General watched our advance. He was large and heavily jowled with reddish hair tinged with gray. A bushy orange mustache sprouted from a face as knobby and knotted as a clenched fist. Emblems of various Midwestern militia divisions decorated his worn fatigues, making him appear like an overage Boy Scout. "Whatcha got?" he called out in a thin, high voice that belied his bulk.

"Trophies," the sergeant reported. "A white woman and the AWOL lieutenant." The excitement in his voice hinted promotion.

"Bring them to my court," the General ordered. He labored out of the old La-Z-Boy as a razor-faced aide opened the door. We entered a room lit dimly by kerosene lanterns and furnished with two patio tables, six rickety aluminum chairs, and a large bench with a throne-like chair.

The General awaited us there. "Sergeant, where did you capture your prisoners?" he asked with an exaggerated sense of protocol.

The sergeant snapped to attention. "In the burn, sir," he reported.

I thought that was obvious since we were covered with soot.

The General looked down at us solemnly. "You're guilty of trespassing on the sovereign soil of the free nation of True America," he said. "How do you plead?"

After a short silence, Deborah spoke. "We were not actually captured," she said.

"Silence, woman," the General snapped. "I am addressing my question to the man. You'll speak only if you're spoken to."

I measured the situation. The General was a bloated bully, a bigot who had bluffed his way into leadership by spouting racist rhetoric and inflammatory conspiracy theories. Someone who delighted in killing as long as his own hands were not bloodied. The aide was a skinny, rat-faced man with garish prison tattoos running the length of his bare arms. A con. A product of institutions. A killer.

"I am addressing you, Lieutenant," the General boomed.

All eyes were on me. "She's right," I said. "We were not captured. We were on our way here."

The sergeant, seeing his promotion slipping away, stammered a protest, but the General, with a wave of his hand, ordered him from the room. The sergeant left reluctantly, drilling me with a hateful stare as he closed the door. The aide assumed guard duty and leveled an Uzi at us.

The General's walnut-colored eyes focused on me. "I have waited a long time to meet you, Lieutenant," he said pompously. "You are a hero here in True America for resisting the Zionist Occupied Government. I assume you have come to enlist. I will be glad to brevet you to light colonel. Making you second-in-command of the Prairie Patriots, the Army of the True America."

I stood relaxed, my eyes staring straight ahead. "I am not a hero," I said. "I am only a guide, and I did not come to join your ragtag army."

"You are rejecting my commission?"

"Yes."

He was angry but he was also determined. "We will talk more about this later." He turned his attention to Deborah. "Who are you and what are you doing here?"

"I am a missionary. I am here to evangelize the inhabitants of the Interior."

"Evangelize!" The General snorted, and his fat lips curled like twin snakes. "We are the true children of God. How can you evangelize us?" Suddenly his eyes widened as if he were seeing Deborah with new recognition. "You," he said. "You're the woman who made the radio spark and crackle the last couple of weeks." He leaned closer and scowled with suspicion. "It's all too convenient, isn't it? The two of you just walking in like this? What do you think, Mr. Simon?" he asked the aide.

"Stinks like a trap to me," the aide said. His face was so ratlike as to be cartoonish, and for a second I suspected I was caught in one of my suppressed dreams. "I think they's some sorta spies."

"That's how I see it," the General agreed. "Some sort of distraction to let the machine-man sneak in, maybe."

"I am who I say I am," Deborah countered. "An evangelist to the tribes."

"Evangelist." The General laughed. "Where's the Lieutenant's pompadour hairstyle and diamond pinkie rings? Where's your hair-sprayed wig and painted face, blondie? Did you drive here in a Mercedes? I should send you to Flowers. Then you would know what evangelists are. Or what they used to be, back when there was still television."

"We Patriots are the true church, woman," Mr. Simon chimed in. "We are the sword of a vengeful Lord."

"I should have you both shot," the General said. "Or I could trade you, girlie, to Flowers. And believe me, you would rather be shot."

The aide stepped nearer and whispered loudly in the commander's ear. "Ah, General, we're getting a mite short on women 'bout here. I kinda think we should keep 'er." Lust dripped from his lips like snake venom.

"But what if she's part of a trap?" the General countered. "She could lead the machine-man here."

"The machine-man knows we're here," the aide replied. "He doesn't attack us cuz we got superior firepower."

It was evident the General was only a figurehead. The crafty aide, Mr. Simon, was the real leader.

"Yes, of course," the General agreed. "You're right. We'll keep the woman. She'll make a good hostage or bargaining chip. But what do we do with the AWOL lieutenant?"

"Certainly he can't be trusted," Mr. Simon suggested, his eyes drilling me with hate. "He went AWOL from one army. He could betray us as well. If we need trade bait, let it be him."

"Who'd want him?"

"The machine-man."

The General lowered his voice to a whisper. "I don't know that I really want to do business with *him.*"

"Let me do it. I'll find a way to lure that ZOG agent in. Maybe we'll kill 'im. Maybe this deserter will get killed in the process."

"I-I-I don't know," the General stammered. "That's risky. Robert's left us alone for the most part. I'd hate to antagonize him."

Mr. Simon licked his dry lips. "The Cannibals, then. We'll trade the two of 'em to that witch in the mountains."

"And who'd be the go-between? You? I don't think anyone here is going to volunteer to barter with the Cannibals."

"Then we kill him and keep her," the aide suggested. "Ain't no way any of us can trust an officer of ZOG. Even an AWOL one. If he had eyes for the truth, he'd have joined us a long time ago."

The General fixed his gaze on me. "You heard Mr. Simon, Lieutenant. He thinks you can't be trusted."

"I can't be," I said.

The General smiled at my candid reply. The glint of admiration in his eye bothered me. I suspected he liked me as much as Mr. Simon liked Deborah. "Take the woman away," the General told his aide. "Lock her in the coal bin and see that no one goes near her. No one. That means you, too, Mr. Simon. Now leave us. I want to have a private talk with the army hero."

"But—" the rat-faced man protested.

"No buts. Lock her up."

I glanced at Deborah. She showed no fear. As the aide led her away, the General untied me and directed me to a chair. "Thirsty?" he asked.

"Yes."

"Bourbon? I have the real thing."

"No, thanks. Water's fine."

The General shrugged, then produced a pitcher of spring water and two glasses. My mouth and throat were parched, and I sipped the cool, sweet water slowly. The General took a seat opposite me and laid his .45 near a kerosene lamp, within his reach but out of mine. "We need to talk," he said. "I need a man like you. I don't want you shot, Lieutenant."

"Is this a recruiting session?"

"Yes." He folded his large hands. The fingers looked like entwined sausages. "You've seen my men. They're loyal but inexperienced. Weekend camps in Michigan didn't make up for real combat. They're amateurs except for Simon. He's professional, but I doubt his loyalty. He's a former Marine who knifed an officer and spent eleven years in Leavenworth. Would still be there except he escaped during the quakes." He cleared his throat and took a long drink. "I've got no officers left," he continued. "The Plague took two of them, one died mining coal, and the last one got pulled away by a bear. All we ever found was scraps of clothing and tufts of hair."

"Your sergeant is bucking for rank."

The General scowled. "He's an idiot. I keep sending him on patrols, hoping he won't come back. Seems like the last time I tried to get rid of him he encountered you."

"He said you had sent him after the Mono."

His voice dropped to a low whisper. "Truth is, I sent him and those other two out to die, Lieutenant. We're running short on food. I figured they'd encounter Robert and that'd be the end of them."

"If your food supplies are low, you don't need me," I said. "I eat too."

He shook his head. "No, I do need you. You could be a hero to these men, Lieutenant. Help restore their vision. They'd work harder. Have a goal again."

"How?"

"We know about you. You're a legend. Set fitness records at Fort Benning that won't ever be broke. Some say you were more than a Ranger, that the Ranger emblem is just a disguise."

"I don't wear any emblems," I said.

He cleared his throat and took another drink before continuing. "I know you were home on leave when the quakes hit. While you were gone, your unit was placed under ZOG command, and you refused to report back. That's mighty heroic."

"It was only a choice. Not heroism."

"The army wants you so bad that they sent the machine-man to get you. You must be important."

"I don't know why Robert is after me."

"Because you're a hero. A man of principle. Besides all that, you brought us a valuable white woman."

"Actually, she brought me."

"Let me put my spin on it, Lieutenant."

"Spin it as you want, General. I don't think she's that valuable to you. You should let her go."

"Let her go where?" he said. "You think she'd survive a day without you? Not with the Cannibals and Irreverend Flowers prowling about. Not to mention her having Robert on her tail. She's more a problem to me than anything, actually. The men will be fighting over her. Lieutenant, I wish you'd never brought her. I'll have to figure out some way to trade her to Flowers or Lady LeClair. But I'm not dealing with the machine-man. If he wants her, he'll have to get her from them. That man's a spook. And he's got gadgets."

"Your Mr. Simon doesn't seem worried about Robert."

The General chuckled. "Simon? Like a true killer he doesn't think he can be killed. He's wrong, and you and I know it. Simon's no help in this area. His blood lust is too intense. He's a mad dog. You're not. You're trained, Lieutenant. You might be the one man that'd be a match for the machine-man." The General rose, stepped behind me and placed his hands on my shoulders. "I need you," he said.

A sexual energy radiated from his greedy touch, and I realized why he'd showed no interest in Deborah. "I take it your army has a 'don't ask, don't tell' policy," I quipped.

"I have my preferences." The General's hands began massaging my neck. "And my privileges."

The handgun was now as close to me as it was to him. I was ready to make my move when someone pounded at the door.

"General," the aide yelled. "You best come outside."

"It can wait," he shouted.

"No, it can't," Mr. Simon yelled back. "You gotta see this."

The commander sighed, reached across the table, and holstered his .45. His sick, insipid eyes lingered on mine for a moment then he took me by the arm and ushered me to the door.

In the compound's plaza a circle of curious onlookers had gathered near the coal bin and a nearby root cellar. From the bin came the sweet sound of Deborah's singing. From the root cellar came wails that sounded like an enraged or wounded animal.

"What's going on out here?" the General shouted. "You brought me out because my daughter's screaming again? Shut her up. She's got half the kids screaming and crying again."

"Listen to 'er," Mr. Simon said. "She ain't ever wailed like this before. I think the woman's singin' is drivin' her nuts."

"She's been nuts," the General said.

From all over the compound came a cacophony of dog howls and barks. Some of the curs strained at chains tethered to the trailers while others ran wild and barked furiously at the door of the cellar. I looked for Dunamis. The white malamute lay quietly where it was tied.

"My God," the General said, pointing at the root cellar. "Can't someone shut her up?" The men all lowered their heads. None of them wanted to approach the cellar.

"What's going on?" I asked.

"It's my girl," the General said. "She isn't right in the head. We have to keep her confined for her own safety."

I then said something that made no sense at all, especially to me. "Put my friend in with your daughter," I told him.

The General gave me a surprised look then rubbed his chin in thought.

Mr. Simon rushed forward in a selfish frenzy. "No," he pleaded. "Your girl might kill 'er, General. She's too valuable a commodity to take that risk."

The General looked at his aide disdainfully. "I think you've got designs on our prisoner, Mr. Simon. That could cause problems. I think maybe we should follow the Lieutenant's advice. Could be he knows something we don't. Besides, this could solve more than one problem." He snapped his fingers and pointed at the bin. Three men obeyed his bidding, within moments bringing Deborah out.

"I'm putting you in that root cellar," the General told her. "My daughter is in there. I want to see if maybe you can help her. Maybe get her to shut up so we can all get some sleep."

Deborah nodded and took a deep breath. She seemed relaxed and resigned to the situation. The soldiers nervously pushed her down wooden steps to a door slanted into the earth. One unlatched the lock and the other two thrust Deborah into the darkness. Then the door was slammed shut and locked.

"My daughter has problems," the General told me. "She's had them for years, but they've been worse lately."

Suddenly an inhuman wail broke from the dark depths of the hole. It sounded twice more, and the people clustered in silent fear. Then there was silence.

"She done kilt her," Mr. Simon said. "That pretty blonde woman is dead."

"We don't know that," the General said. "It could be that it's my daughter that's dead."

The silence hung in the air like smoke. "Well, I ain't goin' to find out," Simon said. A crazed sneer cut across his face. "I'd rather be shot than go in that hole."

"Shut up," the General ordered. "You're talking about my daughter. Crazy or not, that's my flesh and blood in there."

The small crowd slowly eased away from their commander, and the dogs quivered with their tails between their legs.

For fifteen or twenty minutes we waited. The General stood as

stiff as a statue, the light from burning torches reflecting in his transfixed eyes.

Twenty minutes more. Then the singing began.

First it was Deborah's clear voice singing a modern hymn. Then
another voice. The second voice clarified, grew in strength, and began
accompanying Deborah in perfect harmony.

The General's mouth sagged. "That's my daughter," he said.
"That's my daughter singing in there."

The crowd eased closer again.

"Bring them out," he ordered. "Someone go in there and bring
them out."

No one stepped forward.

"I'll do it," I said. I moved down the steps to the door. No one
moved to stop me.

"It's the work of devils," Mr. Simon said. "They done killed the
angel. Now they're pickin' their teeth with the feathers from 'er wings."

The General snorted in contempt. "Hush up, Mr. Simon." Then
he called after me. "Boy, if you die in there, I'll see you get a military
funeral."

I pushed the door open and entered the darkness, unconcerned
with angels, devils, or military funerals. My only thoughts were
for Deborah.

CHAPTER 7

As I stepped weaponless into the root cellar's oily darkness, flash-backs of army assignments zipped through my mind: a dense jungle in Central America, a desert night in Kuwait, a mountainous cave in Lebanon. For an instant, I was truly a Ranger again, and like any loyal soldier I was looking for my partner. Rangers always had partners. But the cold realization was that hadn't been true for me. I was trained alone. Worked alone. Lived alone. No buddy system for me.

The cellar grew darker. My own thoughts grew darker as well.

Then I saw a light. It glowed for an instant before dimming. It must have been a match. "Deborah," I called softly. I sensed movement, the subtle waves of motion rippling through musty air. Within moments her hand was in mine. "Are you OK?" I whispered.

"We're fine," she replied. "Lead us out and we will follow."

I led her from the dank pit, her hand in my mine. With the other hand she led the General's daughter. We stepped into the torch-lit plaza and stunned Militia members gasped. The General's daughter was filthy. Her hair was ratted and she wore rags for clothing, but in the torchlight she glowed with hope and beauty.

"Stephanie," her father called. She ran to the General and collapsed in his meaty arms. "What's this?" he said, sobbing. "What's restored my girl?"

"The mercy of God," Deborah said.

As one body, the curious onlookers gasped and stepped back in astonishment.

The white dog brushed against my legs. I looked down. He seemed to be smiling at me. As the people pressed in, I turned to Deborah but couldn't reach her. The crowd had wrapped itself around its miracle worker. "Deborah," I yelled, pushing people aside.

Amidst that sea of need, she raised a hand and time stopped. "Come to me one by one," she commanded. The people immediately formed a long, quiet line.

"What are you doing?" I called to her.

"I'm doing my Father's business," she said.

"It's not safe," I warned.

"Life's not safe, Daniel." She laid hands on a woman, and instantly the woman shouted and fell in a faint.

I stepped back in a slow retreat, my mind scrambling to make sense of this bizarre scene. It was a carnival, with Deborah the main attraction. It was more than I could understand, more than I *wanted* to understand. But I could not deny one thing: She actually *cared* for the people.

The next few days the sideshow continued. The people pressed on Deborah continually, pleading for her touch and prayers. For many she prayed countless times. Still they returned and she allowed it. They brought their babies and small children to her. Once I even saw her lay hands on a sick dog, and later the same mutt was running around the compound like a pup.

When she wasn't praying for toothaches and sicknesses, she was answering questions about God. I caught bits of her messages and assumed she was teaching from a book, but I never saw a book or notes in her hands.

The General's daughter trailed Deborah everywhere as walking evidence, proof of the truth of Deborah's preaching. The sentries were even drawn from their perches and joined lines that stretched the length of the compound. No one seemed concerned for security.

I hung on the edges of the crowd, alert for danger and unaffected by the wailing, sobbing, laughing, shouting people. To stay vigilant I reminded myself of Robert's nearness. Once, I thought I saw him standing on a distant ridge, as tall and dark as a cedar post, as ominous as death. But it was a momentary glimpse, one caught from the corner of my eye. When I focused, he was gone and nothing remained in his place. No fence post, no tree, no shadow against a rock. Just the thin, dry air of the prairie.

Mr. Simon also worried me. He seemed to resent Deborah's influence and slunk about the crowd clutching his little Uzi like a man strangling a snake. Once, I felt his cowardly stare on my back. I looked

through people until I found his beady eyes glaring from the shadows
with the cold intentions of a weasel. But he wasn't staring at me. He
focused instead on Deborah.

I forced a confrontation with her then, physically pulling her away
from the throngs. "What are you doing?" I demanded. "The longer we
stay here the more dangerous it is."

"What's the danger?" she asked.

"Robert," I said. "And Mr. Simon." I wanted to add the Patriots
themselves if they tired of her words and demonstrations.

"Mr. Simon?"

"Yes. I don't trust him."

She pushed away from me gently. "Do me a favor, Daniel," she
said. "Play with Dunamis."

I couldn't believe my ears. She wanted me to play with the white
dog.

"Make friends with Dunamis," she requested. "The poor boy is
lonely." She returned to the people.

I made friends with the dog by accident, not because she told
me to.

Deciding to quit protecting someone who did not want protection,
I went to the river to fish. The white dog followed me. Dunamis lay on
the bank like a clump of shag rug, his coal-black eyes sparkling with
eagerness, until I eventually stroked his furry head. His tail brushed
the dusty riverbank with enthusiasm. Later, as the sun set through
venetian blinds of red and yellow ribbons, I skipped a flat stone across
the water, and the dog leaped in to chase it. Then I tossed a stick that
he retrieved and dropped happily at my feet, his eyes glistening with
joy. "OK, we play," I said. I tossed sticks until my arm was sore, but I

couldn't wear the white dog out. "Enough," I said finally and returned to the camp, the malamute bouncing behind me. Whether I liked it or not, the dog had bonded to me.

During the day's heat I snatched naps in the root cellar. At night I prowled the starlit ridges or stood silent guard in high, rocky crevices. Deborah shared a bedroom with the General's daughter, and I occassionally glimpsed her shadowy form behind curtains. She was always out of my touch, beyond my reach.

The morning of our sixth day in the compound I returned from a night's watch and found her waiting for me in the plaza. "It is time for us to leave," she said. "My work is finished here." Dunamis was already hitched to the loaded travois.

I was more than ready to go. "So it's check-out time," I said. "Have you paid the phone bill?"

"I put it on my Visa," she retorted.

The General told us goodbye with the thankfulness of a father whose only child had been returned from hell. The rest of the compound remained asleep except Mr. Simon. I glimpsed him staring angrily at us from a window, but when he caught my eye he ducked back.

General Jerry was a blubbering mess as he tried to express his appreciation.

"You needn't thank me," Deborah told him. "I ask only that you welcome those who come behind me."

"There are people coming?" he asked hopefully.

"Yes. Prepare for an invasion by an army of mercy."

"An army of mercy," he said. "We've been prepared for everything except that."

The General tried to thank me too. "Come back, Lieutenant," he urged, trying to pull me into a hug. "Come back and see us."

I stiff-armed him and walked away. Deborah scolded me later. "You could have been more polite," she said. "He was our host."

"That was my best effort," I said. "I didn't punch him or anything."

"You judge too harshly, Daniel. The General's not evil."

"How about his sexual preferences?" I asked. "Or didn't you notice?"

"That's been taken care of," she said.

"Taken care of?"

"Yes. That which was bent has been made straight."

"But—"

"Do you want to know more?" she asked. "Are you ready for deeper questions and answers?"

I shook my head. Somehow I knew answers would require something from me. Something I was not willing to spend. Or share.

"No? Then let's move on. How far to the 'Postates?"

"Five, six days to the southwest," I told her.

"Fine. Lead on, Daniel. And I'll follow."

We walked silently for several miles, but I finally had to voice my opinions. "You think this will be easy, don't you?" I said. "The 'Postates are worse than the Patriots. They hate Monotheists. Flowers is a madman. Besides that, Robert is out there somewhere waiting for us."

She gave me a look as flat as the plains and as turbulent as a thunderhead. "I don't expect things to be easy," she said. "I just expect things to be done."

"You're stubborn," I told her.

"No," she argued. "I'm determined. There's a difference." She continued walking.

And you're lovely when you're angry, I wanted to tell her. But I didn't.

We hiked restlessly through a vastness where houses were rare. When the stars came out, we were miles from the compound, alone on the prairie sea. I noticed she was limping more. "We better stop," I said.

"I'm not tired," she answered.

"I am." We halted on a rocky ridge above miles of nothingness. She leaned back against the travois and gazed up at the canopy of heaven.

"You shouldn't push yourself so hard," I told her.

"I have work to do. Places to go. People to see."

"We are in the most remote part of the Interior. There is no one around for miles."

"There are people around," she said. "Or else I wouldn't be here."

I shook my head in resignation. It was impossible to reason with the woman.

"There are so many stars," she said, still staring heavenward. "You hardly ever see stars in the cities. Too many fires, I guess." She released a long sigh and her defenses lowered like a drawbridge. "It's hard to stare at stars and not dream," she said.

I sensed romance in the air. Opportunity. "And what are your dreams?" I asked.

"I have died to my own dreams," she said. "But I used to dream about having a family. A husband, children. All the things any normal woman would want."

"Why give them up?"

"For a greater purpose." She sighed again and the drawbridge closed. "How about you, Daniel? What do you see when you look at the stars?"

"Little points of light, nothing more."

"No dreams?"

"I only dream of horses."

"Horses aren't a dream for you, they're a goal. A dream is something else, something magical and just out of reach. Something woven together with wishes and faith."

"Then I have no dreams," I said. "I don't believe in magic." But I did have a dream, even then, and she was the focus of it. Even so, I lacked the courage to tell her.

She stretched out an arm and pointed toward a far horizon that cut into the black velvet skyline. "What's that, Daniel?" she asked. "Is there a light on that distant hill?"

I raised my rifle and searched through the telescopic sights until I found an orange and yellow glow. "Fire," I said. "Someone's campfire."

"How far?" she asked.

I looked at her suspiciously. "Three miles," I said. "Maybe four."

She rose with dogged determination. "Let's go," she said. "We need to see who it is."

"But—"

"Don't tell me it's Robert. If everything I've heard about him is true, he doesn't make fires. Besides, he's behind us, isn't he? The fire's in front of us."

"You know it's not safe."

"Life's not safe, Daniel," she said. "Haven't I told you that already?"

We arrived within two hours. "Hello to the camp," Deborah called out.

The six people around the fire stared wide-eyed in our direction. I didn't see any firearms, but I kept mine ready just in case.

"We are coming in," Deborah said. "We mean you no harm."

The three men and three women huddled together, the glow of a large bonfire reflecting in their startled eyes. They all wore robes, and the women's heads were covered with scarves. "Who are you?" a tall, bald man asked. "Are you from this planet or are you the ones we await?"

"My name is Deborah," she said, approaching as if entering a friend's living room. "And with me is Daniel. We are from this planet."

Five pairs of disappointed eyes turned to the bald man, the obvious leader. The fire roared, fueled by a stack of cedar fence posts. Encircling it, a dozen rock monuments stood like stone men. "We've interrupted some sort of ceremony," I whispered to Deborah.

"Good," she said curtly. She approached them. "Are you waiting for someone?" she asked.

"We await the Mother Ship," the leader said profoundly.

Great, I thought. *UFO nuts. Space cadets.* "You're just going to attract Robert," I said. "Do you know who Robert is?"

"He doesn't exist," the baldy answered.

"What makes you think that?" I challenged.

"Because we won't allow him to exist," the man said acidly.

"So," Deborah said, "you've built a fire so the Mother Ship will find you and pick you up?"

"It is time," the leader said. The others nodded rhythmically.

"You're not on your way to New Seattle?" I asked. "New Mu?"

"That's a myth," a woman spoke angrily from the huddle. "It's a terrible deception perpetrated by the government to keep mortals earthly minded. The Interior is full of myths. There's no Robert. No New Mu. No New Seattle."

"That's true," the leader said. "We've been to the New Coast. We took the southern route, aided by the Polygamists. There is no New Lemuria. If you are Pilgrims, I urge you to go no farther. Stay here with us. The Kingdom of Heaven comes in a wheel within a wheel. The Mother Craft, piloted by Ezekiel himself, comes tonight."

"Why out here in the middle of nowhere?" I asked.

The leader looked at me angrily. "They come first only for the elect, the chosen," he said.

"And you're the chosen," I said.

"We are." The dancing fire painted his face with a red glow and cutting black shadows. "Ezekiel returns for us, then we'll return later with more ships for the other believers."

Deborah turned to me, her face like flint. She was ready to roll up her sleeves and go to work. "I think it's going to be a busy night," she said. "What would you like to do? Stay in the darkness and keep an eye out for Robert?"

"That makes sense to me," I said. "I'm not a deacon in the First Church of the Demented."

"You stand guard," she said. "Just don't get too paranoid."

I retreated into the folds of the night, leaving her to the labors of evangelism. Paranoid? What did she mean by *paranoid*?

I stayed awake for hours, certain the bright fire would attract my nemesis. While I watched for Robert, I also observed the curious assembly beside the fire. The tall man ranted and gestured wildly, but

Deborah sat and peacefully reasoned with the people. She was slowly wooing several away from the leader. The ignored fire finally dimmed. My eyes grew heavy and I allowed myself some sleep.

Dawn hinted pink in the eastern sky when Deborah awakened me. "Come," she said. "Let's be going. Quiet. Don't awaken anyone." The six were wrapped like mummies in old blankets and sleeping bags around the smoldering coals.

I felt chagrined for having slept so soundly then awakened by my charge. "Your work here is done?" I whispered.

"I planted seeds," she said. "Others will water."

"Did you sleep?"

"No."

"Aren't you tired?" I asked.

"No," she said. "I feel fine."

We crept quietly away. "So how did you do?" I asked. "Did you convert the space cadets?"

"Those who had ears heard," she said. "But there is no reasoning with the unreasonable." The edge to her answer seemed directed at me personally.

We trudged on, reeling in the landscape as though it were a long roll of brown paper. Deborah didn't seem to tire, but when we stopped to rest during the afternoon I knew she was more fatigued than she showed.

"I hope we find a house tonight," she said. "I could use a good night's sleep."

"You could sleep just as well outside," I mentioned.

"No, Daniel. I sleep in houses. You should try it sometime."

"My house is made of earth and sky," I said. "The stars are my night-lights." I waited to see if my prose had impressed her. It hadn't. She had dozed off.

Hunger was eating me from the inside out. In Ranger training I'd endured days and nights without sleep. Runs of forty and fifty miles across deserts, mountains, and swamps. Meals of insects and plant roots. And I'd always come out on top. But Deborah's paced persistence was wearing me down. I was tired and very hungry.

I left her to find food. We were outside my turf, so there were no more caches to raid. I had to kill something. I also wanted to check my backtrail. I sensed that someone was following us. It had to be Robert. Once again I thought I saw him, a distant, fleeting figure on a far ridge. If the Patriots were right and Robert had orders to kill Deborah, why didn't he simply overtake us and do it? Did he fear me? Respect me? Possibly, but I doubted it. He was only toying with us, justifying his own existence by prolonging the hunt.

The sweet smell of roasting meat drifted on the air. I returned to our camp and found Deborah roasting a large bird over a small fire. "What's this?" I asked.

"Quail, I think. Some sort of quail. I don't know the area birds very well."

"Where did it come from?"

She looked up at me and smiled.

"No, don't say it," I said. "Don't ask if I am ready for answers."

"Are you?"

"No. And I don't care where the bird came from." I ate hungrily. So did Dunamis.

We continued across a dry and colorless canvas of prairie, then chanced upon an old cow camp just before twilight. No mailbox or front gates. Just a shack on the hardpan prairie. Years of windblown sand had stripped it of paint, giving the building a skinned look. The chimney had crumbled to the ground in a small pile of soft, broken brick. Windows of shattered glass and ripped screens stared like vacant eyes, and a porch of broken planks extended an ominous greeting. There was no garage or machine sheds, only a rickety corral and the tumbling remains of a stack yard for hay.

"Who could have lived here?" Deborah asked. "This wasn't much of a home. There are no swing sets or basketball hoops. Not even any power poles."

"No one lived here," I explained. "It was a summer camp for cowboys." When I reached for the screen door, it fell off its hinges. Inside, the wooden floors were warped and faded, and the low ceiling was laced with spider webs. Knife marks notched the kitchen table, and gaping cupboard doors exposed empty shelves.

Two cast-iron bed frames with worn springs and thin, moth-eaten mattresses crowded a tiny bedroom. C. M. Russell prints hung on crumbling plasterboard walls. Their glass and frames were stained with insect droppings.

Deborah followed my gaze around the shack. "A Holiday Inn for cowboys," she said. "Looks like your kind of place, Daniel. This is almost as good as being outside."

I gave her an impatient look. "If you're suggesting I sleep inside, you're nuts."

"Not here, either?" she sighed.

"Not here, either."

"Most men would welcome my company," she challenged. "I would be fighting them off."

"It doesn't have anything to do with you," I said. "Or the weird things you do."

"You're right. It has to do with memories, doesn't it?"

"I don't know what you're talking about."

"The big, brave Ranger who is afraid of houses? Come on, Daniel. Something's not right here."

"I'm your guide. Not your latest project."

She held up her hands. "OK, I give up. And I apologize. If you insist on sleeping outside, I should be thankful and welcome the space." She began her duties.

I stomped outside and sulked. How come the one person I wanted to be close to was so demanding? Why couldn't she be content with the physical world of survival, building, procreating, and planting? Why was she so obsessed with the internal?

Maybe I could meet her halfway. I walked back into the shack and found her sitting in a corner with a lit candle, her head leaning against the wall, her eyes closed.

"I refuse to live in the past," I declared. "Old houses are the past. When I want to stay in a house, I will build a new one."

Her blue eyes slowly opened. "What lightning bolt struck you?" she asked.

I waved my hands defensively, and my rifle barrel struck a wall. "Well, you wanted to know. You're always bugging me about why I won't stay in houses. That's why."

"Is it?" she asked. "What's so bad about the past? What's so scary about the memories? You've seen more tragedy than most people, Daniel, but you've been prepared for tragedy. There's death and destruction everywhere. No one alive today has good memories."

"It's not about memories," I argued. "It's about perspective. I'm looking forward. To goals. To fresh starts."

"You live like a caveman."

I couldn't argue that. "But that's not the point," I said, leaning against the bare wall. I live the way I do—short-term—for a long-term benefit. I'm staying alive. I'm looking for a horse. When I find one, I'll tame it. Then I will use it to hunt game and capture more horses."

"You sound like you're working your way through college."

"And what's wrong with that?"

"Nothing. You're just so goal-oriented."

"Me? How about you? Walk all day. Go to the Patriots. Go to the 'Postates. Find a house. Sleep in it. Your whole life is a series of little goals."

"But my goals aren't about me," she said. "This isn't my dream."

"No," I said rudely. "You're more noble." I saw the hurt in her eyes. "I'm sorry," I said. "That was low."

She patted the floor beside her. "Sit down," she pleaded. "Just for a minute."

"Why?"

"Because I'm asking you. Please."

I sighed, slid down the wall, and sat cross-legged with my rifle across my thighs. "OK?" I said. "Now what?"

"Talk to me."

"We've been talking."

"No. Really talk to me. About yourself. Do you have any brothers and sisters?"

"No. I was an only child."

"Did your father want you to be in the service?"

"Yeah. It was planned for me since the womb."

"We have that in common," she said. "But a different sort of army. I was homeschooled through high school, graduated from college at nineteen, then did a year's training in a church program. A spiritual boot camp."

"So we're the same?" I asked sarcastically.

"Not the same but similar."

The sky darkened, and the room—lit only by the candle glowing between us—grew dim. "I gotta go," I said. "I have to be outside."

She smiled softly. "Thank you for staying as long as you did."

"And for the stimulating conversation," I added.

"Yes. And for the stimulating conversation."

"I guess you have to do your thing now. Or continue doing it. The prayers and stuff, I mean." I was shifting to rise when I heard a soft creak of the boards on the front porch.

Deborah stiffened.

I brought a finger to my lips. "Someone's out there," I whispered.

A faint flicker of fear lit her eyes, and she glanced toward the entryway. The malamute pricked his ears.

A knock sounded on the door.

It was such a usual sound, so civilized, that we looked at each other in disbelief. I moved softly to the door and stood with my rifle barrel against the jamb.

The knock sounded again. The distinctive rapping of knuckles against wood.

I reached for the knob.

CHAPTER 8

"You open it, then step back quickly," I told Deborah. I readied my rifle.

"No," she said. "Open the door but lower your gun."

"Lower my gun?" I whispered in a thin hiss. "It could be Robert."

"It's not," she said. "Trust me."

The knocking sounded again.

I looked at her suspiciously. Then I leaned the rifle against a window jamb and opened the door to the thin, callow face of Mr. Simon. "You!" I pulled him through the entryway and flung him against the opposite wall. Deborah shouted and rushed forward, stopping me from unsheathing my knife.

"Don't!" She grabbed my arm. I could have tossed her aside easily, but there was no threat in Simon's face, only humiliation and fear. I stepped back.

Deborah lit another candle and approached the man. "What are you doing here?" she asked.

His pitiful, stubbled face wrinkled with desperation. "I heard you talkin' 'bout forgiveness back in the compound," he whined. "You suppose God could forgive a man like me? Ah've kilt other men. Several of 'em."

"There are no limits to his mercy," she said.

"You're the one who's been following us?" I asked. "You haven't seen Robert?"

"I ain't seen no one," he said, "'cept those space cadets on the hill. You sure got 'em all stirred up," he told Deborah. "Five of 'em are talkin' Jesus and fixin' to go back to where they came from, but the bald-headed guy is tryin' to make 'em stay."

"You've followed us since we left the General," Deborah said. "Why didn't you approach us earlier?"

He shrugged. "Tryin' to screw up some courage, ah suppose. If you was to say I can't be forgiven there'd be nuthin' left for me, 'cept scroungin' like a Babbler, or endin' it all by huntin' down the machine-man and lettin' him finish me. I can't stay in the compound. They all prayin' all the time and singin', and I stick out like a yeller melon in a garden of greens."

"There is grace for you, Mr. Simon," Deborah said. "It may take time to confess your sins, but we have time. We have all night." She looked at me. "And what are you going to do, Daniel?"

"You know what I'm going to do," I said. "I'll be on guard in the dark."

I found shelter in a corner of the rickety corrals, but it was hard to find solace, knowing the weasly Mr. Simon was pouring out his putrid soul to the woman I loved. That was the first time I admitted it. *I love her,* I said to myself. Then I got up the gumption to whisper it. "I love her." Even as I did, I was afraid someone would hear. Several times during that long night I crept close to the house and peered in. Each time it was the same: Mr. Simon was either on his knees or his face, bawling like a baby, with Deborah kneeling over him, either barking out orders like a drill sergeant or speaking soft and soothingly. This went on for hours.

I was exhausted but slept little. My mind focused on her. My passion for Deborah was becoming a distraction. I had to have her or leave her, but she'd given no indications of sharing my feelings. In fact, she seemed above human love. *She should be a nun in a convent,* I told myself. *If we only lived in times when there were nuns, when there were convents.*

In the morning I found Deborah alone in the house, asleep on a cot, the white dog on the floor beside her. I moved stealthily through the building, searching for the Militia killer, but he wasn't there. Outside I searched the premises. Deborah finally awakened and found me.

"Where is he?" I asked.

"He's gone," she said. "He went back to the Patriots."

"In the middle of the night?"

"Early this morning."

Simon had passed by me and I hadn't known. I cursed myself for my lack of vigilance. He could have easily killed me. Why didn't he? Didn't he detest me as much as I detested him?

"You don't care much for him, do you?" she asked.

"He's a killer," I said. But before I could erect a statue to my own self-righteousness, I saw a single canoe listing in murky water and six Cannibals fading from sight. I was a killer too.

"He *was* a killer," she corrected me. "He is not a killer anymore."

"How do you know?" I challenged.

"Because I know who changed him," she said.

Arguing with her made as much sense as whittling iron. "You should be a redhead," I told her. "You have the disposition."

Her vague look told me that was the strangest comment she had heard in a long time. "We need to find the 'Postates," she said. "You lead and I will follow."

We walked on and on, low on food and sleep. For me the task was a fatiguing duty. An aching weariness had invaded my bones and sucked the power from my muscles. But for Deborah the march was a crusade, a pilgrimage. She looked drawn at times but she never complained or slackened her pace. When the sun rose high, glaring like a torch, we finally rested under the only shelter within miles—a dead cottonwood tree.

"You have been limping more," I told her.

"Have I?"

"Yes, you have," I said. "May I ask how you got it?"

"It was given to me as a sign because the Word says the lame shall be a remnant."

My look must have been as vacant as the landscape. What word? What remnant?

"You don't understand, do you?" she said.

"No."

"You know nothing about the Bible?"

"I was raised by the Uniform Code of Military Justice." I turned the subject back to her infirmity. "You didn't really answer my question."

"Would you believe me if I told you I wrestled with an angel?"

"No. But did you?"

She tossed her head back and laughed. "No, I'm sorry. I was teasing you. It wasn't anything dramatic. I got hit by a car as a kid, chasing a ball into the street."

"I would have believed the angel story," I told her.

"You would have tried to believe it," she said. "Words mean little to you, Daniel. That's OK. In fact, I like that about you." She smiled and I felt my aches and pains begin to wane. "Go to sleep, Daniel. If words mean little to you, perhaps wonders will mean more."

"What are you talking about?"

"Rest," she said. Reaching down, she untied my shoes and removed them and my socks. "Rest," she said again.

I laid back on the dry soil, stared up at the smooth, white skeleton of the tree, and angled my face into the shade cast by its bare limbs. The heat of the day smothered me, its slight breeze born from a furnace.

I'll never sleep, I told myself.

I awakened several hours later, my eyes opening to a canopy of rustling, scintillating green. For a moment I imagined I was in Ranger scuba training, submerged in tropical waters, staring up from warm depths to a surface where sunlight sparkled on slowly undulating ripples. The swirls of green whistled and parted, and a single ray of light stabbed my eyes.

I blinked and looked again. Green leaves. Against my head, where I had rested on the smooth, polished skeleton of a hideless tree, I felt the rough, corduroy texture of cottonwood bark. I rolled over onto my hands and knees and gaped at the tree in stunned confusion. "It's alive," I said.

Deborah was retying the bundle on the travois. "The Word in action," she said.

"How?" I asked. The tree had been dead for years, but the ground beneath me was bare, no sheddings of dry twigs, bark, or branches.

"*How* is not the right question." She rose to continue our journey, but I remained on my hands and knees, doglike in posture, stonelike in my understanding.

"What is?" I asked. *"Why?"*

"No, *Who. Who* is the right question. But come, we must be going. You lead and I will follow."

We traveled for two more days, our pace slowing only because of my exhaustion. While I grew noticeably weaker, both Deborah and the Malamute remained strong. Water was scarce and food seemed impossible. I would have eaten any animal I could find but saw none. I even began wishing wolves would find us. "Have you ever eaten wolf?" I asked Deborah.

She wrinkled her nose. "No. I suppose you have?"

"Several times. During the winter. It's tough and stringy."

"Are you hungry enough to eat wolf now?" she asked.

"I'd eat one raw," I said.

She laughed and petted the white dog. "I think you're making Dunamis nervous."

"I wouldn't eat your dog," I said.

"I know. I was only teasing."

"I don't know how you brought that tree to life," I told her. "But I wish it had been an apple tree."

"The 'Postates will feed us," she said.

"The 'Postates might sell us to the Cannibals."

"Then the Cannibals will feed us."

"No, the Cannibals will *eat* us."

"Really, Daniel," she said. "You can be so pessimistic."

She spent the nights in two more houses, and each time I lingered a little longer before leaving the building. One night I slept on the roof of an old barn and wished I were in the house with her. But I wanted a different *her*. I was scared of the woman who lit candles and prayed prayers I couldn't understand. I was becoming suspicious of the glow that grew after an hour or two of her blessings. Maybe she was some sort of witch. But then, better for her to be a witch, I decided, than a saint I could not have.

Seven days after leaving the Patriot camp we crested a pine-topped hill and looked down at a small semicircular settlement where the people bustled like ants. Subterranean buildings faced the sun-exposed south. In the plaza stood a twelve-foot-high wooden statue of a man with his head and right arm raised to the sky. The carving of Irreverend Flowers, fashioned from a massive cedar tree, rose from a giant granite base. As the people passed by, they rubbed the icon's knees. The kneecaps glistened from the many polishings.

"This is a well-planned community," Deborah said. "They have several wind turbines. Solar heating. Cisterns. Greenhouses. The wind turbines must provide some basic electricity. I wonder what they use the electricity for? What would you use it for, Daniel?"

"An electric toothbrush," I joked. I was not interested in evaluating their technologies. I was more concerned with their defenses.

"All the lodging is underground, so they stay cool in the summer and warm in the winter," she added. "These are very bright people."

"These are very dangerous people," I reminded her. "Dangerous because they're bright. And dangerous because they're dumb enough to follow Flowers."

"Some people just have blocks in their minds, Daniel. Blocks that keep them from seeing and hearing the truth."

"And you're determined to blow the blocks out of these people's minds."

"I don't know what I'm here to do," she said. "I'm only glad that we have finally found them."

"And they've found us," I said, pointing across the way to sentinels in a tree stand. Sunlight reflected off their rifle scopes. "We are in their crosshairs."

Moments later two guards met us. They were better armed than the Patriots—one had a customized Colt AR-15 with a thirty-round clip, the other a Mauser bolt action with a heavy barrel and a twenty-power sniper scope—but I preferred the Patriots' clothing. These men wore blue floral-patterned robes tied at the waist with a scarlet sash. Below the sash a heavy leather belt carried ammo packs, knives, and handcuffs. The taller guard, the one in command, had salt-and-pepper hair and beard. The shorter one was a redhead with cold green eyes.

"Who are you?" the leader asked us politely. His full beard was trimmed to about an inch, and his teeth were clean and white. "What are you doing here?"

As Deborah extended her hand in greeting, the guards eyed her suspiciously. "My name is Deborah," she said, her hand still extended. "And this is Daniel. We have come to visit Mr. Flowers and his people."

"*The Most Irreverend Flowers*," the redhead corrected her.

"The Most Irreverend Flowers," she said and smiled.

The taller of the two men shook Deborah's hand.

I offered neither of the guards my hand, nor did they offer me theirs. I had already evaluated my ability to kill them if necessary.

"What are your names?" Deborah asked.

"Our names are not important," the leader answered. "Come along." He took the point, and his subordinate fell in at the rear.

There was an order and uniformity in Flowers's camp that the Patriots had lacked. No barking dogs. No sulking underlings or emaciated wives. No faded camo clothing. All the people wore colored robes indicating their status or duty, we learned. Laborers, such as the men busy on a construction project, wore navy blue robes tucked into their belts. The men and women working in the greenhouses and gardens wore green robes. All the men sported full, precisely-groomed beards, and the women's brightly scrubbed faces showed hints of lipstick and eye shadow.

The premises were tidy, landscaped with rock fascia, vines, and flowers. A stream flowed through the center of their camp. I memorized the layout and looked for possible escape routes. There were few. The compound was designed to funnel traffic toward armed sentinels. Only the men wearing scarlet sashes carried weapons, an eclectic assortment—besides the AR-15 and Mauser, I saw a Ruger No. IV with a Nikon scope, a Ruger Mini 14 similar to my own, and two Browning automatic rifles. Only the leaders, or officers, carried handguns. Glocks. Model 17s.

We passed beneath the carved totem of Flowers—the guards rubbed a kneecap in homage—and stopped in front of the main building. At the guards' request, I handed over my rifle and knife. They asked if I had anything else. When I shook my head, they nodded and walked away.

The door opened and a tall, slender man with gray beard, silver hair, and piercing black eyes stepped out. His robe and sash were golden. I'd seen Flowers on television years before, but he hardly looked like the same man. His hair was brown then and swept back in a pretentious pompadour above a full, fleshy face.

"Greetings," he said. His full, deep voice was more recognizable than his appearance. "Please come in."

"My dog?" Deborah asked.

He waved his hand and two young men with green sashes trotted over.

"Your animal will be fed, groomed, and watered," Flowers said. "We like animals."

His speech and actions were decidedly polite, but I knew that beneath the gold robe lay a devious, lecherous heart that beat with the cold calculations of a wolf. I feared for Deborah.

Flowers led us to a large sunken room—a classroom or meeting hall—with padded concrete slabs as pews. The surrounding walls held a garish exhibition of photographs of Flowers with young women and children of the compound. There were no pictures of him with any of the men. Flowers seated himself and gestured for us to sit across from him.

Almost magically, from one of several dark hallways, a woman in a red robe appeared, carrying a tray with three large drinks. She served Flowers first, then Deborah and me. We both thanked her, but she neither met our eyes nor responded. She simply slipped away on slippered feet.

"Drink up," Flowers said. "There are no formalities here." He sipped slowly, his eyes staring through a thin veneer of sophistication that masked a ribald savagery.

The glass was smooth and cool to the touch, and I was so parched I drank eagerly, disregarding any threat of poisoning or drugging. The drink was an herbal tea with a dash of lemon juice.

"We thank you for your hospitality," Deborah said.

He held up one hand. "Shh," he said. "You can thank me later." Two pretty young girls entered, carrying a large tray of dried fruit between them. They stood silently before us, their heads bowed. "Partake," Flowers said. We nibbled on dried apple and banana chips. I was ravenous, but I felt uncomfortable eating with the two girls standing there like statues and Flowers staring at us. When we had eaten our fill, the girls left, then quickly returned with stainless steel water bowls and towels. They began removing our shoes. I was shocked. I knew my feet, shoes, and socks smelled like rancid coyote bait.

Flowers noticed my embarrassment and smiled. "It is their pleasure to wash your feet," he said. "Enjoy it."

Deborah accepted the act gracefully, but I remained uncomfortable. When our feet were clean and dried, the girls brought fresh water and washed our hands and faces with soft, delicate pattings, then left noiselessly.

"Are you refreshed?" Flowers asked.

"Much better, thank you," Deborah answered.

"Now, then," Flowers said, "to what do I owe the honor of a visit from the infamous Lieutenant and his pretty young companion?"

"You know who I am?" I said.

"Our mutual friend, Catfish, has described you to me," he explained. "Besides, you wear faded military clothing, but you're too strong and bright to be a Patriot." He turned his eyes on Deborah. "And you must be the Mono," he said. "The missionary to the vast wasteland of the Interior."

"My name is Deborah," she said.

"You are a beautiful woman," he told her.

I wished I could slit his lascivious throat.

She did not respond.

He turned his eyes back to me. "You know, Lieutenant, I had imagined you as a larger man. A man of—how do I say this?—a more *physical* presence."

"I was bigger once," I said.

He laughed. "You have retained a sense of humor, Lieutenant. That's a sign of physical and mental well-being. I have heard much about you—you are a legend in this land. It's rumored you've been to the New Coast. I would be most interested in hearing your stories. What does the New Coast look like?"

"It looks like the old one," I said. "Except it's five hundred miles to the east."

"And Lady LeClair, how did you avoid her and her Cannibals?"

"I gave them a wide berth."

"You must have passed near here as well," he noted.

"I gave you a wide berth too," I said, letting him see the contempt in my eyes.

He smiled condescendingly, leaned back, and folded his hands. "You're not gifted with social skills, are you, Lieutenant? How about Robert? Can you tell me stories about him?"

"I know little about him."

"Oh, is that right? I am most intrigued by the stories I've heard. Some say he lives in a concrete dome that looks like a gumbo hill, but inside it's filled with high-tech equipment. Supposedly the power is provided by an amplification of his own brain's electricity. Have you heard this?"

"Sounds like a story Catfish told after he'd eaten his own muffins," I said.

Flowers laughed. "And good muffins they are. But back to Robert. We know his infrared face shield can magnify objects miles away, in daylight or at night. But what interests me most is his buckle. Have you heard about the buckle, Lieutenant?"

"I've heard a couple of tall tales," I said.

"Well, let me explain it to your friend," he said, winking at Deborah. "Robert's belt is linked to his nervous system with the buckle engrafted into his skin. When he's torturing someone, a dial on the buckle slowly rises, like a thermometer on an oven. When it hits the red zone, he kills, and synthetic adrenaline and endorphins are released into his body. A plastic orgasm, if you will."

"You seem to know a lot about Robert," I said. "But do you know the myths or the truths?"

Flowers countered my parry. "It's no myth that Robert is terrorizing the Interior because of you, is it, Lieutenant?"

"Then why hasn't he found me?" I asked.

"Yes, why not? You must be very skilled, Lieutenant. Some even believe that Robert is afraid of you, that you are capable of even killing him."

"You find this fascinating, don't you?" Deborah interjected. I wasn't sure if her question was for me or for him.

Flowers grinned. "Of course, I do. My flock is based on control and pleasure—my personal pleasure. This Robert individual, with or without his magic belt, seems to embody control and pleasure. I envy him."

"Perhaps you can recruit him," I said sarcastically. "Are you accepting new members?"

"There's always room for more," he said. "Robert would make a valuable addition to my security staff."

"And us?" I asked. "Are you going to recruit us?"

His smile darkened the room. "No," he said. "I am going to kill you."

"Both of us?" I asked.

"No, Lieutenant. Just you. I have other uses for your pretty friend."

I repressed an urge to strangle him, knowing he was too clever not to have armed guards nearby. Their weapons were probably trained on me at that moment.

"If you must kill, kill me," Deborah said. "Let Daniel go. He is only my guide."

"Only a guide?" Flowers said, mocking us. "All that time out there, just the two of you, alone beneath the prairie sky, and he is only a guide? My, my, Lieutenant. Perhaps you are not the man I thought you were."

"Do what you have to do," I told him.

"What I have to do," he said, "is crucify you. Upside down. And burn you alive. We're having a little toga party this evening—I'll be

Nero, of course, or perhaps Caligula—and you shall provide our illumination."

"And me?" Deborah asked.

"More illumination!" He laughed and patted his hands together. "The Lieutenant will illuminate our garden party with his physical sacrifice. You, my lovely young Mono wench, shall enlighten it with your mind." Restraint had broken in Flowers's mind, and craziness was spilling out.

"What do you mean?" she asked.

"A debate. Like Mars Hill." He looked at me. "That's a biblical reference, Lieutenant, in case you are scripturally illiterate." He turned back to Deborah. "You and I will debate while your friend roasts. Monotheism against polytheism. Of course, I'm not really a Poly but it's illegal to be anything else. I'm a Mono, too, actually. I worship Self. Namely my Self, not anyone else's. But I will win the debate because I'm the judge. Afterward you will be reeducated and initiated into our little group. Fresh bloodlines are needed here. The power is in the blood, you know."

"You have fallen a long way," Deborah observed.

He gave her a cold stare. "I have not fallen at all," he said. "I have risen. I have risen from the deep, dark pit of shallow and intolerant theology to a liberating and vibrant truth. But enough!" he shouted. "We will not talk of that now. Save it for the debate, Mono. You will need all of your cleverness then." He began to rise.

"Grant me one request," she asked.

He looked at her with mock acquiescence. "Certainly," he said. "I can surely condescend to your petty desires. What do you want? Time alone to pray?"

"A wager," she said. "On the outcome of the debate."

"A wager?" He laughed. "I've already told you I am the judge. You have no way of winning."

"Bet me." Her eyes were cool with challenge.

He smiled with the excitement of a predator smelling blood. "OK. What are we wagering?"

"Daniel's life," she said. "Let him live until the debate is over, and set him free if I win."

"If you win? How vain. You can't win."

"Bet me," she insisted.

Flowers turned to me. "The woman would rescue you, Lieutenant," he said. "And I thought you were supposed to be the hero. If you married her, she'd have you sweeping floors and doing windows."

"I'd gladly sweep her floors and do her windows," I said.

The possessiveness in my voice angered him. "Say goodbye to your Mono friend," he growled at me. "My security staff is coming for you both."

"What about the bet?" Deborah asked.

"It's on," he snapped. "The bet's on. But now there's work to be done. You, woman, will be bathed and made presentable. And you, Lieutenant. You have a date with a cross."

He clapped his hands twice and guards entered the room. I was taken one way, Deborah another.

"Be at peace," I thought I heard her call after me.

Be at peace? A crucifixion awaited me.

Be at peace?

CHAPTER 9

The two guards who had first arrested Deborah and me escorted me to a single-room cell. "Strip," the redhead ordered.

I pulled off my shirt and fatigue bottoms.

"Everything," he said. "Buck-naked everything."

I removed all my clothing, and the guards began sewing me into the garment of my dreams. Horsehide. The irony made me smile.

"What's so amusing?" the guard with the gray-flecked beard asked.

"My goal has been to catch a horse," I told him. "Now it appears the horse has caught me."

He scowled with a grave, disbelieving look and waved the other guard away. "Go get some men to wheel the cross to the plaza," he told him.

The redhead glared and started to argue. "Go," his superior said. The subordinate turned and left. The guard captain waited a few moments until the man's steps receded and a door closed. Then the captain looked up at me with intense eyes. "Do you understand what is about to happen to you?" he asked.

"I'm the evening entertainment," I said.

"And why do you take this so lightly? Are you as crazed as everyone else?" He tugged tightly on whang leather that laced the horsehide tight between my shoulders. I suspected he was breaking protocol by talking to me.

"Who are you?" I asked. "You're not one of Flowers's disciples."

"My name's Stinson," he whispered. "I'm ATF. I infiltrated the cult years ago when Flowers was still based in Atlanta."

"ATF? And you've stayed with them?"

"Where am I to go? I'm a city boy, I can't survive alone in the hills like you, Lieutenant. I'd feel safer facing Robert than facing wolves, bears, and starvation."

"Being prey is humbling," I offered.

"Then you must be a humble man," he said.

"No, I'm not." I thought of Deborah and realized I knew nothing of true humility. "What are your orders?" I asked.

"Who knows? I've lost all contact with my superiors. I have no idea if the ATF even exists anymore."

"If they do, they are probably under UN control," I said. "That's why I went AWOL. I found out I was serving the wrong master."

He came around to the front and laced the hide tight against my chest. He was similar to me. Five or six years older, but the same height, build, and professional carriage. "If I can help you escape, will you take me with you?" he asked.

"The woman has to escape too," I said.

He shook his head. "That's a long shot. Flowers will keep her under tight wraps."

"She must be part of the deal," I insisted. "And if we get out of here, we are going on to the Cannibals."

"The Cannibals! You're going farther west?"

"She leads. I follow."

He shook his head sadly. "Then there's nothing I can do to help you," he whispered. "I was hoping you and the woman were sane, but obviously you're not. You have to figure your own way out of this mess, Lieutenant."

"At least give me an edge," I said. "What's their plan for the evening?"

"Roman theater. A carnival of cruelty. You'll be lashed upside down to an inverted cross and burned alive. If you're lucky you'll die of smoke inhalation first. But Flowers doesn't like that. It's too quick."

"He wants to torture me to death?"

"He meditates to the screams of the dying."

"I don't plan on screaming."

"He'll find a way. He says the screams feed energy to his soul and inspire his poetry."

"He's a poet?"

"A terrible one. Twice a week we have to gather around his statue for his public readings. I'd almost rather be burned alive."

"No, I think you'd choose the poetry reading," I said.

His face clouded. "Sorry," he said. "I forgot this is real for you. To me it all seems like a bad dream, one I can't awaken from."

"Go with us when we leave," I said.

"Leave?" he scoffed. "You think you'll be leaving? You're crazier than Flowers." His tone sounded like the closing of a door.

Stinson led me in chains to the plaza and secured me to the cedar statue as workers rolled an inverted cross, mounted on a wheeled cart, from a hilltop arbor of pine trees. I must have disgusted Stinson because he left me in the redhead's care.

"You keep one of these things around?" I asked him, referring to the mobile cross.

"Tortures R Us," he answered, a self-pleased smile cracking across his face.

The workers hoisted the cross off its cart and into a waiting hole. They refilled the hole, tamped the dirt firm, and moved the cart away. "It's your time," the redhead told me as he unlocked the chains. Four men took me by the arms and legs, carried me to the cross, tipped me upside down, then lashed my legs to the vertical beam and my arms to the horizontal beam. My belt was fastened to a small hook that suspended me about two feet above the ground.

"How's the view?" the redhead asked.

"Lovely," I told him. "A real Kodak moment." My Ranger survival skills activated in case my faith in Deborah was premature. I had hoped for an ally in Stinson, but I was ready to settle for an enemy. "What's your name?" I asked the redhead.

"Elroy," he said.

"Elroy? Man, I bet you hated your parents for that."

He smiled. "Save your breath. You won't have it much longer." He left for the party.

I observed the bacchanalia upside down as the village bustled to life. From the surrounding buildings men, women, and children dressed in white togas emerged, carrying tables, benches, tablecloths, dishes, pots, and baskets of food. The carcass of a young goat roasted on a spit over an open fire. Earthenware vats of wine appeared, and the cultists partook of it liberally as they worked. I looked for Stinson but couldn't see him. The redhead was drinking with some young men his age. I called to him. "Hey, Red," I yelled. "I'm thirsty."

"No, you're dead," he said. "You only think you're thirsty." He lowered his stoneware beaker into a large vat. "Dandelion," he said. "Best dandelion wine in a thousand miles." He drank it in one long gulp, then reached for a different vat and refilled the beaker. He walked over to me and smiled. "Chokecherry," he said, drinking greedily.

"I'd rather be burned alive," I told him, "than have the hangover you're going to have in the morning."

He splashed the remnant of his wine in my face. "I've got news for you, Lieutenant," he said. "You ain't never been burned alive before. You don't know what you're talkin' about." He turned to walk away.

"So tell me," I yelled at him. "Tell me what it's like, Elroy. What's it like to burn?"

He turned and gave me a cold smile. "I know your game, Ranger. Taunt the enemy. Get him mad. Make him do something stupid that'll give you a break. What you don't know is you ain't the first dummy I've helped burn. And you won't be the last." He rejoined the revelry where everyone, including the children, was drinking with crazed abandonment. Adolescent girls danced like nymphets, and naked toddlers—all resembling Flowers—wandered about unattended.

"Push," someone shouted behind me. It was Stinson directing workers moving a portable platform into place. Secured to the platform were two podiums. The stage for the play.

"Stinson," I called to him as he walked near. "Where's my friend? Is she OK?"

He ignored me. There was no way out for me. I was down to trusting Deborah for my release.

A terrible racket, like the buzzing of large crickets, sounded. I twisted to see a half-dozen drunk musicians tuning fiddles, guitars, and banjos. Then someone brushed against me. At Elroy's command small children began piling twigs under my head.

"Do you doubt it now?" Elroy asked me. "Do you still believe this isn't happening?"

"My boy Elroy," I mocked him. "A figment of Flowers's imagination. When he dies, you will cease to exist."

He spit wine in my face and walked away.

The blood rushing to my head was giving me a pounding headache. I tried to relieve it by lifting my neck and shoulders.

Suddenly there was a trumpet blast, and Deborah appeared at the far end of the compound, escorted by a trio of handmaidens. She wore a scarlet robe and carried a large shepherd's rod, obviously a stage prop. Her hair, piled high, had garlands of tiny flowers woven into it.

Two more trumpet blasts and Flowers emerged from his domicile with beefy guards flanking him and young girls spreading flower petals in his path.

"Annasoh! Annasoh!" the people shouted. "Annasoh! Annasoh!"
A teenage girl wandered near me, shouting this strange refrain.
"What's *annasoh?*" I asked.

She looked at me as if I were the incarnation of stupidity. "It's *hosanna* backwards," she said. She ran to join the procession that followed Flowers to his dais.

Clothed in a silver toga embroidered with gold sequins, he ascended the platform. His white hair was slicked and curled, and he held an inverted bronze cross in his right arm. He paused at the podium, looked across at Deborah, down at me, and out to his people. "Children," he said in his loud, full voice. "Children, we are children at play, and oh, what games we have for tonight." His followers, which I guessed numbered between ninety and one hundred, cheered wildly.

"Television!" he yelled.

"Television!" the people shouted back.

"Tell us a vision," he shouted.

"Tell us a vision," the people responded.

"I will tell you a vision," he said. "Pay-for-view. Imagine tonight's festivities on pay-for-view. The Intolerant Monotheist versus the Spark of the Divine Within. How many millions of homes? Fifty, sixty, seventy? Nay, seven times seventy. Four-hundred-and-ninety million homes. That is the vision. Tell us the vision. Television is the vision. Flowers shall bloom again."

"Flowers shall bloom again," the crowd chanted.

"Where will Flowers bloom?"

"Television!"

"And what web will he weave?"

"The World Wide Web!"

"Flowers in every home," he shouted.

"Flowers in every home." The crowd responded as if this were a standard liturgy.

He held up his hand to silence them. "Now, children, celebrating is fun, but this is a serious moment as well. Are we capable of being serious? Can we be children and be serious too?"

A foreboding hush fell on the small crowd.

"Monotheism is illegal. The penalty is death. But are we like all the others? No, no, no. We are a gracious, loving people. We will allow freedom of speech to the woman. But if the Spark of the Divine Within does not bear witness to her words, then she will be reeducated. Reminded. Redeemed. Released. Reprieved." He pointed a long arm and finger at me. "More dangerous than a Monotheist is one who guides a Monotheist. This is the blind who leads the blind. It is he who has led the Mono astray. He must be purified. He must be refined."

"Purify! Purify!" the crowd yelled.

"His darkness will be lit with fire," Flowers said. "But first the woman will be allowed to speak. If her words do not quicken with life, then we torch the man. We dine. We drink. There will be games of sport for the men, and the woman shall be the prize."

The men cheered lustily.

A handmaiden rushed to Flowers and knelt at his feet. "Speak, my little flower," he said more quietly.

She rose, he bent, and she whispered in his ear. Then she ran away.

Flowers raised both his hands to the sky. "Hear this," he proclaimed. "From the mouths of babes, from one of the handmaidens who waited on our esteemed guest, hear this. The Monotheist is a virgin."

The followers gasped, then hissed.

"Is there any crime so great as not to share one's body?" he shouted.

"No!"

"Is it the unpardonable sin?"

"Yes!"

"Can a body locked in ice reveal anything but a heart locked in ice?"

"No!"

"Is the flesh warm?"

"Yes!"

"Should the heart be cold?"

"No!"

Like a devilish maestro, he again quieted the crowd with the wave of a hand. "She is a tormented being," he said. "She has been raised since a baby to wear shackles and put shackles on others. We are children raised to be free and to grant freedom to everyone. Let there be light."

"Let there be light." Explosions of color painted the sky as flares and torches were lit simultaneously throughout the plaza. Music played and the people began a wild array of dances, some men with men, some girls with girls, but most simply gyrating individually to a drumming heard only within themselves. Flowers danced by himself at his podium, his head thrown back and his glazed eyes staring to the heavens.

I searched through the melee of twisting, contorting bodies until I could see Deborah. She stood quietly transfixed, her eyes closed, and her head slightly bent. This bizarre, aerobic ritual continued until the celebrators slowly began collapsing, spent.

For several minutes everyone lay quietly, then Flowers sprouted to his feet. The others followed except those who had passed out from the drinking and the frenzy.

"Time for discourse," he shouted.

"Discourse," a few shouted back.

He swept his arm grandly toward his nemesis. "Ladies first."

Deborah cleared her throat softly and looked out at the people. Their white togas were now dirty, stained, and disheveled. I had seen mobs before in The Sudan, Haiti, and Mexico, but I had never seen a people so thirsty for blood. I knew Flowers's whims were the only thing keeping the two of us alive.

"Proceed, woman," he ordered. "Orate."

"I have a request first," Deborah said loudly.

"Ask what you will," Flowers responded.

"Bring me a mirror," she said.

Flowers looked at her suspiciously, then grinned and waved for two of the handmaidens to do her bidding. They returned in moments, holding a full mirror between them.

Deborah stationed them in front of the people. "Come. Look at yourselves," she said.

One drunk woman laughed, rushed forward and began making faces in the mirror.

"All of you," Deborah said. "Line up. One by one. Look at yourselves."

"This is not discourse," Flowers protested.

"Are you worried?" she asked.

"I most certainly am not," he retorted.

"Then tell your people to form a line and look long and hard in the mirror."

"Do as she says," he commanded, and the white-robed cultists formed a sloppy, weaving line that resembled a collection of overaged trick-or-treaters.

One at a time they stood and looked in the mirror. As each gazed, the party spirit began to die, and the people sobered. Elroy saw his reflection, then collapsed backward in a faint. Stinson stared in the mirror thoughtfully, then lowered his head and walked away.

From where Flowers stood he apparently could not see what his people were seeing. Neither could I nor Deborah. "What is this trick?" he whispered to her angrily. She looked at him but did not answer.

Some of the people drew back in shock after looking at the polished glass. Others cried hysterically. Two women and another man fainted and were dragged away. In single file they paraded past. Then they gathered in a sad, jaded group, their faces staring in stunned confusion toward the platform.

"What are you seeing?" Flowers asked, but none of his followers seemed able to answer. "I shall see for myself," he said, stepping away from his dais.

"Wait," Deborah said. "Discourse."

He stopped and stared at her. "Discourse?"

"Discourse first."

"But I must see what is in the mirror."

"Discourse," she challenged.

Her tone insulted him. "Certainly." He stiffened and returned to his podium. "Discourse is civilized. We will be civilized. You begin."

"You once preached to thousands—" she began.

"Millions," he said. "Tens of millions, actually."

"To a multitude."

"A biblical multitude," he said proudly. "As the sands cover the shore."

"And what do you have now?" she asked. "Homes dug into the

earth like badgers. Dozens of little children claiming you as their father. The murder of those who oppose you. Is this how you intended it to be?"

"I did not write the script," he hissed.

"When did you break communion?" she asked.

He shook a clenched fist toward her. "That deity of yours broke communion," he snarled. "He broke the deal. I preached and toiled and labored like a slave in fields white with harvest. I preached the good news, and what did your god do for me? He killed my only son through the Plague. He took my homes and my wife in the quakes. He let the government remove tax exemptions from ministries. He made me appear a fool to the media."

"You preached the good news?" she challenged. "The good news of personal wealth, health, and escape from hardship."

"Sounds like good news to me." He laughed, but the people did not laugh with him.

"You predicted the rapture on a certain date," Deborah said. "A date that is years behind us."

"I did," he bragged. "I even wrote a novel about it. A novel that sold over 300,000 copies."

"And you deceived thousands, tens of thousands."

"Nay," he said, sweeping his hand as if brushing her comments aside. "Millions. I deceived millions."

"All because you were so certain when the Lord was going to return."

"Well, he told me," Flowers chided. "He told me he was coming and that I was to be his end-times witness. Me and me alone. I had the keys to his kingdom. I was to usher in the deliverance of his bride and his wrath upon the sinner. He told me and I listened and did what he said. And what did I get out of the deal? Laughed at. Mocked. Belittled. I listened but he lied."

"Perhaps it was not his voice you heard," Deborah said.

Flowers's face reddened and beaded with sweat. "I heard!" he screamed. "I heard from God, and I know him for what he is."

"You heard what you wanted to hear," she challenged. "Hear this now: Repent and you will be spared, for his mercy endures forever."

"Repent?" He laughed and looked to his stunned people for support. "Why should I repent?"

"Your heart knows."

"Why should I repent?" he ranted. "Why should I?"

Resignation came across Deborah's face. She had had enough. "Look in the mirror," she said, her voice sad but authoritative.

Flowers cast her a cruel and cowardly glance. "What kind of trick is this, you little witch?" He hissed again. "You must be a witch, a sorceress. You have cast a spell upon the mirror. Maybe you are Lady LeClair herself coming in another form." He turned to his people in mock panic. "It is her, it is her," he shouted in warning. "It's Lady LeClair, the witch, in the form of a young maiden. She has come to eat us all."

They stared at him dumbly.

"Look in the mirror," Deborah said again.

"'Look in the mirror,' she says. 'Look in the mirror,'" he mocked. Flowers pulled himself to his full height, straightened his toga, and stepped pompously off the platform. "What do I have to fear? I have no fear. Nothing scares me."

The people drew back as he approached.

"Are you afraid of me?" he asked them. "Am I some sort of beast? I am your father. I am the Spark of the Divine Within. Just call me Sparky," he joked, imploring their support.

Stinson stepped out from the assembly and stood before Flowers. "Just look in the mirror," he said.

Flowers puffed angrily, looked down his nose at his guard captain, then whirled and stared at the polished glass as if he were diving from a pier into a pool.

His face grew ashen. Terror spread from his face in a blue hue of sudden realization. His lips began to form a scream, but before his protest found voice he jerked backward into the air, as if grabbed by unseen hands. He hit the earth like a book being slammed shut. Then he lay still. Not a twitch or a shudder.

The people drew back another step. No one pressed in to care for the fallen Flowers.

Deborah pointed toward me. "Release my friend," she said.

Stinson and two other men cut me down. Blood returned, rapid and painful, to my torso and limbs. I staggered toward Deborah, my mental gyroscope still realigning itself, my arms and legs lit by thousands of pinpricks. "What happened?" I asked her.

She stood over Flowers's body. "He's dead," she said calmly.

"How?" I asked. "What did he see? What did *they* see?"

She looked at me with blue eyes ablaze, and I felt as Babbler must have the first time he stared into her face. Dumbfounded. Amazed. I had to force words to form. "What's . . . in . . . the . . . mirror?" I asked.

She shook her head. "I don't know," she said. "I haven't the faintest idea."

"You don't know?"

"No," she said. "Perhaps we'd better look."

CHAPTER 10

"No! No! Don't look!" A woman fell in front of Deborah and me as we stepped toward the mirror.

The faces of the cultists reflected a mixture of sorrow, terror, and confusion. Some huddled together like sticks bundled from a dead tree. I caught Stinson's eye, but his expression told me nothing.

Of course, I knew I was going to look. I would look because Deborah would look. What did I think I would see? I was afraid I'd be shown a slow, rolling river and six Cannibals rising from its depths.

Deborah gently eased the begging woman aside. "It's OK," she said. "We'll be safe." The woman collapsed in tears. Deborah and I stepped before the mirror as a couple, almost like a bride and groom posing for a photographer. I expected to die as quickly as Flowers had.

To my amazement there was nothing reflected upon the shiny surface except our own images. My face was flushed, stubbled with beard, and framed by a ragged haircut. I looked tired and older than my years.

Deborah's face shone and her eyes were crystalline, but she was not as beautiful as I'd thought. Her hair wasn't platinum. It was only sun-bleached. And her face held a simple plainness, like the prairie.

Her luster was a spiritual transcendence that Babbler had seen from the beginning, but it had taken me weeks to break through its surface. I had seen her through my own vain imaginings as an ideal. Now she appeared more complete than I could have imagined. Complete because of her humanity. Because of her imperfections.

The mirror showed truth, but I saw little about myself. I was simply rough and ragged.

"What do you see?" Stinson asked.

"We see only ourselves," Deborah said.

"Only yourselves? There's no name, no lettering on the mirror? There's not two people?"

"Yes," she said. "Two people. Daniel and me."

"No," Stinson said, speaking for the group. "Aren't there two people who are not you? Two strange people?"

Deborah turned from the mirror and faced them. She gestured to Stinson. "What did you see?" she asked.

"A name," he said. "Ananias. And two people I did not recognize."

"I saw the name Sapphira," a woman volunteered. "I also saw two people, and they fell over as if they were dead." The others concurred.

I took Deborah gently by the arm and whispered in her ear. "What are they talking about?"

"Ananias and Sapphira were a man and a woman in the Bible," she said. "The Book of Acts. They were struck dead for lying to God."

"Biblical stuff again," I said. "So the mirror trick wasn't just for our rescue. It was a prelude for you doing your thing."

"Yes. I suppose you can say that. Why don't you stick around? Watch and listen."

"Can't stand crowds," I said. My main concern was to locate my weapons. I felt naked unarmed.

"You're going to go find your gun, aren't you?"

"That's right."

"Well, maybe you should go shopping for a new wardrobe while you're at it," she added.

I looked down and realized I was still in the horsehide. I hadn't even noticed it in the mirror. As I slipped away, the people began peppering Deborah with questions.

"How did you know to ask for the mirror?" Stinson asked.

"I didn't know," I heard Deborah answer. "It was just an impression I had."

"We have lied to God," a woman wailed.

"No," Deborah corrected her. "Flowers lied to God. You have only lied to yourselves."

The crowd was so mesmerized that Flowers's body lay unattended beneath his shrine. His face, as lit by a full moon, was carved in fear, his eyes open as if fixed on something timeless and terrible. I dragged him to a root cellar and covered him with a tattered canvas tarpaulin. His Shroud of Turin.

Then I went investigating. I found my rifle and knife in a closet near my holding cell. But what to do for clothes? A robe certainly wasn't my style. I searched Flowers's private quarters. His stone-wall bedroom held a giant circular bed with mirrors lining the ceiling and walls. Ironic, I thought, that a mirror would be his downfall.

Water ran cool and silver from a sink tap. I helped myself to his toiletries, shaving with scented soap and a disposable razor, and brushing my teeth with a packaged brush and real toothpaste. I considered trimming my hair but decided I'd only make matters worse. In Flowers's dressers I found clothes that must have belonged to a son. They were my size. I chose a pair of blue jeans, a yellow T-shirt emblazoned with a marathon logo, and a crisp blue cotton shirt.

Under a stack of linen and silk pajamas I also found a large leather-bound photo album. I expected family photographs but found instead a record of Flowers's career. Photos of his first small pastorate in Georgia. News clippings of his faculty appointment to a school in Oklahoma. Revivals in stadiums. Social events with senators, Hollywood stars, famous athletes, and Presidents. The last page displayed an article announcing Flowers's prediction for Christ's return.

I tried to remember what I was doing on the date Flowers had prophesied. It was graduation day from Ranger school. My father was there. I hadn't seen him in two years. I smiled and put the album back under the silk pajamas. "You were right," I said. "God did come back that day."

I searched his quarters for items I might use, but there was nothing I wanted. Everything connected to Flowers seemed stained. All I really wanted was to leave with Deborah. Let the cult members put their own lives back together.

Her time with the cultists ended about midnight. By then I'd secured a hilltop post, built a bed of freshly cut pine boughs, and gone to sleep knowing I owed her my life. What, if anything, would she want from me? What could I give her?

She would want me to talk and spend nights in empty houses. Could I give that?

I doubted it.

In the morning we had a quiet breakfast with Stinson and a few others. We were fed bowls of a gritty and grainy meal lightly soaked in powdered milk. I'd eaten worse. The travois was then loaded with provisions, and the people gathered around Deborah, begging her to return.

"The Lieutenant told me where you plan on going from here," Stinson said. "Is it true? Are you going to the Cannibals?"

"Yes, we are," she said.

"Then we may never see you again. You could be killed and eaten."

"Missionaries have taken the Word to cannibals for centuries," Deborah explained. "Some have died for the faith."

The people pleaded with her to remain. I say *her* because none of them pleaded with *me*. I seemed inconsequential, of little more value than the white dog, if that. I tossed Stinson a challenge. "How about coming with us?" I asked. "We could use another gun, and your work here is done now."

"No," he said. "My work here has just begun."

"But Flowers is dead," I said softly. "Your assignment is over."

"You don't have to whisper," he told me. "The people know what I am. I told them last night."

"Then come with us," I argued. "It may not be safe for you here."

"No, you don't understand. Deborah anointed me to stay and be the new leader. And the people have accepted that."

"Anointed you?"

"Yes. She prayed over me and anointed me with oil. I have a new calling, a new assignment."

"Daniel," Deborah called, interrupting us. "Are you ready to go? You lead and I'll follow."

I was glad to be leaving, but I wasn't thrilled about our direction. Every step took us closer to Deborah's greatest challenge. Lady LeClair awaited us.

We hiked through rolling hills dotted with ponderosa pine and scrub cedar. Grasshoppers jumped everywhere beneath our feet. I knew they were one reason for the 'Postates survival. The insects were high in protein and easily caught with netting. "Do you remember our cereal being a little crunchy this morning?" I asked Deborah.

"Yes. I suppose they need to conserve their powdered milk."

"It wasn't the lack of milk," I said. "And those weren't nuts we were chewing on. They were dried and chopped grasshoppers."

"Oh?"

"That doesn't bother you?" I asked.

She shook her head. "Why should it? John the Baptist lived on locusts and honey."

"Who was he?" I asked.

She smiled in wonderment. "Maybe it's a blessing you know so little. You won't have much to unlearn."

"I'm not sure I want to know anything. I like my life simple."

"You mean *simplistic*," she challenged. "Kill or be killed."

"Whatever. I know better than to argue with you, Deborah. Besides, we should stop talking. It makes us thirsty."

"And it makes us human," she chided. "We can't have that, can we, Daniel?"

I ignored her remark. "We'll leave these foothills soon," I told her. "And enter a long farm valley. In a few days we'll be at the edge of the mountains. We could probably see them from here if the sky weren't so hazy with dust."

"Will the going be rough?"

"At times. That area was hit hard by the quakes. Some streams run into the ground and disappear. In other places geysers can erupt without warning. There are more bears. More lions."

"Do you expect us to meet people on the way?" she asked.

"I'd be surprised if we did. Anyone we meet will be dangerous. No one with their wheels spinning right is going to go anywhere near the Cannibals."

"So our wheels are not spinning right?"

"We are definitely out of alignment." The edge to my voice was sharper than my knife.

"You don't need to go on with me, Daniel," Deborah said. "Draw me a map. I can find them."

"I've gone this far. I might as well see how the last chapter reads."

She put her hand on my forearm. The touch turned my eyes to hers. "You don't owe me anything," she said.

"Owe you?"

"Yes. For what happened back there while you were on the cross. It had nothing to do with me. You owe me nothing."

"No, I do owe you," I said. "You saved my life. I need to pay you back."

"You can't be in debt to a woman?"

"It's not that."

"Then what is it? Just accept the fact that you owe me nothing."

"I can't do that."

"Why?"

"It's not how I was raised."

"Then be something different."

"It's not that easy."

"Fine. Then you can owe me. But don't try to save my life, OK? If you have to pay me back, you know what I want you to do."

"I'm willing to try," I said.

"You're willing to start sleeping in houses?"

"If it's that important to you. And I can't figure out why it should be. You obviously don't need my protection, and it certainly isn't a hormonal thing, is it?"

For the first time I saw her blush. "Last night was a strange way to have one's virginity announced," she said.

"I'm sorry, I didn't mean to—"

"No, no. It's all right. I'm twenty-six years old, Daniel. And I'm a virgin. I consider my chastity a blessing. The world just thinks me strange."

I tried to make light of the situation. "Well, I'm not a virgin, but I might as well be. You're the first woman I've even been close to for a couple years. 'Course, I guess if I took a bath more often. . . . "

"I was going to comment on the change of clothing," Deborah said. "You look nice. Almost civilized."

"I stole them." I said.

"No, they were provided for you."

"Whatever. Clothes won't make much difference to the Cannibals. I wonder how I'll taste. I hope I'm tougher than rawhide."

Deborah parried my poor humor. "You will probably be very tender," she said. "Maybe a little crusty on the outside, but as soft as butter inside." She rose from where she was sitting and slapped her leg as a signal. The malamute got to his feet, threw his shoulders into his burden, and began pushing west. Sometimes I marveled at the white dog. The animal was so obedient, so willing to please.

By early evening the houses became more numerous as we left the ranchland and descended into the once-lush farmground of the Yellowstone River Valley. Soon we were walking down a paved frontage road with houses on each side.

"This bothers you, doesn't it?" Deborah asked. "All these houses, the signs of civilization. I can tell by the way you're walking. You're tense."

"I should be," I said. "Any of these houses could lodge a threat. A bear, lion, some madman. I like the prairie better because you can see for miles in every direction."

"It's almost dark. I'll need to pick a house soon. Are you going to stay inside?"

"I gave my word that I'll try. No promises that I'll succeed."

She picked a western-style log cabin. We turned at a mailbox and walked down a gravel lane. The doors to the home were open, and all the furnishings were gone.

"Looted," I said. "Are you sure you want to stay in this one?"

"This one's fine." She began unhooking Dunamis from his travois.

"I suppose you will want to do your thing. You know, whatever it is you do. The sweeping or whatever you call it."

"I'll cleanse the house," she said. "Why don't you light some candles."

"You want me to light the candles?"

"Sure. It's getting dark. They're in my pack next to my journal."

"You keep a journal?"

"Yes."

"When do you write in it? I've never seen you write."

"At night," she said. "It's the last thing I do before I go to sleep. It's sort of a diary, sort of a prayer journal. Why are you so interested?"

"I don't know. No reason, I guess." I went to her pack for the candles and matches. Dunamis watched me curiously. "There are only three candles," I said. "Where are the others?"

"What others?"

"The other candles. I've watched the houses you've stayed in. They always light up just before everything goes dark. You must have more candles."

"Three are all I've ever had," she said.

"Then how do you explain the extra light?"

"I can't."

"You can't?"

"No. So, are you going to talk tonight, Daniel? I mean real talk, not just an inventory of my light sources."

My chest became heavy, and my mind began to accelerate. "What kind of talk?"

"Well, the you-tell-me-about-yourself kind of talk would be nice. I still don't know much about you. Tell me about your Ranger training."

"Why?"

"Because it's you. It's who you are. You're an Army Ranger."

"I'm an ex-Ranger."

"So what went wrong?"

"With the military? It didn't live up to my standards. Unisex barracks, unisex bathrooms. Sensitivity training on gay and women's issues. Police action against people like you."

"People like me?"

"Yeah. You know. Monos."

"So you went AWOL?"

"It just sort of happened," I explained. "It wasn't really planned or anything."

"Your body might be AWOL, Daniel, but your heart is still with the service."

"Maybe," I conceded. "I know I can't see myself as a deserter. I'm not a runner."

"Aren't you?" she asked.

"What am I running from?"

"Yourself."

"No, I'm not. I'm just trying to survive."

"Just survive? How about play? Do you ever play at anything?"

"Play at what? Babblers play. They stuff prairie dog skins with rags and pretend they're playing soccer. Kicking stuffed skins into prairie dog holes. Is that what you mean?"

"Whatever's fun," she said. "What do you do for fun?"

"I don't have time for fun."

"What if you did? You're a Ranger. You must be able to do a lot of things. Sky dive. Scuba dive. Rappelling."

"I can do all those."

"But they're not fun, are they? More duty. More training. I'm talking fun, Daniel. F-U-N. Fun."

"If I'd stayed in the army, there are units beyond the Rangers. I guess my fun would have been to climb the ladder, see how far I could go."

"What units?"

"Special Forces. Green Berets."

"That's it? Just two steps."

"No." I began to get a dull ache in my head.

"No? Then what else?"

"There are other units. Delta Forces. Others. Units so secretive nobody knows anything about them."

"Even you?"

The headache increased in intensity. "Even me."

"Are you OK, Daniel? Does it bother you to talk about the army?"

"I just have a headache. Let's not talk about me for a while. What do you do for fun? Heal the sick? Raise the dead?"

She emitted the prettiest, most musical laugh I had ever heard. It was like water rolling across a creek bed of piano keys. "Yeah," she said. "That's fun. Pure joy. But for human, mortal fun—" She pulled her candle closer so I could better see her face. "Are you ready for this? I knit."

"You knit?"

"Yeah." She giggled.

"That doesn't sound like you."

"Well, it's me. I make doll clothes that I give to little girls. And blankets and scarves that I give to old people."

"And that's fun?"

"Sure. It gives people pleasure. We all have to do things to help others."

"Well, I guide missionaries." A burp of laughter rose in my throat.

"You almost laughed!" Deborah hooted. "Watch out or you'll lose control."

"No, I won't," I argued. "I won't lose control."

She giggled and the light in her eyes lit the room. "Oh, Daniel. You are too much."

"I am?" I said. "Sometimes I think I am not quite enough."

Her countenance sobered. "What do you mean?"

"I dunno. It's just the expectations. What my father expected of me, what the army expected of me, what many of the inhabitants of the Interior expect of me." Why was I talking so much? It was like someone had turned on a spout.

"What do they expect?"

"They expect me to kill Robert," I said. "Like I'm some sort of Pat Garrett and he's Billy the Kid."

"It always comes down to this with you. You and Robert. Kill or be killed. If no one has seen Robert and lived, how does anyone know that he even exists?"

"We have seen his victims," I said. "*I* have seen his victims."

"But no one has seen him."

"Maybe we have. He could be a master of disguises. Sometimes I've thought Babbler was Robert."

"Babbler's a victim," she said. "Everyone is Robert's victim as long as you all live in fear of him."

"What do you know about Robert?" Anger edged my voice.

"I know that eventually you are going to kill Robert or he is going to kill you."

"Do you know which one of us lives?" I asked.

"No."

"Would you tell me if you did know?"

"Probably not."

My anger turned to sarcasm. "Tell me this then, Miss Mono, missionary to the tribes, can Robert be saved?"

For once she seemed short of words and didn't answer. She stared at the wall for a few minutes then rose. "It is time for me to pray," she said. She left me sitting alone in the room.

Very alone. Even the dog got up and left.

Maybe Deborah had realized that talking to me wasn't so great after all.

CHAPTER 11

Dawn did not find me inside the log house. I lay outside in the grass with no remembrance of leaving the building. Candlelight flickered through Deborah's window. Her prayer light. I waited outside, somewhat chagrined, until she came out.

She did not mention my failure.

Our southwesterly course took us down a farm valley frozen eerily in time. Tractors rusted in fields. Cars blocked driveways. Birds fluttered in the leaves of large cottonwood trees. At any moment I expected a dog to bark, a child to yell, or an old woman to bang a screen door, walk out on a porch, and wave a hello. "Y'all hungry?" she'd yell. "Come in for breakfast."

We crossed the Yellowstone River on a crumbling concrete bridge near the shell of a small, windblown town. Looking down at the murky water reminded me of my friend Catfish—and of six Cannibals in a sinking canoe. Had any of them survived? Could they identify me? It didn't really make any difference. The Cannibals ate their guests regardless of past sins or virtues.

I also wondered if Deborah knew about my drowning the Cannibals. Could she see inside me?

Probably.

And what did she see? Probably more than I saw in myself. I was an outward man. My vision focused on the next horizon. Somewhere, over the next hill, was a herd of horses. Or a bull elk for the winter larder. Looking inward reminded me of looking backward. Behind me was Robert.

At that moment the only thing I was looking for was meat. My body craved protein. Had I found a horse I might have eaten it.

Food mattered little to Deborah. She ate it when it was available but showed no irritability when it wasn't. She seemed to draw strength directly from the air. And daily she outwalked me in spite of her slight limp.

We paralleled a clear stream that cut through rolling foothills like a slash of liquid light. I wasn't used to clear water. Thick stands of scrub willow bordered the stream on both sides.

Something about the thicket bothered me. "Stop," I said. The short hairs on my neck rose.

"What's wrong?" Deborah asked.

I brought my finger to my lips, then popped the ten-round clip out of my Ruger and replaced it with a thirty rounder. I pointed toward the willows. "Back away," I whispered.

Dunamis emitted a low whine and pricked his ears toward the trees. I cast the malamute a scolding look that it ignored. Deborah softly coaxed the dog to retreat with her.

The thicket stirred as if a whirlwind was forming in its center. Then came a whistling snort, like an engine firing to life.

"Buffalo," I warned.

The bull burst from the foliage like a cannonball, its broad head lacquered with blood. The hide of the hump was peeled back like a lid, exposing a fly-pecked mass of fat and muscle. There was no time for running or aiming. I broadened my stance and fired from the hip, sending forth a hot rope of hollow-pointed bullets. The brass flew in the air like a swarm of metallic wasps.

It took seconds but seemed like days. The big bull drank bullets. Its head and neck erupted in fissures of blood, but it never slowed. It charged me at full speed. At the last instant I pivoted like a matador and felt a horn rip through my shirt. The bull spun me like a top. I cleared my head, gained my balance, and steadied myself to fire the last few rounds of my clip.

The bull was charging Deborah.

Halfway up a steep bank, she fought to keep her footing. The malamute shielded her, his hair bristling and teeth bared. Though anchored to the travois, Dunamis was willing to fight and die for his master.

But fighting wasn't necessary. The bull fell dead at the dog's feet. The hunk of torn hide streamed behind it like a convertible top.

I popped out my clip and quickly reloaded. "Stay alert," I told Deborah.

She looked down at the bull. Then her eyes darted to each side. "Why?" she asked. "It's dead."

"Grizzly," I said, backing slowly, keeping one eye on the thicket and the other eye on the buffalo in case it was only stunned. It wasn't. The bull's eyes had already glazed.

"A bear too?" Deborah whispered.

"Somewhere around here," I said. "A wounded one." I pointed my rifle barrel at the buff's torn hide. "Something nearly tore this guy apart. Only a griz could do that."

We stared at the willows but nothing else stirred. Dunamis showed no sign that danger was near. "I think we're OK," I said.

"What are we going to do now?" Deborah asked.

"Harvest some meat. Do you know how to butcher?"

"Not really."

I handed her my knife. "Learn," I said. "I'll talk you through it."

Deborah sliced ribbons of steak from the bison, following my instructions, while I watched for the bear.

She noticed my torn shirt. "Are you hurt?" she asked.

"No. I was lucky."

"It wasn't luck. There is no such thing as luck."

"You're right," I said. "That bull could have had me, but it seemed to be after you."

"It was," she said.

"This is one of those mysterious things, right? You think the buffalo was sent on a mission."

"What do you think?" she said.

"I think I don't want to know."

We walked as if on eggshells the rest of the day. I not only feared the wounded griz, I was also afraid the scent of the meat would draw wolves or lions. Or the gunfire would draw Robert or the Cannibals.

By nightfall the strain of staying alert had exhausted me, and I was actually glad to see a house.

"You do what you have to do," I told Deborah. "I'm going to start broiling steaks." She set about cleaning house while I started a fire and roasted meat. I called her when the steaks looked done. Meat charred on the outside and raw in the middle tasted delicious to me. I gulped it down faster than the dog did. Deborah nibbled on hers. "How is it?" I asked.

"Different," she said. "Good flavor but a little tough."

"You must not be as hungry as I am."

"I'm not," she said. "I don't require much food."

"Or much rest." I wiped my fingers on my jeans.

"I get my own rest." She paused. "By the way, where are you sleeping tonight?"

"I'll try the house. But I'm not making any promises."

"You seem nervous, Daniel."

"I put 27 bullets into that bull," I said. "That leaves me 13 rounds. Not many for Cannibal country."

"We're not here to kill them," she said.

"You're not. But I kill before I get eaten. Besides, you're forgetting about the bear. Or are you here to save its soul too?"

"We might not even see the bear."

"I think we will," I said. "I've got a feeling."

"Well, it's nice to know you have feelings."

"I would trade the feelings for a larger caliber rifle and a hundred rounds of ammo."

"Bad trade," she said. "Keep the feelings."

The night was cooling. "I suppose we better go inside," I told her.

The house looked more intimidating to me than a charging bison.

Deborah seemed to sense my worry. "You sleep where you need to," she said. "We're even. You saved my life by killing the bull."

"It's not about debts now," I said. "It's about personal challenges."

Deborah and Dunamis took a bedroom. I unrolled a blanket and curled up on the carpeted floor of the living room. I was as full as a gorged coyote, and I thought I might last the night inside the house.

I didn't. Long before dawn I awakened on the porch roof. I lay and listened for sounds. All I heard were the soft babbling of the stream and the occasional, punctuating hoot of an owl.

At daylight I broiled the last of the buffalo steak. Dunamis joined me, but Deborah announced she was fasting.

"You need to eat to keep up your strength," I said.

"Do I seem weak?"

"No." Her perseverance certainly wasn't an issue. "I didn't make it through the night inside," I confessed.

"I know. I heard you get up and leave. Did you dream?"

"What do you think?" I said. "You know I don't dream."

"Everyone dreams," she said. "I dreamt about the bear."

"I'm not surprised. You had a traumatic experience with the buffalo, and you're mind was reliving it."

"No, I don't have anxiety dreams. I have visions. I saw the bear. It has a slash down the right side of its face and a puncture wound in the stomach. It's really big and sort of silver in color."

"Grizzly," I said. "A wounded griz."

"No, it's not wounded. Not anymore. It's been healed."

"Healed?"

"Yes. By Lady LeClair."

"You know this?"

"Yes, but don't worry about it," she said.

"Worry keeps me alert."

"Worry keeps you tired."

As we progressed toward the mountains I felt a subtle pull, like the magnetic draw of the Cannibal Queen's dark heart. The land became cold and silent. There were tracks of animals but no sightings. We saw nothing of the bear, yet I could always feel its eyes.

At dusk we looked at houses like earlier travelers had inspected motels. "You pick," Deborah said.

I chose a small vacation cabin on the banks of another stream. The water was clear and quick. "The mountains are close," I said, bending to wash my face and hair. "The water's getting colder."

"If they're so close, why haven't we seen them?" she asked.

"They're still covered by some sort of haze. Dust, maybe. Smoke from a fire. Or ash from a volcano."

"It's not dust or smoke, Daniel. And it's not ash, either."

"Then what is it?"

"It's just darkness. It's an evil that radiates from Lady LeClair."

"You're speaking metaphorically, right?" I didn't want to admit that I, too, had felt a force reeling us in like lures on the end of a fishing line.

"No, I'm speaking realistically."

"We're entering a black fog of bad vibes?"

"Something like that."

"Then you better pray," I said. "And I will scout for supper."

In the carport rafters I found an old fishing pole and a handful of flies. I fished the stream while Deborah did her domestic duties. I pulled five brook trout from deep, quiet pools while Deborah's songs broke hauntingly over my shoulder. I even felt the candlelight increase until I imagined it warming my back.

"You have a way with houses," I kidded her when she came down to the stream. "What a housewife you would make."

"Thank you, Daniel. I'm flattered."

The tone in her voice embarrassed me. I'd been joking, but it struck something deep and resonant within her. To break the awkwardness I called the dog and fed him one of the fish. He licked my fingers gently when he was finished.

"Do you want me to cook tonight?" Deborah asked.

"We don't have any aluminum foil," I said. "We're going to have to try and fry the fish on a flat rock."

"I can do that."

"I thought you were fasting."

"I am. But I can cook for you if you want me to."

I hesitated.

"What's wrong? Are you afraid of my cooking?"

"No. I'm just not used to seeing you act so domestic."

"You suppose too much, Daniel. Find me a flat rock."

She fried and I ate. The fish were dry and rubbery, but it was the most perfect meal I could remember. When I finished, she sat beside me. It was a beautiful evening. The haze had lifted, the stars shone, and the stream gurgled and splashed.

"You almost seem relaxed," she said.

"I am. Part of it is Dunamis. I'm getting used to having a dog."

"Great," she teased. "And here I thought it was my cooking."

I smiled. "That too. But to be honest, I'd never usually sit by a stream like this. It's too noisy. You can't hear if someone is sneaking up on you. But I'm learning to trust Dunamis's senses."

"Well, that's a start," she said. "We all have to grow and change."

"How about some change for you?" I asked. "How about you sleeping outside tonight?"

"Outside? But we're just getting you housebroken."

"I've made my attempts and failed. But you haven't tried sleeping outside. It's prettier out here. Look at the stars tonight."

She didn't look up. "I have more work to do in the house, Daniel."

"Does it take all night?"

"Sort of," she said.

"But after your chores you eventually sleep, right?"

"Yes."

"So do whatever you need to do then come out here."

"I don't know, I—"

"Deborah. How much have I asked you for?"

"Not much," she admitted.

"Then do this for me, one time. Don't worry, I'll respect your space. You can trust me."

"It's not a matter of trusting you, Daniel. You're actually about the most trustworthy person I've ever met."

"Fine, then you'll do it?"

"You don't know what you're asking."

"I'm asking one little favor," I said. "Try sleeping outside. If you get uncomfortable and have to go to the house I'll understand."

She brought fingers pensively to her chin. "Let me think about it," she said. "But I have to finish my prayers and journal entries first."

"Hop to it."

"One thing. If I do sleep outside tonight, you still have to talk."

"Agreed," I said.

The nights were cooler near the mountains. When Deborah returned, I was wrapped in a blanket, leaning against a pine tree. I moved the blanket to make room for her. "Come on in," I said. She hesitated for a moment then sat down and leaned against me. I covered us up. Fire embers danced inches from our feet. We both stared at the glow as if mesmerized. Her head rested against my shoulder, but I didn't dare reach for her hand. Besides, I was still holding my gun.

"I shouldn't be doing this," she said finally.

"Doing what?"

"You know. This. Being here with you."

"You mean under a blanket? Deborah, we're friends. We've traveled together for weeks. We've risked our lives together."

"I know," she said. "But somehow I think I'm risking even more right now."

"I won't touch you," I said. "I promise."

"That's not the problem."

"Then I'll make sure you don't touch me," I joked.

Her head turned and she looked up into my eyes. "Promise?" she asked. Her seriousness surprised me.

"I promise."

"Thank you." I felt her body relax and settle closer to mine.

"It's no big deal," I whispered. "There's no one to see us. Except maybe Robert or Lady LeClair."

"It's not that," she said. "There's always someone to see. But it's

OK. Let's not talk about it. Talk about something else, Daniel. Tell me about where you grew up."

"Which place?" I said. "I was a military brat, remember?"

"The main one. The one you'd call home."

"It's east of here on the Tongue River."

"Is it a pretty house?"

"It's OK."

"Do you have good memories of it?"

I shifted and knew my nervousness was being transmitted like a spark through jumper cables. "Some good, some bad," I said. "Like most people."

"How long did you live there?"

"We moved there when I was twelve. That's when my father retired from active duty, but he continued with the army as a civilian consultant."

"The military must have been everything to him."

"It was. And he wanted it to be everything to me. He tried to get me appointmented to West Point, but it didn't happen. He said politics blocked it. I did get an ROTC scholarship, though."

"That was quite a speech for you, Daniel," she said. "I bet you said almost fifty words."

"It's easier to talk when you are close to me."

"Don't con me, Daniel."

"I'm not conning you. I like having you close."

"I once went a full year without talking," she said.

"You? You're kidding."

"No. It was a 'word fast.' Three of us did it. We went twelve months without speaking. We signed—" she gestured with her hands in sign language "—and wrote notes. I even wrote out my prayers though I think God hears our thoughts whether they come out in words or not. But words are better. For prayers, anyway."

"Your parents must have thought you were nuts."

"Actually, my parents encouraged it."

"And what did you learn by not speaking?"

"I learned to hear," she said.

I nodded in agreement. "I can understand that. That's one reason I'm silent. I need to hear what's going on around me."

"No, no. You don't understand. I learned to listen for things inside me, not around me."

"Inside you?"

"Yes. The voice of the Spirit. It is a very still, quiet voice. Sometimes I can hardly hear it at all."

"Like when it tells you to get a mirror."

"That's right."

"But it doesn't tell you why?"

"I didn't need to know why."

"You said three of you did it. You meant the ones who you said started this journey with you."

"Yes," she said sadly.

"And they're dead?"

"Yes. Martyred in the Dakotas."

She offered nothing more. The end of our conversational rope had been reached, and we dangled there, gripping the knot. "Daniel," she said finally. "I have a difficult request."

"More difficult than guiding you to Cannibals?"

"Yes. I want to sleep beside you tonight—"

My heart nearly ripped through my chest. "Say that again."

"I want to sleep beside you. Not with you. Do you understand?"

"I think so," I said. "But moments ago you wouldn't come under the blanket."

"I know. Will it bother you? I don't want to be a tease. I really don't. It's just that I've never been close to a man before. Not all night."

"It's OK," I said, gently pulling her closer. "I know what you're saying. It feels odd for me to hold someone too. And if I have to, I'll get up and sleep in that cold stream."

I felt her face smile. "I don't want you to do that," she said.

"I don't particularly want to either."

She scrunched down and laid her head against my chest. "If *I* get up and leave, it has nothing to do with you," she said. "It will be . . . because I have to."

"I know."

"I can hear your heart," she said quietly.

"Nice to know I still have one."

"You have a big one." She yawned.

Deborah slowly drifted to sleep. I felt her soft breath against my neck. I should have been the happiest man in the Interior, but I wasn't.

Secretly I had to wonder. Was Deborah relaxing her standards because she was in love with me? Or had she seen something in the mirror she had not told me?

Had she seen her own death?

Or mine?

CHAPTER 12

I awakened to an empty feeling. My arms were filled only with a gun and a dog.

Dunamis rested against me peacefully. I didn't remember Deborah leaving or the dog taking her place. Had it been a dream? Had she ever been there at all?

She had. But the white hairs on my shoulder had been shed by a malamute, not by the woman I loved. Our relationship seemed star-crossed. I couldn't stay in houses, and she couldn't stay out of them.

I went to the stream and splashed cold water on my face. *Prepare to lose her,* I told myself. *She is too good to hold. Too pure.*

As I knelt by the water, she came up quietly behind me and put her hand on my shoulder. "I'm sorry," she said. "Please forgive me."

"Forgive you for what?"

"For teasing you, then leaving you. I should either have stayed with you or never come to you at all."

"It's OK." I reached up and put my hand on hers. "I haven't done any better at meeting your expectations."

"I just want to be honest with you, Daniel," she said. "I don't want to manipulate or deceive you. Or have any expectations at all."

"Expectations happen."

"I can't afford them."

I rose, faced her, kissed my fingers, and touched them lightly to her cheek. "You are the best person I've ever known," I said. "I can't help but love you, but I realize I might not ever have you."

"Daniel, it's not because I don't love you too."

"I know, it's—"

"It's something bigger than either of us, or the two of us put together."

I nodded. "Maybe we better go now." I hitched Dunamis to the travois, and we began our trek to the southwest, following the rapid, narrow stream as if it were a ribbon tied to the glaciers of the mountains. As if it were a string tied to the cold domains of the witch's stronghold.

We walked in silence until the silence began to eat at me. I needed to hear her voice. Nearing the ending of our journey caused me to think of its beginning. Of a man named Storch lying partially eaten on the prairie, his life's blood slowly draining into the sod. "Do you remember Storch?" I asked.

"Who?"

"Storch. The guy with the vehicle. You crossed paths with him a couple days before finding me."

"Yes, I remember him. Why?"

"I watched him die," I said. She gave me a confused look. "How about Babbler?" I asked. "Do you remember Babbler?"

"Babbler? Now who are you talking about?"

"An older man. Filthy. Not all there upstairs. He carried little traps around his neck."

"Oh, yes. He was sweet. He was fascinated with my eyes. Why are you bringing up these people, Daniel?"

I shrugged. "I don't know. I guess I'm allowing my memory to function."

"You expect to die, don't you?" she said with surprise and concern in her voice.

"Yeah, I expect to die. And be eaten. We'd have a better chance against Robert than we do just waltzing right into the Cannibal camp. We might as well salt and pepper ourselves and bring our own forks."

"We don't know what lies ahead for us."

"You're not afraid?"

"No, but it's not because I'm brave."

"No? What is it then?"

"It's because I'm peaceful," she said.

There were so many things I wanted to ask her. How did the Slinger come back to life? How did a dead tree grow leaves? What did she really see in the mirror? The questions were holstered in my heart, but I could not draw them out.

As we crested a tall, grassy ridge, she suddenly stopped and pointed. "Look!"

I raised my gun, expecting the grizzly or the Cannibals, but she was pointing at the Beartooth Mountains. The peaks broke through a cloud-dappled sky like upraised hands of granite. "What a cathedral," she said. "What an awesome display of God's greatness!"

"Haven't you seen mountains before?" I asked.

"No. Not mountains like these."

"It means we're close," I said. "Closer than I thought."

"They're so high. There's even snow on the peaks."

"And the ocean is not far away either," I said. "Just past the mountains are salt water bays and islands. Parts of what used to be Idaho and Utah."

She stood as if transfixed on the scene before her.

"We could go there, you know," I told her.

"Where?"

"To the ocean. There will be Pilgrims there. People you can minister to. We can bypass LeClair."

"No," she said. "We can't. There is no bypassing Lady LeClair."

"Why not?" I pleaded.

"She is the ruler of this darkness, Daniel. And she is summoning me."

"You don't have to answer her summons."

"Yes, I do."

"Why? Do you really think she can be changed or converted?"

"I don't know. I won't know until I see her."

"Well, believe me, you can't—"

She hushed me with a raised hand, and I knew by the look in her eyes that she was listening to an inner voice.

"What is it?" I whispered.

"The bear," she said.

A sharp tingle climbed my spine, and a chill settled on my shoulders like snowfall. I flipped the safety off my Ruger and slowly scanned the area with my eyes. For the buffalo I had shot from the hip. That was poor technique. Not very professional. I brought the rifle to my shoulder. My body froze for an instant. Then I heard the bear growl. I turned slowly toward the sound, my eyes following the muzzle. I was ready to expend the last of my bullets, but I was not ready for the sight that came to my eyes.

"Daniel," Deborah said, her hand touching my arm. "Do you see what I see?"

"I see it," I said. "But I don't believe it."

Emerging from a grove of aspen was an enormous sow grizzly. Astride the beast's back was a naked woman with flowing black hair. On each side of the bear and its mistress walked three armed men, wearing only flesh-colored jock straps and running shoes. The legs, arms, chests and heads of the men were dark, not with hair, but with tattoos. "Lady LeClair," I whispered, "and six of her eunuchs."

The woman raised a hand, and the bear and bodyguards halted. She pointed, and two of the eunuchs advanced toward us.

Deborah's body stiffened as if she were righting herself to face the challenge.

"What do we do?" I asked her.

"I don't know," she said.

Lady LeClair remained mounted on the griz like a general on a war horse.

Even from a distance I felt the cold probing of her eyes. "I could kill them all," I whispered. "All but the bear. And I might even get it if I'm lucky."

"Forget luck," she said. "You have no authority over her or the bear. You could only kill the men, and we're not here to kill."

My repulsion grew as the eunuchs approached. Though no stranger to horror, I'd never seen anything as despicable as Lady LeClair's slaves. They were the vomit of humanity, their eyes more animal than human, their movements almost reptilian. I looked past them. In comparison the witch Queen was a creature of beauty, her raven hair glowing with a blue-black sheen, her naked body lithe and powerful.

She smiled at me. Then she directed her mount with a pat to the neck, and the bear waddled into the aspens like an oversized, hairy pig. Four eunuchs trotted beside it like savages from a distant century. The other two eunuchs continued toward us.

"Where is she going?" Deborah asked.

"Back to her castle," I surmised. "She doesn't consider us worthy of her glory." I nodded at the approaching eunuchs. "Let me take them out," I said.

She put her hand on mine, and my arms went weak. My hands loosened on my weapon until it dangled limply from my fingers.

LeClair's grotesque boy-toys approached with M-16s leveled. Necklaces of human ears and teeth dangled against their chests, and their shaved heads were a palette of swirling colors. Drawings of goat heads, naked women, wolves, and bats illustrated their torsos and limbs. One sported a flying saucer rising out of his navel, somehow a familiar image. Their bodies were also pierced with gold rings in their noses, eyelids, ears, nipples, and navels. At twenty feet they stopped and stared at us quietly. I scanned the surroundings, looking for other warriors. I could see none.

Strange, I thought, for Lady LeClair was known to have seventy to eighty men.

"We come in peace," Deborah said, her voice steady and clear. "My companion will give you his weapon."

A small sneer dimpled the cheek of the saucer-man. "We don't want it," he said. "His bullets have no power over us."

I desperately wanted to test his theory.

"Please take us to your camp," Deborah said.

They looked at each other and laughed, then their rifles prodded us forward down a trail barely wide enough for Dunamis and the travois. We moved through the aspens into a narrow gorge thick with ponderosa pine, then climbed a rise that overlooked a small valley enclosed by jagged mountain peaks. The natural beauty of the meadow belied the evil that awaited us. In the valley's center a circular stone building rose from bear grass and scrub willow like a fortified grain silo. Smaller stone buildings were dispersed among the trees. At first sight the compound looked simpler than the 'Postate camp. No wind turbines, solar heating, gardens, or greenhouses. I had no time to study the layout. With a push in the back from an M-16, we marched on to the rock castle and stopped at its large double doors.

The doors opened and a wrinkled little man stared at us. "Please come in," he said. He was as skinny and hairless as a baby rat, his markings few and faded. I guessed him to be in his seventies.

"Tenderize 'em, houseboy," the saucer-man said. Then he and his companion left, shaking with laughter.

The little man paid them no attention. "I am Quito," he said, smiling through stained and broken teeth. "Allow me to take your weapon." He asked for it as if it were an overcoat.

"I would just as soon keep it," I said.

"As you will. I am the handservant of the Queen. Follow me."

We stepped into a room clouded with a hot, acrid steam that obscured the stone walls and ceiling. "The castle is heated by a geyser," our guide explained. "This is our boiler room. It is used for cleansing baths." The steam stung my eyes and bit at my mouth and lungs.

Quito opened another door, and we stepped into the clearer, cooler air of a tall, circular chamber bare of furnishings. The stone walls stretched twenty feet to a small railed balcony. That balcony and the door behind us were the room's only exits.

"I would offer you chairs," Quito said, "but we have none. Except the Queen's throne, of course." He gestured upward to the witch's perch. "I will gladly take your dog and care for him," he said to Deborah.

I looked down at Dunamis. Once again the malamute had followed so faithfully and quietly that I had forgotten all about him.

"Thank you," Deborah answered. "He may be hungry."

"The animal will be well cared for," Quito said. He turned to me. "It would be better for you if I relieved you of the weapon," he said. "It's useless. There is no escape from this room."

"No way," I said. "Until you pry my cold, dead fingers from it."

"Quaint," he said. "Have it your way. I will be back later." He shuffled quietly through the door, and it closed solidly behind him. I heard a dead bolt secure it.

For minutes Deborah and I stood with our attention riveted on the small balcony. "She's up there," I said. "In a room behind the railing. I can feel her." A chill descending from the balcony seeped through my skin. "Do you feel that?" I whispered.

"She's probing us," Deborah said. "Reading us."

"What is she looking for?"

"Our essence. Our identity."

"What is she finding?"

"She finds nothing in me," Deborah said. "She can only detect the workings of death."

I felt the power bite and burn inside me. "Great," I said. "I must read like a set of encyclopedias."

Deborah put her arm around me and the pain subsided.

"What did you do?" I asked.

"Covered you," she said.

"I know that. But what did you do?"

She ignored the question. "She's about to appear." Deborah's arm remained around my shoulders.

Lady LeClair, a tall, stunning woman, stepped onto the balcony wearing a shimmering silver dress. Her hair spilled over her shoulders like an ebony waterfall. Quito followed with a chair. She seated herself and he disappeared.

"What's your inner voice telling you?" I whispered to Deborah. "Is it time to ask for a mirror?"

"Silence!" Lady LeClair shouted. Her voice swirled and echoed down the stony, cylindrical room like the cries of a swarm of bats. "I know who you are," she continued. She pointed at me. "Behold the man," she cried out. "The infamous Daniel. You bring me good seed, Lieutenant." She shifted her gaze to Deborah. "And behold the woman. I will bathe in your blood, Mono."

"Very melodramatic," I called out, hoping to divert her attention from Deborah. "But how do you know who we are?"

The witch laughed. "I control the wild things. The crows and ravens brought word of you. I know why you are here, and I know you are overwhelmed by futility, frustration, fear, depression, and despair."

"All Ds and Fs," I said. "Not very good grades."

"Add *failure* and *death* for the Mono," she added.

"And me?"

"You might still make a passing grade, Lieutenant."

"C for *castration*?" I asked.

"Possibly. Or maybe B for *breeder*."

"Is she for real?" I said quietly to Deborah.

"Yes and no," Deborah responded. "And I don't think you should be antagonizing her."

I considered my weapon. "I could pick her off from here," I whispered.

There was no possible way the witch could have heard me, but she did. "Pick me off?" she mocked. "Do you really believe you have any control over me at all? Allow me to give you a demonstration." She clapped twice, the door behind us opened, and the broad head and silver-haired bulk of the female grizzly entered.

We were trapped in a stone tomb with 1200 pounds of death. I didn't even think about raising my gun. The animal ambled slowly around the room. Waves of fat and muscle rippled beneath her thick, loose hide. She glanced at us as if we were nothing but marmots.

Lady LeClair clapped three times and the bear stopped, rose slowly to her hind feet, balancing awkwardly with her front legs bent for balance, and roared loudly. A patch of bare skin glistened on her belly, and a scar ran from one eye to the throat.

"My baby was injured," Lady LeClair said. "She tangled with a buffalo. As you can see, I healed her. I heal all the animals that come to me." The Queen clapped again, and the brute dropped to all fours.

Lumbering to within a few feet of us, the griz stopped. I stared into her small, piglike eyes and smelled the stench of rotting flesh on her breath.

"One word from me and the two of you are appetizers," the witch said.

We stood so still we scarcely breathed.

"But the Mono's blood is too precious to be wasted," Lady LeClair continued. "Do you know how hard it is to find a virgin these days?" She clapped a command, and the bear turned and waddled out the open door. The door slammed shut.

"It is time," LeClair announced, "for the two of you to begin your preparations."

"Is she going to castrate me?" I asked Deborah. "If she is, I'd rather shoot myself now."

Deborah shook her head. "No," she whispered. "Just the opposite. She wants you for a mate."

Astonished, I glanced at Deborah, then back to the balcony. The chair was empty. The witch had disappeared. "A mate?" I said.

"I think so, Daniel." Her hand reached out. Before we could touch, the door opened and Quito reentered the chamber.

"The young woman must come with me," he said.

"What about me?" I asked.

"You stay."

"Where are you taking her?" I demanded.

"Don't be alarmed." He gestured with his arm for Deborah to go before him. "The young woman will be well cared for."

I pulled Deborah to me. "I will get you out of this," I said.

"It's not in our control," she answered. Her arms encircled my neck, and she kissed me lightly on the cheek. "This test is yours," she whispered. "Keep the faith."

"I have no faith."

"Find some." She moved toward Quito, and they left.

I was alone. For a long time I stared up at the small balcony and waited for the raven-haired witch to return. I aimed my rifle there, knowing I could snuff her with a single shot. Then I paced. Pacing was not a good idea. I needed to conserve my strength. I seated myself on the cool stone floor. I probably sat for hours before deciding I might as well sleep.

I rested as the army had trained me. Asleep but not asleep. Twice I felt the Cannibal Queen step onto the balcony. The fingers of her powers pricked my consciousness. Both times I awakened, my finger on the Ruger's trigger, but in both instances she was already gone. I ultimately fell into a sleep as cold and hard as the stone around me.

When I awakened in the morning, a bowl of warm food and a wooden spoon waited beside me. My breakfast was a creamed wheat cereal moistened with water. I stirred it suspiciously, then tasted it slowly and carefully. It was bland but hearty. I ate it to keep my strength. The moment I finished, Quito entered the room. "How long will I be staying here?" I asked as he took the bowl away.

"I do not know," he said. "As long as our Queen deems it necessary."

"Where is Deborah?"

"I cannot tell you," he said. "Because you might think it possible to rescue her. And it's not possible."

"I still have my rifle," I said. "I could make you take me to her."

"No," he said. "You cannot make me do anything at all."

"You would die for your Queen?"

"Yes. In an instant. All of us would."

"All of you?" I asked. "I have not seen very many people. Where are the rest? Where are all of LeClair's followers?"

He turned his gentle eyes downward and sadness covered his face. "There have been losses," he whispered.

"Losses?"

"Yes. Bad karma. In fact, a few weeks ago we sent out our six bravest warriors, but only five of them returned."

I suppressed a reaction. "What happened?" I asked.

"Quarro, the one with the flying saucer tattoo, said Robert attacked them and he alone escaped."

"Robert lets no one escape," I said.

"Quarro said so. Of course, he lies sometimes." Quito began shuffling nervously toward the door. "I talk too much," he whispered. "It is my shortcoming."

"Quito," I said. "I want an audience with your Queen."

"You will have one," he said, closing the door. "You will have one soon."

"When?" I demanded.

"Sooner than you wish," he said, and the door closed behind him.

I turned and looked up at the balcony. Once again I could feel her penetrating stare. "I'm waiting for you," I stated quietly.

"No, I'm waiting for you," I thought I heard her answer.

CHAPTER 13

The second morning I awakened to find my rifle, knife, and fanny pack gone. When Quito came with the porridge I asked him where my belongings were.

"I took them away," he said.

"You took them without waking me?" It didn't seem possible that an elderly, weak, knock-kneed eunuch could rob me while I slept.

"I'm very quiet," he said. "Except when I talk. And I talk too much."

"But why take them? No one seemed worried about my weapons."

"They were taken to protect you," he explained. "The Queen was afraid you would hurt yourself."

"Suicide? I'm not so scared or depressed that I would kill myself."

"Not yet." He bowed politely and left with my chamber pot.

I ate my porridge, then began tracing the room carefully, my hands and eyes exploring for a weakness in the masonry or for a series of finger and toe holds that might allow me to climb to the balcony. I'd done this before and was no more successful this time. The rock and mortar were strong, the walls smooth and sheer. I gave up, but rather than lapse into lethargy, I exercised. I stretched and did pushups and situps. I visualized being free with Deborah, the two of us returning to the prairie.

Be alert, I told myself. *Be patient. Your time will come.*

I looked up at the empty balcony. *I can beat you,* I challenged the invisible witch. *Test me.*

Foolish me.

I had no idea what I was asking for.

The testing came in the middle of the night. I don't know how to explain it. I am a natural man, trained in the five senses. What happened was not of the natural world. One moment I was adrift in a light sleep, like a sailor on a raft. The next moment I was teetering on a precipice above the eternal. Reality crumbled under my feet, and a bottomless abyss beckoned below. Shades of darkness swirled and rolled within the pit like the wings of a million crows.

This is a dream. Command it to stop! I told myself.

"This is no dream." The darkness itself spoke to me.

Waves of depression and shame rolled over me. Life became gray and meaningless. There was no order, no goals, no answers. No horses. No weapons. My survival instinct drained like blood from a slit artery.

"Curse God and die," the darkness called to me.

The deep pit became a black river, and I saw the faces of dead Cannibals rising from the roiling depths. Their mouths opened in silent screams.

A force as firm as a large hand pressed against my lower back, pushing me from the edge. The dead Cannibals reached for me with long, bony arms and fingers.

This is all an illusion, I told myself. *Create your own illusion.*

I imagined a golden thread the diameter of a spider web descending from above. This was my love for Deborah and everything she represented.

As I reached and clung to this lifeline, I felt myself being lifted upward. But suddenly the dark force of the pit exploded with fury, a missile of energy struck the thread, and my imaginary line broke. I began falling.

I fell through a blackness that soaked into the pores of my soul, filling me with heaviness. I became gravity itself. I gained mass and density as I spiraled downward, but I had no hope of ever hitting bottom. There was no bottom. The cries from my throat were ripped away like paper pages. They floated upward, thin and powerless, until they dissipated.

In the army I'd endured torture from enemies and my peers, but I had never known pain like this. I needed help. I needed a deliverance. Or a deliverer.

"Call for me, and I will come to you." The words floated in the darkness like a small school of fish. *"Call for me."* The witch was bidding me.

No! I resisted from the very depths of my willpower.

"Suffer this!" the darkness shouted.

Suddenly my mind seemed to cleave, and the halves spun off separately, entering their own descending orbits like abandoned satellites. I was two people at once. Both in pain. Both insane. My mind was leaving me, but flames of pain surged through my body. I felt muscles being torn from my bones. Had death been available I would have embraced it. But the absence of death was the fullness of my futility. There was no ending. No escape. No end of time or suffering.

"Call for me!" came the cry again.

I saw the two hemispheres of my mind racing toward each other on a collision course. Permanent insanity would result from their impact.

I cried out. I don't know what words I used or if I used words at all, but I cried out. I conceded. The falling continued, but now an ending loomed below me like a distant landing pad. A finality. A floor.

I awakened on the cold stone of the chamber, trembling, totally spent, soaked with cold sweat. I opened my eyes and saw the witch standing on her balcony.

"Do you want more?" she asked.

I rolled onto my stomach, too exhausted to speak. I only grunted. My muscles were racked with soreness, and my mind felt torched. I closed my eyes and hoped she'd go away.

What did I cry? I wondered. *What did I agree to?*

I knew the witch could read my mind, but she refused to answer my questions.

Numbness blanketed me.

Later Quito came in with food and water. He lingered near me, concerned for my well-being.

"Quito," I whispered, gesturing with a finger for him to draw closer.

He glanced upward at the balcony, then bent down to my lips. "What happened to me?" I asked.

"You saw the abyss."

"What is it?"

"It's part of her kingdom. The deathless death."

"I can't go back there," I mumbled, trying to restrain myself from sobbing.

"It is not the worst she has to offer you," he said. "Her ecstasy is worse than torment."

"An ecstasy that leads to self-mutilation?" I asked.

"Yes."

Nothing in Ranger training had prepared me for this battlefield. I was a materialist. This was a war within ethers and vapors. Lands I had never scouted. This was Deborah's type of war, and I could not survive without her help. I knew I was in peril if I even spoke her name. "Quito," I pleaded. "How's . . . ?"

"She's fine," he said. "I keep her comfortable."

I needed an ally, and the old eunuch was my only hope. There had to be something I could use to gain his empathy. "Quito. The eyes. Have you ever seen eyes like . . . ?"

"No," he admitted. "They are beautiful." The tone of his voice told me I had discovered the key. Beholding Deborah's eyes was like discovering hidden treasure. Misfits, like Babbler and Quito, found solace in the warmth of her light.

"You've seen the Queen's eyes?" I said.

"Yes. I see them daily."

"Compare them." I gasped for breath to pursue my ploy, but my energy was gone. "Quito. I'm feeling strange. I don't care to eat. I'm getting dizzy."

"It is her. She is calling you again," he said.

"I don't want to go," I cried.

"You have no choice."

I passed out.

I came to, not in the stone chamber but in a tub of hot water. Steam hung heavily in the air, obscuring my vision, but I sensed I wasn't alone. There was another tub in the room, and someone was in it.

"Ah, my pretty little army boy. You have awakened," the Queen said from behind a misty veil.

I shook my head to clear my senses, but it didn't help. The steam was my main disorientation.

"The water feels good, doesn't it?" she said. "How long since you had a hot bath, Lieutenant?"

I focused on her voice. Slowly her form took shape in a stone tub about ten feet away. The steam began to dissipate, and I beheld her face as through a light fog. She seemed strikingly beautiful. Her eyes were large and green, framed by hair so black it nearly glowed purple. Her lips were red and full.

"Sore from your little trip? The hot water will relieve your pain."

"What?" I said. "What do you want from me?"

She pointed a finger at me. Her nails were long and painted. "I need you, Lieutenant. You see what I have around me for men. Faithful little Quito. The foolish and brazen Quarro. And the others. Not a man among them."

"You . . . took . . . their . . . manhood." My words fell leaden to the floor.

"Yes. They gave it to me." She laughed coldly as from a throat of icicles. "Silly of them, wasn't it?"

"Where's . . . ?"

"Silence. You will not mention that name."

"I won't . . . mention it," I said. I was afraid, not for myself, but for retribution against Deborah.

"No, but you will think of her," the Queen snapped. "But when I'm done with you, you'll forget you ever knew her."

"What's your plan . . . for me?"

"I offer you my kingdom," she said.

"I bet . . . you say that . . . to all . . . the boys," I quipped.

"You're right," she said. "I do." She stood in the tub in a subtle but somehow frank display of her nakedness. For a moment I thought I was looking at a goddess. She lingered purposely, allowing me to fully appreciate her beauty. "It can all be yours," she said. Stepping from the tub, she disappeared into the steam.

The next thing I knew I was again lying on the cold stone floor of the chamber. Minutes later her manservant entered. "Quito," I said softly. "Was I in a hot bath?"

"Yes," he said. "The Queen ordered it."

"And she was there?"

"Yes. You were in her quarters." He nodded upward.

"How is—"

"Don't ask," he said.

"I must know," I said. "Tell me."

"She's OK," he whispered.

"You have thought about her eyes?" I asked.

He lowered his head and wouldn't answer.

"What do you see in her eyes, Quito?"

He turned away and his frail shoulders shuddered.

"Quito, what's wrong? What's bothering you?"

His eyes shot up at the balcony, then down to me. "She draws your friend's blood soon," he said.

"What does that mean? Surely the Queen won't kill her."

"I don't know," he said, backing toward the door. "The Queen is very jealous. I think she might take all of her blood at once."

"Quito. You must help us."

"There is nothing I can do."

"Quito. How can I save her? What does the Queen want from me?"

"She wants your unfailing love. She wants to possess you."

A deep trembling erupted within me as if I were again falling into the abyss. "Tell her she can have me," I said. "I will pledge my love for the life of the young woman."

"Don't do that," he warned. "You will lose her respect. You have already passed one test. Don't fail now."

"What test? How did I pass it?"

"In the abyss. When you cried out. You did not cry for the Queen. You cried for . . . "

"For her? I cried for her?"

"Yes. And it has made the Queen very angry." He paled and seemed to shrink in front of my eyes. "She will test you again. She needs you badly."

"Quito, the game is almost over, isn't it? There is only you and Quarro and a few others. Has she eaten everyone? Where are they?"

I had pressed too far. Truth made him panic, and he fled the room as fast as his old legs could carry him.

My next visitor was Quarro. The flying-saucer man walked in and pointed my own weapon at me. "Get to your feet," he barked. "We're going outside."

The air was pungent with the smell of pine, and light stabbed my eyes. I squinted for minutes before I could see. The blue sky was so distant it seemed unworldly, the atmosphere of another planet. The natural world no longer seemed real since I had stared into the jaws of the abyss. When I could finally focus, I looked around for Deborah.

The saucer-man would have none of that. "Get going." He pushed me in the back with the rifle and directing me to a stand of aspens. In the center of the trees an area had been cleared, and a beautiful black horse stood haltered to a post. It pawed nervously as we approached.

"Stand here," Quarro said.

I stood about fifteen feet away from the animal. Quarro disappeared into the trees. For fifteen minutes or more the horse and I stared at each other. From his long, fine legs to his smooth and sculptured head, he was the animal of my dreams, the pursuit of my soul.

"He's beautiful, isn't he?" a voice said from the trees. The witch's voice.

I nodded.

"He's yours," she said. "If you can ride him."

I waited for her next command. At that moment horses meant nothing to me. I wanted to live. I wanted to find Deborah. Nothing else mattered, but I would ride the horse if she asked me to. No sound came from the trees. No commands.

The stallion snorted and wildness flared white in his eyes. Was it my test to ride the horse? Would that be seen as an attempt to escape? I knew at least one rifle was trained on me. Could I rush to the horse, untie him, swing to his back, and stay mounted long enough to get off the mountain?

I doubted it. I was a soldier not a cowboy. Was I being tested to run or not to run? To ride or not to ride?

Ride the horse. Get on the horse and ride away. The urge within me grew so great my legs began to buckle.

The horse stared at me as if awaiting my approach.

Ride the horse. Ride away.

I took a deep breath and started forward when a warm breeze hit my face. A wind of warning. It pushed me back. Something, or someone, did not want me near the horse.

Suddenly Quito emerged from the trees with the rifle pointed at my head. "Get out," he urged. "Get away."

I turned my back on the black horse. The saucer-man marched me back to my stone prison, pushed me in, and locked the door behind me.

I sat down and stared up at the balcony, waiting for the witch to appear. What had the test with the horse meant? Did I flunk or pass?

Finally I stood and shouted at the top of my voice. "Lady LeClair, Lady LeClair." This continued for several minutes until she finally stepped onto the balcony in a shimmering black dress and veil.

"What do you want?" she called down. "Do you want the horse?"

"It's not a matter of what I want," I said. "It's a matter of what you want. You want me and I'm here."

"You do not know what I want," she said.

"I think I do," I replied. "Give me an audience with you. Let's talk."

"Men!" she said. "You are all so demanding. When I want you *I* will call for *you*." She left.

That night I dreamed. Black horses raced across a dark landscape, their manes and tails aflame and smoke streaming from their nostrils and eyes. The Queen and I rode the lead horse, the stallion, from the aspen grove. I sat behind her with my arms around her waist. Other horses pressed against us. The stallion nickered hideously, and the Queen threw back her head and nickered shrilly in response. We were stampeding toward the abyss.

Do not remember this dream, something demanded from within me. *You have succeeded in forgetting all others. Forget this one too.*

"No," came another voice. "*It's time to remember.*"

CHAPTER 14

I awakened on a bed covered with satin sheets. I knew whose bed it was. Her scent and presence permeated the air and covered me more heavily than the blankets.

"Sleep well?" she called from an anteroom.

"How did I get here?" I asked. My clothes were piled in a corner. I slipped out of the bed and began dressing.

"My little porridge is effective, isn't it, Lieutenant? Weren't you trained not to eat strange food?"

Drugs, I thought. *Or some sort of poison.*

"My garden grows the finest mushrooms," she said. "And toadstools and cactus. I must show you someday."

"How long have I been here?" I demanded. "What did we do?"

"What's wrong, Lover? Are you afraid we consummated our covenant?"

I heard water splashing. She was soaking in her tub. "We have no covenant," I said. "Not yet." I couldn't remember any ecstasy. Certainly this wasn't the test Quito had warned me of.

"Today I bathe in water," she taunted me. "Perhaps tomorrow I will bathe in the blood of your beloved."

I had refused her. Somehow she had drawn me to her bed, but I had spurned her advances. I understood none of this, but somehow I knew Deborah's prayers had protected me, and the Queen was sulking in anger, trying to entice me into her next web. She wanted me to lose my temper.

"Mono blood is wonderful for the skin," she said. "It's very rich."

Anger made claws of my hands. I moved forward to strangle her even though caution warned me away.

"I will need an attendant when the blood is drawn," she cooed. "You will be that attendant, Lieutenant. You will put the first needle into her veins."

Kill her! one part of my mind screamed.

Flee! cried the other.

Just do something, I told myself. Two quick bounds took me to the balcony, and I vaulted over the railing. The stone floor rushed up at me. By twisting in the air I hit in a parachutist's crouch, rolled over my right shoulder, and slapped the floor with my forearms to absorb the impact. Total blackness.

After I came to, it took minutes for my head to clear. Propped against a chamber wall, I found Quito sponging my forehead with a cold, wet cloth. My forearms were swollen and aching.

"How are you?" he asked.

I could only grunt.

"Shh," Quito said. "You are very sore."

"Leave him," the Queen screamed. Her voice cleared my mind like a cold wind. Quito hastened to his feet and scurried from the room.

"You arrogant army fool," the witch shouted from her balcony. "You would deprive me of my pleasure by trying to kill yourself? How cowardly."

"It wasn't suicide," I said.

"It was certainly stupid," she replied. "I hardly think you are good genetic material, Lieutenant."

"I'm not," I said. "I'm weak and stupid."

"Then we certainly can't have you perpetuating your bloodline, can we? Quito is old. He won't live much longer. I will be needing a new houseboy, Lieutenant." She turned to leave.

She didn't want me anymore. I was a reject, no longer had any bargaining power. "Wait," I cried. "I want to make you a deal."

The witch stopped. "A deal? What could you possibly have to offer?"

"Robert," I said. Strength drained from me by merely mentioning the name.

"Robert? The machine-man?" She traced the balcony railing with a finger as if deep in thought. "You think you can bring me Robert? Alive?"

"Yes," I said. "For her release."

"How can you capture Robert? Do you know where he lives?"

"No."

"Then how can you find him?"

"He will find me," I said.

"And you think you can master him?"

"I will have to."

"That would make you stronger than Robert," she said sagaciously. "That means I would have to have *you*, Lieutenant, not the machine-man."

"No. He and I will fight to the death. In this chamber. Bare hands. You get the winner. But you must set the woman free before we fight."

"An interesting scenario," she said. "I appreciate your dramatic sense."

"It's a good trade, Queen. The Mono does not have an unlimited amount of blood. Kill her and she's gone. Robert you could have forever. Besides, he's probably a virgin too."

"Robert a virgin? What makes you think that?"

"Has anyone seen him with anyone? Are his victims ever raped?"

"That means nothing."

"His sole purpose is to kill," I said. "He would let nothing else distract him."

"But you can't prove that a man is a virgin," she argued.

"His blood would prove it. The blood of virgins keeps you young and beautiful. Draw his. You would not only stay young and lovely, but imagine having his strength."

I could tell I caught her interest.

"Believe me," I continued. "You would have the rarest of creatures. A male virgin. A virgin warrior."

"You are quite the salesman, Lieutenant. If multilevel marketing still existed, you would have quite a future. I'll give your proposal some thought." She left the balcony in a swirl of self-importance.

I slumped against the wall, sore from head to toe, my head aching and my mind not believing my own words. I had wagered Deborah's life against my ability to capture and return with Robert. A virgin Robert at that.

Later Quito returned. He shuffled in stealthily and handed me several thin breadsticks. "Eat," he said. "You will need your strength."

"Quito," I whispered. "You shouldn't be here."

"You must not deal with the Queen," he said. "She lies."

"I know she lies."

"She will not keep her end of the bargain," he insisted.

"I know that. I'm trying to buy time."

"Do you really think you can capture the machine-man?"

"I don't know," I confessed. "I couldn't think of anything else to offer her."

"It was a good plan," he said. "She has fantasies about Robert. She has told them to me in detail. But it was a bad plan too. She will never release the Mono, and she would never permit you to leave the mountain alone."

"She will let me go after Robert."

"Maybe. But not intact. She will take your manhood first."

"No. She knows I will need all my strength to capture Robert."

"It's a huge risk."

"It's not a risk at all. I have nothing to lose. No other choices."

Quito crouched beside me like a small, hairless child. A child with a secret. "It is true what you suggested earlier," he whispered. "We are very few in number. You have seen all of us there are to see."

"Where are the others?" I asked.

"Dead. Some from illness. Some committed suicide. I suspect

others were killed and eaten. And we are eunuchs. We do not repro-
duce, so there are no children."

"Why do you tell me this?"

"Because—"

"Quito, you have looked in Deborah's eyes again?"

"Yes, just moments ago."

"And what did you see?"

"I saw life."

"And you've talked with her?"

"Yes. We talked."

"What did she say to you?"

"She told me that all have sinned and come short of the glory."

"What else?"

"She told me to be brave."

"We must all be brave, Quito. Did she tell you anything else?"

He rose to his feet. "I can't say. I must go. The Queen will soon
come to give you her answer. I must wait on her. I am the one who pre-
pares her for her audiences."

He left quickly and quietly. I kept my eyes on the balcony. Eventually the Queen appeared, wearing a headdress of silver plumes and a
long, white satin dress. A wedding dress.

"So, my little army boy, are you ready for my decision?"

I stood. "Yes," I said. "Give your command and I will bring you
Robert."

"But you do this for your little Mono wench and not for your
Queen?"

"The Mono and I are weak," I said. "We are undeserving of you.
Allow me to bring you the one you deserve."

She laughed. "How clever you are, Lieutenant. Perhaps I will keep you after all. A bird in the hand, you know."

"I will bring you Robert," I said. "Then there will be two birds in your hand, and you can choose between us."

"How entertaining you are." She moved closer, leaned against the railing, and stared down at me. "Actually, there is no way that I can lose, Lieutenant. I am not going to let you leave here alone."

I thought of Quarro. "No," I said. "Your warriors would only hinder me."

"Warriors? No, no. I'm sending my baby with you."

"The bear?"

"Yes. The command has already been given. If you make a mistake, she will kill you. You have twenty-one days, no more. Bring me the government agent alive, or your precious little Mono becomes bubble bath."

"If you harm her, I promise I will kill you."

She shrieked a cold laugh. "As if it were even possible," she said. "Only mortals die, Lieutenant."

Then a blur appeared at the door behind her. Something fast and flesh-colored rolled toward her like a tanned bowling ball. She turned and raised her hands. A shout rose in her throat, but it was too late. The object hit her in the small of the back, knocking her against the railing. She teetered, then toppled over, falling toward me, shrieking like a wounded lioness, her plumed headdress fluttering like a bird trying to take wing.

I stepped back and she hit with a sick thud at my feet, her head splitting like a cantaloupe. A stream of blood coursed through the white plumes of her bonnet.

Looking up, I saw Quito standing alone on the balcony, his bald head peering over the railing. "Is she dead?"

"I think so." I rolled the lifeless body over. To my surprise I discovered she wasn't young and beautiful at all, but hideous. Her skin was wrinkled and dotted with liver spots, her hair thin and gray at the roots, her eyes pale and clouded.

The Queen was an old crone. As I watched, she seemed to shrivel in death as the forces that had empowered her left to find another hostess.

"Your illusions were incredible," I said to her as her blood pooled at my feet. "But truth has uncovered you."

Soon Quito stood beside me. "I have killed the Queen," he said.

"She's so ugly, Quito. But I thought she was beautiful."

"She was a powerful witch," he said. "She used trances and steam to create illusions. That and a huge supply of cosmetics. And plastic surgery. Only I knew the truth. I was her beautician."

I suddenly realized the witch's death freed me from enchantment. "Deborah," I said. "I must get to her."

Quito looked at me with sad, confused eyes. "She's gone," he said.

"Gone? You mean, dead?"

"No. Gone. I went to her before attending the Queen. I let her escape."

"Take me," I said. "Where was she going? How do I find her?"

"She was worried for you," Quito said. "She went to do your job."

"My job?"

His eyes widened. Yes," he said. "The Queen bragged to her about your plan. Your friend has gone to do what you were going to do."

It can't be! I thought. *He can't be telling me what I think he's telling me.*

"It's true," he said. "She's doing it for you. She is going to find Robert."

CHAPTER 15

Lady LeClair was dead.

Deborah was free and searching for Robert.

I was standing defenseless in a stone room with a eunuch tugging at my arm.

"C'mon, c'mon," Quito said. "We have to get out of here. Quarro and the others will be coming."

"My weapons," I said vacantly, my eyes still riveted on the dead queen. "Where's my rifle and my knife?"

"No time, no time." Quito shuffled maniacally toward the door, his bald head glistening with perspiration.

My rational mind was still trying to explain the mystery of Lady
LeClair. She had appeared alluring. Gorgeous beyond belief. Confident
and powerful. Now she was a hideous pile of rags and bones. Somewhere there was a lesson in all this for me.

"C'mon!" Quito yelled. "I can hear the others coming."

Even in death the witch had a spell over me. I was nearly rooted to
the floor. She was holding me for her minions.

I tore myself away, bolted from the room, and followed the old
eunuch up a narrow stairway to the Queen's steam room. We passed
through another door, down a shadowy hallway, and into a cubicle no
larger than a prison cell.

"This is my room," Quito said. He moved a pile of blankets
and pried at the floor with his fingers. "The Queen has me sleep
here to guard the passageway." He pulled back a small square of
plywood to reveal a single, shiny pole. "Slide down," he said. "This
is the way Deborah went. Below you will find a ladder that leads to
a tunnel. The tunnel comes out in some bushes about thirty yards
beyond the castle."

"Quito," I said. "You're coming too."

"No, no. I am old and infirm. I would only slow you down."

"They will kill you if you stay."

"Yes, if they catch me," he said. "No one knows the castle like I
do. I can slow them down for you, Lieutenant."

"Quito, if they catch you, blame it on me. Tell them I killed their
queen."

"No, I'm going to tell the truth," he said firmly. "Deborah told me
to be brave and truthful." A distant howl echoed through the stone
chambers of the castle. "They've found the Queen," Quito said. "Hurry,

you must go. She only has an hour's start on you. She shouldn't be hard to find."

"The dog?" I said as I gripped the pole. "Did she take the white dog?"

"I don't know. He's penned near the tunnel entrance."

"I'm taking the horse," I said. "Where's the horse?"

"What horse?" he asked, impatient with my delays.

"The Queen's stallion. The horse in the aspen grove. Where is he?"

"She has no horse," he insisted.

"I saw him."

"You saw an illusion, Lieutenant."

I wanted to prove the eunuch wrong, but there was no time to argue. Instead, I reached over and gripped his shoulder. "Thank you, Quito," I said.

His was the face of a dead man, but he had accepted his fate with dignity. "One thing," he said, grasping my arm. "When you look into her eyes, Lieutenant. What do *you* see?"

Steps were sounding nearer as Quarro and the others searched the building. "I see what we were all meant to be," I said. Then I slid down the smooth pole fifteen feet to a floor. Groping in the dark for the ladder, I descended to a small chamber and a hole just large enough for a man to crawl through. I scurried through the tunnel and emerged in a thicket of bushes. As Quito had said, the castle was about thirty yards away, but there was no activity outside yet. Quarro and the other eunuchs were probably interrogating Quito.

A soft whine sounded behind me. Parting the bushes, I beheld Dunamis's white face and pale blue eyes staring back at me. The door of his wire enclosure was latched with a snap, not a lock, so I slipped it open, and the malamute trotted out gratefully.

The aspen grove was close by. With the dog at my heels I ran through the pines to where the horse had been tethered. I approached the clearing carefully.

There was no horse, only a thick collar and heavy chain attached to a cement post, an area of pressed-down grasses with claw marks in the dirt, bones picked clean, and bear scat.

Illusion. Her ultimate power. Her finest trick.

There had never been a black stallion. She had deceived me. I had almost tried to ride her bear!

And the bear was loose.

"Let's go," I commanded the dog. "Pick up the scent of your master." I turned and ran for the pine-covered foothills, confident that the eunuchs couldn't overtake me. But could I outrun the bear if it followed the Queen's commands from the grave? I would have to. Compounding my frustration, Dunamis showed no bloodhound instincts. He was content to follow me wherever I went. I ran on.

On a rocky knoll I turned to see if I were being followed. Six armed Cannibals rushed toward the dog pen. Quito, I imagined, was already dead. I watched as the big bear ambled out of the castle door. It stopped, sniffed the air, and looked in my direction.

I needed no more motivation. Pursuit gives strength to the prey. I set a ground-eating pace, unencumbered by weapons, certain I would overtake Deborah by backtracking our previous trail. I hoped I would reach her before Robert got her. Or before she got to him. I also had to stay ahead of the bear until I found a weapon capable of killing it.

A big weapon. A cannon.

Deborah had left no tracks. As I ran, I scanned the dust in the foot trails and the stream banks but didn't notice a single print. Had she stayed at the castle? Perhaps she'd thought she could rescue me from the Cannibals. Maybe they had her. I was tempted to return to the witch's fortress.

Then I remembered the houses.

Deborah would return to the last home she'd slept in. The cabin by the creek. If I found the cabin, I might find her. I couldn't explain the absence of a trail. But reentering reality after living in illusion, my senses were not yet razor sharp.

One sense that remained keen, however, was my awareness of Robert. He was no longer behind me but somewhere ahead. For once I was chasing him.

I reached the cabin by the stream just after nightfall and entered by the front door. I called out Deborah's name softly, like a husband home from work. There was no answer. Dunamis stepped in curiously behind me.

"Deborah," I called again. Her presence in her prayer room lingered so strongly it rocked me against a wall. I could almost see the glow of candlelight. "I'm resting here," I told myself aloud. "I'm sleeping in Deborah's room."

And I did. I curled up in some old blankets and imagined her in the room with me. I dozed.

My mental alarm clock went off after an hour or two, and I awakened to find the most beautiful blue eyes staring at me. They were framed by nearly snow-white hair.

"Deborah," I said.

My face got licked. It was the dog. I had slept with one arm around Dunamis.

"I never realized how much your eyes look like hers," I told him. My stomach screamed for food, but I could not still its cry. I had nothing to eat. *Put food out of your mind,* I told myself.

I had to reach the next house. With Deborah gone I was now drawn to houses. I stepped outside to listen to the night yet heard no sounds of pursuit. But how do you hear a bear following you in the forest?

I reached the next house by noon. The sun was at a broil. I searched the building, hoping against hope to find some evidence that she'd been there. I entered the room where she'd prayed, and fatigue suddenly overwhelmed me. I leaned against a wall, then slid to the floor. I slept like a worn child put down for his afternoon nap.

I had a dream and I remembered it. I dreamed I saw Deborah in the clouds, and she was motioning me to follow. "Where are you going?" I shouted.

She smiled at me and said nothing, but I knew what she was doing. She was going to the tribes. To the 'Postates first. She was returning to the work of her ministry. She would lead and I would follow.

But how could she still be ahead of me? It was not humanly possible that I hadn't overtaken her.

Was there danger for her in the 'Postate camp? Was Stinson really who he said he was?

When I awakened from the nap, I quickly resumed my jogging. I considered going cross-country, gambling that I could reach the 'Postate camp ahead of her and deal with any potential threats there. But the houses pulled on me. It was as if my course were already charted. I was caught in a current flowing through a channel carved ahead of me.

The moon peered over my shoulder by the time I reached the next house, the first one we'd stayed in after leaving the Flowers camp. I had no expectations of finding her there, but I knew I would find her presence. And I did. The room she'd slept in glowed with a brighter light than the other rooms washed by moonlight. I collapsed to the floor as if exhausted. Dunamis came to me, licked my face once, and lay down beside me. "Ole white dog," I mumbled. "I'm going to starve us both to death at this rate."

Sleep hit me like a hammer.

I awakened alone, rose on weak and sore legs, and struggled outside where Dunamis lay, his head on his paws, waiting for me. "We'll make it to the 'Postates today," I told the malamute. His eyes glazed with a weary sadness. "They'll feed us," I said. "And Deborah will be there."

We pushed on.

My fast jog turned to a running stumble that became a faltering walk. How many miles had I already covered? Sixty? Eighty? When was the last time I had eaten? I didn't know. How many days had it been since I'd actually seen Deborah? How many days was I imprisoned in the castle? All the days and miles muddled around me.

Wolves hounded my trail. I could hear their distant howls. They'd seen my faltering steps and knew I was weak or wounded, but they would wait until I went down before making their rush.

I would show them. "I will not go down," I said aloud. "I will not be another Storch lying on the prairie, slowly being eaten to death by a pack of snarling carnivores."

No, I will be a madman first, I thought. *A Slinger dressed for battle but without a weapon.*

Keep it up, my racing mind said, *and you will become a Babbler. A foolish scavenger pecked at by his own fears.* Vultures would nest in my hair. Magpies would tear at my exposed heart.

About that time the sky darkened with great clouds of ravens and crows coming from the southwest.

Lady LeClair has sent them, I thought. *These are her scouts. They guide the bear.*

The flocks rolled closer and closer, and their shadows covered the ground.

I turned to face them. If I was to be torn apart by birds of the air, I wanted my body found with wounds to my front, not my back. I stared at the sky and screamed.

The rolling darkness in the sky was not hordes of ravens and crows but slow and low clouds. Rain clouds.

The drops began striking me hard in the face.

Rain. It never rained this time of the year in the Interior.

It fell harder, forcing me to turn my back. The drops hit like hail against my head and shoulders and peppered my legs like buckshot. A cool breeze sprang from the northeast, and within minutes the temperature plunged thirty or forty degrees.

This is not happening, I thought. *It's an illusion.* I forced myself to turn and face the storm. "This is The Season of the Burning Sun," I shouted. "This rain is not real."

The drops hit my face like marbles. Dunamis whined and ran for shelter. *If the dog says it's real, it must be real,* I decided. I followed Dunamis to a cove of sandstone. We huddled there as rainwater poured off the surrounding ledges in miniature waterfalls. "I've never seen anything like this," I told Dunamis. His wet, white fur pressed against me.

The dog seemed to watch the rain with unusual interest. I imagined that he, too, had never seen anything like it.

The rain fell hard all day, then the heavens sighed and the downpour became a light drizzle. We continued the march even though the ground was slick and muddy. I fell several times. The dog and I were both wet, cold, and plastered with mud.

Long after dark I stumbled into the 'Postate compound and collapsed in the plaza. I looked up at what I thought was the statue of Flowers, but it had been replaced. I lay at the foot of a cross. One that was not inverted. My head rested against a woodpile. This was what remained of Flowers's shrine to himself.

I slept. Or maybe I simply passed out.

Dunamis and I were discovered in the morning, carried to a shelter, and laid on cots. Stinson attended me. His face was clean-shaven, and pants and shirt had replaced the robe. I tried speaking to him. "Deborah," I said. My voice was so weak he could hardly hear me. "Deborah," I said again.

His face crinkled into a smile. "She's been here," he said. "She left yesterday."

Come and gone already? It was impossible. I struggled to rise, but Stinson restrained me. "You need food and rest," he said.

They fed me and I slept. I awakened in a bed beneath sheets and blankets. My wet clothes were gone, and I was wearing a heavy cotton robe. I got out of bed mechanically. New clothes were laid out on a chair, and my shoes had been cleaned and dried. I dressed, then followed cool hallways to the kitchen, where I found Stinson making breakfast.

"I was going to bring this to you in bed," he said.

I was not in a gracious mood. "Where is she?" I demanded.

He put a plate of bread and elk steak on the table. "She's gone on to the Patriots," he said.

"You must be lying," I told him. "She had only an hour's start on me. How could she stay so far ahead?"

My antagonism didn't bother him. He only shrugged. "Deborah's a hard one to explain," he said.

I made myself sit and eat, even though I wanted to set out immediately to find her. "Did she say anything about me or Robert or Lady LeClair?" I asked.

"No. We were all curious about the Cannibals, of course. She just said that everything went well. I asked about you. She said you were following her."

Part of me did not believe anything he said. Part of me knew he was telling the truth. I looked up at the ceiling. The underground shelter was so well insulated it took me a minute to realize it was raining again.

Stinson seemed to read my bewilderment. "Yes," he said. "It's raining. It's been coming down for hours."

"This is very odd," I said, as much to myself as to him.

"Lady LeClair must be dead," he said.

I looked up in astonishment. "How did you know that?" "Deborah said Lady LeClair was the power that blocked the rains from the west. When she was pulled down, the rains would come."

"Impossible," I said. "A person can't block rain."

"Is the witch dead?" he asked me.

"Yes. She fell at my feet."

"And now it rains," he reasoned. "It's great for our gardens. Deborah told us to prepare for those who will come after her."

"But she said nothing else about me or Robert?"

"No. At least not to me."

"Are you him?" I asked.

"Who?"

"Robert," I said. "Are you actually Robert?"

Stinson laughed. "No, Lieutenant. I can assure you I am not Robert."

I stared at him gravely. Even if he were Robert, how would I prove it? "Did Deborah warn you about a man named Quarro? A eunuch with a flying saucer tattoo?"

"No . . . " His answer was slow and drawn out as if he were applying brakes to where I was leading him.

"Did she mention a bear?"

"A bear . . . ?"

"Yes. Lady LeClair rode a bear. The bear's following me."

He looked down at the table, then back up at me. "Daniel, I think you need more rest."

"No," I said, pushing the plate away. "I need a gun. A big gun."

"Stay here," he insisted. "Let us take care of you."

"No," I demanded. "I need a rifle and a raincoat. And some food."

"You're going to leave no matter what, aren't you?"

"You can't stop me," I said.

He shrugged again. "Very well, follow me." He led me down a concrete hallway to a series of vaultlike chambers. "These were our fallout shelters," he explained. "We'll use them in the future to store vegetables." He opened a steel door and shone a flashlight on walls lined with weapons. "This is all junk to us now," he said. "Hundreds of guns and tens of thousands of rounds of ammunition. Most of it was to be used against people, not bears." He went to a far corner and picked a gun case off a rack. "You might like this," he said, handing me the case.

I pulled out a long, heavy rifle with a laminated stock. "Dakota Arms," I said. "Custom-made 30/378." A ten-power Leupold scope, Harris bipods, and a Butler Creek suspension sling completed the rig.

"A man like you can kill a bear at 500 yards with that gun," he said, handing me a heavy box of cartridges. "And these are extra-hot loads. With proper bullet placement they could drop an elephant."

"Or Robert," I added.

He stared at me. I didn't like the weight of his eyes.

"Someone has to do it," I said.

Stinson shook his head. "I really wish you would stay, Daniel," he said. "I think you like your old life too much. The running, the constant quest, the thrill of being both hunter and hunted."

I wasn't listening to him. I felt empowered holding the heavy rifle. "This is a special weapon, Stinson," I said. "I will bring it back to you."

"No," he said. "I don't want it. When you're done with it, toss it in a river."

I looked at him as if he were nuts, but he was serious.

"Keep the gun, Daniel," he said, leaving the vault. "Keep it if it makes you feel secure."

"Come with me," I called after him. "Help me find Deborah."

Stinson turned, his face barely distinguishable in the darkened hallway. "What makes you think she needs our help?"

Having outfitted me for my journey, the 'Postates told Dunamis and me goodbye. They wanted the malamute to stay, but the dog whined when they held him. Dunamis insisted on following me.

The going was slow. The ground was too wet for jogging, and Stinson's rifle weighed a ton compared to the little .223 I was used to packing. But desperation spurred me on. I had food, and water was running everywhere, so I took shortcuts through rough country. By dark I'd found one of Deborah's houses.

Wax droppings from her candles gave the only physical evidence she'd ever been there. The unnatural evidence was the soft glow of her presence in all the rooms she had cleansed. I didn't fear staying in houses anymore. They reminded me of her.

Daylight broke bright and shining. The air smelled clean, and the trilling of a meadowlark was the first songbird I'd heard in years.

About noon I reached the old cottonwood tree. The tree Deborah had brought back to life—still fully dressed with green leaves. It was no illusion.

As I stared up at its massive boughs, I was startled by a low distant rumbling, like the sound of incoming aircraft. But it was thunder. Seconds later, lightning flashed and heavy rain drops riddled the ground like bullets. Dunamis and I huddled in the shelter of the tree as the rain fell in liquid black curtains.

In a short time several inches of rain came down. The hardpan soils were soaked, coated with a heavy, gooey mud stickier than wet cement.

The progress we made was punishing. My legs became leaden, and my arms ached from carrying the heavy rifle. Even Dunamis struggled.

At dark we made it to a house I didn't recognize. One Deborah hadn't slept in. I went inside but I couldn't stay there. The place was cold, dark, and lifeless. There was no glow. So Dunamis and I spent the night in a cramped cave littered with the bones of small animals.

The morning dawned warm and sunny again with puffy cumulus clouds floating in the sky. Prairie grasses were greening with resurrection, and more meadowlarks chimed. We mucked northward for hours before resting on a high butte to eat the last of the 'Postate provisions. Sunshine seduced us both and we slept.

I awakened with the sense of being watched. I rolled onto my stomach with the rifle in my hands and scanned the countryside below.

I feared the nightmare of the bear. But the scene below wasn't my nightmare. It was my dream.

A band of wild horses. Six mares, four colts, two yearlings, and a chestnut stallion drank from a pool of rainwater less than a hundred yards away. The breeze blew in my favor, and the horses had not detected me.

In different circumstances this would have been the moment I'd lived for. Had the ground been dry and my body rested, I still wouldn't have had any way of capturing one, but the pursuit would have been on.

But now they might as well have been unicorns in a fairy tale. I was too exhausted, the ground too muddy, and my time controlled by another quest. I watched them intently for fifteen or twenty minutes before the stallion lowered his head, pinned his ears, and herded his harem away.

They never knew I was there.

The horses grazed toward a high divide, then lined out on a trail to the south. On the ridge, the stallion stopped—a thin, black silhouette with his ears pricked toward the west. He watched something. Then he flicked its tail and disappeared.

I lay as quietly as a sniper, searching the prairie and badlands through the ten-power scope of Stinson's 30/378.

I finally saw what the stud horse had seen.

A grizzly came lumbering up a long coulee, its head swinging slowly from side to side. It seemed to be following the spoor left by the dog and me.

I couldn't tell if it was the witch's pet or not. I leveled the rifle on its bipods and trained the crosshairs on the bear's chest. Eight hundred yards, I guessed. I breathed out softly and let the grizzly come closer. Seven hundred yards. I flipped the rifle's safety off. Six hundred yards. Five hundred.

Now, I thought. *Kill it now.*

CHAPTER 16

I began to slowly squeeze the trigger.

Then the big bear stopped, lifted a hind leg, and urinated on a greasewood bush.

It was a male. The grizzly was not the witch's trained sow. Could it still have been sent by her, or was it a rogue male following us on his own?

At three hundred yards the grizzly turned and looked in the direction the horses had gone. He seemed to study his options for a moment before veering to the west, away from us.

I wanted as much country between the bear and me as possible. We pushed northward with renewed vigor.

As I went to sleep that night in the cow camp where Mr. Simon had surprised us, I wondered what had happened to the Militia killer. One way or the other, I suspected our trails would cross again.

Just before dawn I passed the charred remains of the space cadets' fire. At first there was no sign of them. *Perhaps Robert got them,* I thought. Or maybe they'd been right and the Mother Ship had returned. Then a mile farther I found the leader by himself, shivering and nearly delirious.

"Where are the others?" I asked him.

He looked through me for several minutes before deciding I was really there. "You from Osiris?" his voice pled.

"No, I'm from here," I said. "Have you seen the woman who talked with you?"

"Osiris?" he repeated.

"No, not Osiris. Have you seen the woman?"

"Osiris?"

"Where are your followers?"

He turned slowly and pointed east.

I moved away from him.

"Osiris?" he called after me.

I reached the badland pinnacles of the Missouri Breaks late that afternoon and slept in a cave overlooking the Missouri River. Early the next morning I entered the Patriot compound by the same narrow trail Deborah and I had walked as prisoners. I noted the absence of sentinels.

The camp was cleaner, busier, and friendlier than before. Women and children waved hello and even the dogs were groomed and better behaved. I went straight to the General's headquarters. There a young man weeding a vegetable patch informed me the General and his daughter were on the lake fishing.

Suddenly the headquarters door opened, and a man rushed out shouting my name. It was the sergeant whose ear I'd sliced off. I prepared myself to drop him.

He ran toward me unarmed.

I raised the rifle and hoped he realized it could put a hole through him the size of a bowling ball.

He smiled and pushed the rifle aside. "So good to see you, Lieutenant," he said. "We've all been worried about you."

"Deborah," I demanded. "Where is she?"

"She left last night," he said. "She was here several days. It was great having her—"

"Several days!"

"Look at this," he said, pointing to the ear I had sliced with my knife. The ear was whole. "Deborah prayed for it."

"Where did she go?" I demanded, raising the rifle again.

"I don't know," he said, taking me by the arm. "Maybe Mr. Simon knows. He's down at the chapel teaching a class."

"The chapel?"

"Yes. It was the armory, but we remodeled it and put the guns in the coal bin."

"Simon's teaching?"

"Sure is," the sergeant said, leading me across the plaza. "Deborah spent most every minute with him while she was here. It seems like her special way of teaching got transferred onto him."

"You said she was here three days!" I said. "She left the 'Postates just three days ago."

"Well, imagine that," he said, not missing a step. "Well, she was. She taught and ministered to all of us, of course, but mostly to Mr. Simon. She said we'd need a teacher after she was gone."

I noticed for the first time that none of the men were wearing uniforms anymore. "Your clothes," I said.

He patted his flannel shirt. "Yeah, civvies again. Great, isn't it? Deborah told us to quit playin' army."

The chapel group was breaking up as the sergeant and I entered. Simon saw us and approached me with a hand out in greeting. He no longer looked like a weasel. His hair was trimmed and combed, and a peaceful self-assurance filled his eyes.

"It's good to see you, Lieutenant," he said. "Deborah said you'd be right behind 'er."

"She did?"

"You look tired and hungry. Here, let me carry that for you," he said, taking Stinson's rifle from me. "C'mon. We're on our way to the chow hall."

I let him carry the weapon.

Inside the mess hall, an old Quonset building, the entire compound had assembled, sitting at wooden tables. They chatted happily while workers filled bowls from a large vat of stew. The place quieted and everyone stood when they saw Mr. Simon and me.

He seemed embarrassed. "They're not standin' for me," he whispered. "They just know it's time to say grace." He directed me to a table and spoke to the sergeant. "Would you do the honors today?" he asked.

The sergeant offered a long and loud benediction, thanking God for everything from catfish stew to the healing of a baby to the downpours of rain. As everyone was seated, I sat between the sergeant and Mr. Simon.

As famished as I was, I craved information even more. "Where did she go?" I asked. "Why didn't she stay here?"

Mr. Simon looked at me patiently, like a kind father evaluating a son. "She said she had more work to do," he explained.

My body now demanded attention, so I lifted my bowl, drank the stew in several gulps, and wiped my mouth on my shirt sleeve. "What kind of work?"

"I think she's looking for Robert," he said matter-of-factly.

I stared at him in disbelief. "She said that? She said she was going after Robert?"

"She didn't mention him by name, but she's reached the major tribes. The only person left for her to evangelize is Robert."

"You think she plans on *preaching* to Robert?"

A young man came by and refilled my bowl.

"Of course, what else?" Mr. Simon said. "I can't see her doin' anything different, can you?"

"How will she find him?"

"I don't know. How does Deborah do anything? She said there was a Babbler down by Yellowstone she wanted to see again."

"You remember him," the sergeant chipped in. "You guys were eating snakes the day you sliced my ear off. Seems like a lifetime ago now, doesn't it?"

"The big dogtown," I said. "Saks on Fifth Avenue."

"That's probably where you'll find her," Mr. Simon said. "Say, isn't this rain something? I've never seen it rain like this in these parts. I'm used to searing heat. The other morning it was so cool the rain started turning to snow."

"How does she stay ahead of me?" I asked. "I'm traveling as fast as I can."

"Miracles," Mr. Simon said. "Just miracles. That's all."

I looked at them suspiciously. The Patriots were not making sense. If they were going to be irrational, it was time for me to leave. "Can you spare some provisions?" I asked. "A little jerky, maybe. Just something to get me to Saks."

"You can have anything you want," Simon said. "Our hunting's been uncommonly good. The fishing too. But why rush off, Lieutenant? We're having a song service this afternoon."

"No, I have to catch up with her," I said, rising from the table.

"You should hear Mr. Simon play the fiddle," the sergeant offered. "Was tone-deaf before. Now he plays like a master."

Idiots. The woman they revered so highly was marching toward her own tortured death, and they wanted to sing songs. "I'm not much for music," I said. "I have to stop Deborah from reaching Robert."

The sergeant laughed. He acted like it was all a big joke. "You're not going to stop Deborah from doing anything once she's set her mind on it," he said. "Robert's quite a challenge, but she's up to it."

My pent-up anger and frustration finally erupted. "You fools!" I shouted. Everyone in the mess hall turned to look at me. "How could you let her leave? Don't you care if she dies?"

Mr. Simon rose slowly. "Deborah's welfare is very important to us," he said quietly. "But she's taught us to look beyond her to the God she serves and those who follow after her."

"So you sacrifice her to Robert?" I said.

"No, we respect her decisions. Whatever she does has a purpose in it."

"You're all crazy," I shouted. "All of you." They had let Deborah leave. Now I had many more miles to cover. So many that I questioned my ability to do it.

"We're sad for you, Lieutenant," Mr. Simon said.

"Sad for me? Why?"

"Because you refuse to open your eyes. You keep charging forward, chasing something you can't catch and overlooking what's all around you."

"I don't know what you're talking about," I said.

"That's sad too."

"I need food."

"Come on, then," he said. "Let's get you and the dog some food for your journey."

I crossed the burn with Dunamis, glad to be putting the transformed militia behind me. The burn was no longer a wasteland of soot and ash. Instead, a short carpet of grass was growing. Only the black stalks of charred brush indicated an earlier prairie fire.

The entire prairie was slowly changing before my eyes. Native grasses sprang from the ground. Creeks, coulees, and reservoirs brimmed with water. I had never seen the Interior like this.

As different as it was in appearance, it was still my turf. I was home now with caches of food and weapons available to me. I seriously considered abandoning the 30/378 because of its weight, but the bear still haunted my thoughts. Two sights burned into my memory: the abyss and the spectacle of Lady LeClair mounted on a grizzly. I suspected the bear still trailed behind me.

That evening we came across the carcass of a recently killed bison calf. Bear sign was everywhere, and the length of the claw marks indicated a griz.

Later, during the night, a pack of wolves trailed us. Once they came so close they appeared like wisps of smoke floating through starlight. I was not concerned about them. This was my hunting ground, and they knew me and my capabilities.

The dog and I denned for a few hours in a badlands crevice where I'd cached canned food, bandages, a knife, and cartridges for my Ruger. The cartridges were the wrong caliber and I didn't need the bandages, but we ate the canned sardines. Before I left, I strapped the knife on my belt.

The next morning we came upon a small herd of bison. They were upwind and so engrossed with green grass that we walked right through their midst. I could have dropped any of them with Stinson's gun.

A few miles later we surprised a large bull elk, his sweeping antlers still in the furry stages of velvet. The bull wasn't much more observant than the bison. Green grass made the grazers careless.

Then we came to a creek that was normally dry but now roared like a small river. I had no choice except to try and cross it. I waded in, holding the rifle above my head. The dog paddled beside me. Halfway across, the current knocked me off my feet. I had to drop the gun to swim for my life. The water was thick and brown, and whole trees floated in its pull. I relaxed and became like another log, a log that kicked for the opposite bank. When I finally came to shore I was hundreds of yards below where I entered.

I pulled myself up on the bank, then remembered Dunamis. At first I couldn't see him and was certain I'd lost Deborah's dog. But then his white head came bobbing toward me, and he lunged out of the water. I had Dunamis but the rifle was gone.

I was now weaponless in the Interior except for a small hunting knife. My hair and short, scrubby beard were matted with mud, I was dripping water, and I had gotten so skinny I was afraid I'd lose my pants. The white dog looked better than I did. You might have wondered which of us was the animal and which was its master.

I heard the prairie dogs before I saw them. Their little chirps and barks sounded like noisy children on a playground.

I had reached Saks. Deborah had to be near, but *how near* was another matter. The massive dogtown stretched five miles wide and eight miles long. I struck through the heart of it. The incessant chirping of thousands of rodents drove all thought from my mind. I couldn't think. I could only walk and look. But I was finding nothing. I spent the entire day walking the length of Saks. "We're shopping till we drop," I told the dog.

When darkness fell, I began navigating the dogtown's width. "Supermarket, aisle three, aisle four," I sang softly to myself, trying to repeat Babbler's stupid little ditty. Dunamis trotted behind me, paying no attention to either the scolding prairie dogs or my musical foolishness.

In the moonlight the earthen mounds took on a soft glow as if each were a magic doorway to an underground world. Twice I startled other animals in the darkness without knowing what they were. Probably badgers. Prairie dogs were hard to catch, but Saks was so huge the predators couldn't help trying. Everyone can get lucky sometime. I was hoping to.

I slept while I walked. I didn't realize it until I stepped in a hole, fell, and woke myself up. It was daylight, and from the landmarks I knew I was on the south edge of the dogtown. I had traversed all of Saks and there was no sign of Babbler or Deborah. Or anyone else.

Not only was I still alone, I was wet again. It had rained on me, and I was tired, hungry, and miserable. I stumbled on until the day became warm and humid. Then, overcome by discouragement and fatigue, I curled up with the white dog and went to sleep.

Several hours later I was rousted awake.

"Daniel, Daniel," the voice said. "Get up. It's going to rain."

My mind drifted up from exhaustion, and I looked into the face of a handsome, older man, his cheeks pink from a fresh shave, his hair brushed neatly back. "Who are you?" I said, pushing him away.

"Daniel, it is me, Jones," he said.

I shook the sleep from my mind. "I don't know a Jones," I said. "Who are you?"

He extended a hand and assisted me to my feet. "It's me, my friend," he said. "Just imagine me scruffy and dirty."

I cleared my eyes and looked at him closely. "Babbler," I said. "What happened?"

"I am whole and healed," he said. "My mind is well."

I knew there could only be one reason. "Deborah?"

"Yes. The one I called 'the pretty-eyed one' returned and found me. My mind is now sharp and clear. I remember things."

"Where is she?" I demanded. "Where is she, Babbler?"

"My name is Jones," he announced. "I was born in Iowa City, Iowa. I was a postal employee for many years in Sioux Falls. I was married and had three girls and a boy. My wife and daughters were lost in the Plague but my boy lives. Somewhere my boy is alive."

"Babbler," I said, shaking him. "Where is Deborah?"

"I'm not Babbler," he insisted. "I am Jones. Deborah left this morning. We prayed in a house together. Then she told me to wait for you."

"Why didn't she wait? Babbler, where do I find her?"

"The name is Jones. She said she didn't have time to wait for you. She's going south. She said she would lead and you would follow."

"South? But where? Did she say anything about Robert?"

"She said she knows where Robert lives. She is on her way to his house."

"To his house. Babbler, think. Where is it? Where is this house?"

"I don't have to think," he said. "Because I don't know. Really, Daniel, you're acting crazy. I would tell you if I knew. Deborah has gone south. She said she knew where Robert lived and you would follow her."

"But how am I supposed to find her?"

"Just go," he said. "Somehow you will get there."

I sighed and stared at him with sad resignation. Babbler was now more sane than I. He was my protector and advisor. "And what about you, Bab—, uh, Jones? What are you going to do now?"

"I'm going east," he said. "I know the country between here and Sioux Falls. Deborah has instructed me to meet the ones who are coming. Exciting, isn't it? A few days ago I was incoherent. In a few more days I will be leading pioneers west."

"Yes," I said numbly. "It's very exciting."

"Like a wagon boss," he said, smiling. Then he sobered and put a protective arm on my shoulder. "But, Daniel, you worry too much about Robert. He's like New Mu—he's more myth than reality."

"No," I said. "He's not like New Mu. New Mu never existed. Robert exists."

"Yes," he agreed. "But he's overrated."

I brushed his arm away. "He's a killer," I snapped. "And Deborah is walking right into his trap."

The old man beamed a gentle smile and shook his head. "No," he said, "He is walking into hers."

CHAPTER 17

My hopes were dashed again. I'd thought when I found Babbler I would find Deborah, but she was thrust by a propulsion I could not match. No matter how hard I pushed, she stayed at least a day ahead of me. No matter where I arrived, she'd been there and gone. She told Babbler I was to follow, but follow where? The intermittent rains made tracking impossible. And she left no signs or directions. She could at least have waited for me.

Had I not been hopelessly in love with her, I would have resumed my normal routine of hunter and wanderer. Wild horses were easier to find and catch than a woman on a mission.

The night after leaving Babbler I huddled with Dunamis in the corner of an old barn. The plank walls whistled with the wind, the roof leaked in a chorus of drips, and ovations of thunder clapped overhead. Lightning, flaring through broken windows, cast stark shadows against stall timbers. Dunamis nuzzled against me heavily.

The storm raged furiously as if the heavens were at war.

But the day dawned bright, and the land almost hummed with new growth. By staying on higher ground we made reasonable time but hunger threatened. The rain had washed away two of my caches so completely that there was no sign they'd ever existed. I steered my course toward Catfish. The old man would have food.

I reached the Yellowstone River by midafternoon, sloshing through knee-deep water in what was usually a dry slough. I had already decided that if Catfish wasn't there I would help myself to his gardens and setlines, but a thin wisp of smoke rising from the willows told me he was home.

"Hello to the camp," I yelled weakly. No one appeared or called back. I approached warily. A fire was burning outside the hut, but there was no sign of the old man.

Hunger spurred me to his garden, and I was picking and eating radishes when I felt a shotgun thrust against my head.

"Make one wrong move, Cannibal, and I blow your head off."

I raised my arms and slowly turned around. "Catfish, it's me," I said.

He squinted and scowled. "Who are you?" he demanded.

"Daniel," I said. "It's me, Catfish. The Lieutenant."

He lowered the shotgun. "Daniel? What's happened to you? You look like you're dead and don't know it." He guided me by one arm into the hut where I collapsed on the dry earthen floor.

"What set upon you?" he asked. "Where are your weapons?"

"Food," I said. "Got anything to eat?"

"Got a banquet cooking," he said. "But you look like you could use something immediate." He took a wooden bowl down from a simple shelf and mashed three or four tomatoes into a pulpy soup. "Drink this down," he said.

I didn't need further encouragement. The vegetables strengthened me almost immediately, and I sat up.

"We'll have a real meal in a little while," he said. "I got a ten-pound sucker bakin' in the coals. Not only that, but a case of preserves washed on my shore the other day. Homemade stuff. Chokecherry. Strawberry. I already ate half of it, but I stuck some inside that ole fish. Baked fish with marmalade. Don't know how that'll work, but we'll find out."

"Baked fish," I said. "You must have aluminum foil."

He reached under a tattered coat and brought out a crisp new roll. "Lookee," he chimed. "Looks new right off the supermarket shelf, don't it?"

"Where did you get that?" I asked.

"The girl gave it to me."

"The girl?"

"Yeah, the Mono that you was talkin' 'bout before. The one with the pretty eyes."

"Deborah?" I said. "She's been here?"

"Deborah? Whatever. She never told me her name. She just waltzed into my camp yesterday like she owned the place. I was a little whacked out. Been samplin' some of my hemp harvest. For some reason I knew who she was right away, so I asked about you. 'Didya find the Lieutenant?' I says, and she says yes, that you were a ways behind 'er."

"Where did she go?" I asked. "Which way?"

"I'll get to that. Don't rush me. Anyways, to continue my story, I was sittin' there stoned outa my gourd, and she starts askin' me questions, like 'Do you want to be free from the chains of darkness?' or somesuch. I just stared at her, too ripped to be rational. I think she finally got the drift of what planet I was habitatin', 'cuz finally she just looks at me and says, 'Silver and gold have I none, but this I do have,' and she reaches into a little pack she was carryin' and brought out this roll of aluminum foil. It was a sight to behold! I rolled out a long sheet and it twinkled and shined like liquid silver. I guess I stared at it for some time because when I raised my eyes to look for her, she was gone. Being too mellowed to get to my feet, I just sat and looked around. Thought she'd reappear but she didn't. Maybe the Cannibals scared 'er off. That's all I can guess."

"Cannibals?" I exclaimed.

"Yeah, those colored-up mutations of Lady LeClair's came back right after the girl left. Capsized their canoes up the river a ways. Floated onto my bank like a string of drowned rats. Only this time I was waiting for 'em. Me and Bertha, that is." He patted the stock of his shotgun. "Got the drop on 'em. Looked like the same bunch that raided me before. Six of 'em again."

"No," I said. "Not the same bunch. Not entirely."

"Well, one was the same. The real ugly one with the flying saucer soarin' outa his belly button. I remembered him. He acted like the leader. Anyway, the river's running mighty high and swift, and it was more than those boys had bargained for. Figure a whirlpool sucked their crafts down. Lucky for me they lost all their weapons 'cept a revolver. I took it away from 'em."

"What did you do with them?" I asked. "Where are they?"

He shrugged. "I dunno. I just put the run on 'em. I wasn't scared of 'em this time. They was cold and sick and seemed to be goin' somewhere in particular. We struck a deal first though."

"Struck a deal? What sort of deal?"

"Dope," he said. "They saw the cannabis I had hangin' to dry, not to mention the stuff I had bagged up already. I told 'em I couldn't give 'em any, that it was all for Flowers."

"Flowers is dead," I said.

"So they told me. I got the feeling they'd already been to his camp and got run off. The flyin' saucer guy told me the Mono girl had killed Flowers. Not only that, but he said she'd killed ole Lady LeClair too."

"That's not exactly true," I said.

"Well, I didn't believe a word of it. The blue-eyed girl a killer? That's a mite of a stretch. But my economy's hurt if Flowers is pushin' up flowers, that's for sure. Be a glut on the dope market now, so I figure why not trade with the Cannibals? 'You boys stay outa my hair,' I told them, 'and I'll give ya a big bag of dope. But you come nosin' back around here again and I'll shoot ya full o' holes.' They took the dope and skedaddled. I saw 'em outa Dodge, so to speak."

"Which way?" I said. "Which way did they go?"

"I sent 'em up the Tongue. Figured I didn't want 'em on my river, so I sent 'em south. They crossed on that old bridge east of here. I threw a setline and some bait into the deal and told 'em to get goin'. Figured they could fish their way south. If I'm lucky, they'll run into Robert, and he'll cut their throats for me."

"Robert? Has there been any sign of Robert?" I asked.

"Nope. Been pretty quiet on that front. Hear three Pilgrims were found dead a couple weeks ago. Two women and a man. That mighta been Robert's doin', but other than that, this part of the Interior's been a right respectful place."

"Catfish," I shouted. "The girl. Where is she? Where did she go?"

He tugged at his gray whiskers. "Well, I don't know for sure. But there was one thing. Don't really know what to make of it."

"What?" I demanded, tempted to shake him. "What was it?"

"I remember her sayin', just before she up and left, that life and death were in the power of the tongue. She repeated it. The power of the tongue."

"Yes, so?"

"Well, it mighta been a coincidence, but when I escorted those Cannibals southward, I saw a fresh track in the mud. Made by a woman's foot. And I thought, ain't that a hoot? She says life and death is in the power of the tongue and here she is walkin' the riverbank. The Tongue River, get it?"

"The Tongue. You mean she went the same way as the Cannibals?"

"No, they went the same way as her. She had a lead on 'em. 'Course they might not ever have picked up her track themselves 'cuz I sure didn't mention it. I figure if they blamed her for killin' LeClair they might not be too predisposed to hospitality if they found 'er."

"You sent the Cannibals after Deborah," I said. Anger nearly choked the words from my throat.

"No, no," he said. "I sent them up the Tongue, and she was already goin' that way, headin' towards Wyomin', I figure. I didn't set 'em after 'er on purpose. I sorta liked that gal."

"Catfish," I said, "I need a weapon and I need food."

"Sure, sure," he said with a vacant smile. "I'm just your one-stop shoppin' headquarters." He rose and went outside where the fish was baking in the hot coals. "Life and death's in the power of the Tongue," I heard him singin' to himself. "In the power of the Tongue. Can ya beat that?"

CHAPTER 18

Cursed rain. It was too much of a good thing. It never seemed to stop. The wind whipped the rain inside the hut, splattering against Catfish and me as we ate.

The old man didn't seem to notice. "I'm the best cook on the river," he bragged. "Who else would think of stuffin' a carp with jelly?"

"You should open a restaurant," I said.

Catfish chuckled. "With peace comin' to the Interior I just might have to do that."

"Peace?" I said. "What makes you think there's going to be peace?"

"Well, Flowers and LeClair are both dead. The militia's been pacified."

"There's Robert," I said.

"His day's comin'," Catfish said. "Sooner or later something will happen. Maybe an accident. Maybe we'll all get lucky."

"Maybe you eat too many muffins," I said.

"No, the way I figure it, you're gonna kill him, Lieutenant. I always thought it would come down to you against him, and I think you're the better man."

"I hope you're right." I wasn't hoping for my sake but for Deborah's. I licked my fingers clean and glanced over at Dunamis. The white dog, stuffed with his share of baked carp, was curled up asleep in a corner. "I'm going to follow the dog's lead and get some sleep," I said "I'll be out of here before daylight."

I wanted to hit the trail by moonlight. What moonlight? When I rolled out of the blankets, the sky was black with clouds and a thin sheet of rain continued to fall. "You coming, Dunamis?" I said. The dog was ready to go.

The old man stirred from his blankets. "You'll be needin' a firearm," he said, offering me my choice of his pump shotgun or the eunuch's revolver.

"You might need the scattergun," I told him. I took the pistol, a Ruger Blackhawk 357 Magnum. I checked the cylinder–five bullets and one spent casing—and stuck it in my belt.

"I got some good dreams to get back to," Catfish said, rewrapping himself in bedding. "Good luck, *mi amigo*."

I pulled on my rain poncho and headed south. It was so dark I read the path like braille. If branches poked me, I was off course. The rain fell in a light, misty spray that hung in the air like wet lace. A corrosive chill seeped into my bones, and a weak, rasping spot formed in my lungs. Pneumonia was setting in, but I couldn't let a little sickness stop me. I had to reach Deborah before she found Robert. I knew *he* wasn't sick. He'd probably been resting for days, keeping warm and well fed.

Daylight only exchanged a black blanket for a dense, gray one. A thick foggy mist enveloped the land, reducing visibility to less than thirty feet. I forced myself to jog. The only weight I carried was the revolver and the burden of urgency.

Once, I crossed a single imprint from a narrow foot. I knew Deborah's tracks well. It was hers. Twice I passed signs that I supposed were the Cannibals', but the mud and rain made it impossible to tell.

The farther south I went, the more a killer instinct rose in me. I had five shells and at least seven enemies: six Cannibals and Robert. But there was no hesitation or fear. With cold, calculated resolve, I summoned any strength and cunning stored in my depths, as if raiding another cache.

I had a course to follow. The Cannibals were but speed bumps on my way toward a showdown with Robert. If I encountered them, they would be extinguished like a row of nightlights leading to center stage, where a single spotlight fell.

I turned my fear of Robert into a motivating force. I had run from him too long. Before I'd had no reason to stand and fight. Now I had every reason in the world: Deborah's life.

With each step I became more the warrior my father and the government had trained me to be. No longer AWOL, I was on duty, on assignment. I had a job to do.

By midmorning the fog lifted, and the landscape became increasingly familiar even though I never spent time south of the Yellowstone

River. Robert would have expected it. So, though I knew where the trail had taken me, I was still unprepared for the destination.

Then the skies suddenly cleared, the sun broke out, and I was standing on the bank of the Tongue River, staring at a brick house on a hill. The home of my childhood. The house of my parents.

I approached it cautiously. It appeared like a cathedral with its stout red-brick walls, sun-exposed loft that rose like a mezzanine, and proverbial hilltop location sheltered by cottonwood, ash, and Russian olive trees.

It was a fortress.

Memories did not flood over me as I approached. No thoughts of mowing the lawn, hiking to the river to fish, or lunches on the redwood deck. The house sparked nothing in me. It was an empty shell like all the empty houses I had avoided for years. I circumscribed it slowly, looking for sign of either Robert or the Cannibals. I crept past a small set of corrals and stables to a blacktopped lane bordered by a white, synthetic wood fence. The paved lane ran uphill to form a circle in front of the house. A cement sidewalk led to the front steps. To the right of the door was a large picture window.

Behind the window stood a woman.

At first I thought it was a memory. Or the ghost of my mother. The apparition wore a flowing cotton dress my mother had often worn on cool summer evenings.

Reflections on the windowpane obscured the woman's face, but I knew it wasn't a ghost. It was Deborah.

I walked up the front steps to the door. She opened it. "Welcome," she said. Her face glowed with love as if she were a wife receiving a husband home from a long journey.

I stood pensively in the doorway as Dunamis wagged his tail and barked a greeting to his master.

Deborah bent down and hugged him, then stood and looked at me. "Aren't you coming in?" she asked.

I was overjoyed to see her, but danger had to be dealt with first. My eyes stared, direct and hard, and my right hand gripped the butt of the revolver. "Where's Robert?" I asked.

"He's here," she said.

I pulled the weapon from my belt and cocked the hammer. "Where?"

She nodded toward a wooden staircase that ascended to the loft. My father's study. "Up there," she said.

I gave her a defiant look. "I have to kill him," I said.

The slight nod of her head surprised me. "I know." She stepped back so I could approach the staircase.

With pistol drawn I climbed the steps slowly with the confidence of a man prepared to die.

The fact that Deborah was unharmed meant she had either eluded him or he was setting a trap. My life for hers. A good exchange.

Doubt hit me. What if Deborah had conspired with Robert all along? I had a sudden compulsion to turn and shoot her. My head jerked with the impact of the thought. Then I discarded it.

Deborah was the only person I trusted. She would never betray me. She would never lead me into a trap.

I stepped onto the loft floor. Sunlight streaming through southside windows washed the room. My father's desk and file cabinets sat against the west wall. A bookcase filled the wall behind me. To my left, in the northeast corner was a closet, small bathroom, and a simple bunk bed. I saw Robert nowhere. The door to the bathroom stood open, but the door to the closet was closed.

The closet.

Holding the pistol in my right hand, I turned the doorknob with my left and pulled the door open. The closet was bare except for two hangers of clothes and some items on a top shelf. I heard soft steps on the stairs behind me. I pivoted smoothly and held the gunsights on the head and shoulders rising slowly to the landing. Deborah. I uncocked the weapon. "I thought you said he was up here," I challenged.

She stepped closer. "He is."

"Where?"

"What have you found in the closet?" she asked.

I turned and looked again. One hanger held a dark turtleneck sweater made from a material like Spandex, only heavier. I recognized a lightweight body armor lining the chest and back. The other hanger held a similar set of bottoms and a headpiece. I took the latter in my hand. It was a tight-fitting helmet made of the same material but with an attached face shield. I looked at Deborah curiously.

"Look on the shelf," she said.

I reached for the items there. Night goggles. Infrared binoculars. A small laptop computer. A radio with transmitter and receiver.

"The radio is solar powered and wired into the metal framing around the windows," Deborah explained. "The framing also serves as the antenna."

I put the objects back on the shelf. "So this is where Robert lives," I said. "But where is he?"

Deborah took a step closer, her eyes firm and level. "He's here," she insisted.

"Where?"

"Daniel," she said. "You are Robert."

I squinted, then stared at her, waiting for her to smile or laugh. It was not like her to joke like this.

"You are Robert," she said again.

I laughed a short, shallow, nervous chuckle. "Quit joking," I said.

"I'm not joking, Daniel." Her eyes flared like phosphorous. "You are Robert."

I felt as if I'd been thrown against a wall. My mouth gaped, and my heart dropped to my stomach like a hot stone. "No," I said.

"Yes," she said.

"No." Cold fingers of fear were tearing my spine apart.

"Yes."

Then I began screaming it. "No, No, No!"

She came forward, took my hand, and led me to a small mirror by the bookshelves. We stood before it. "What do you see?" she asked.

I saw a sick, tired, ravaged man staring out from hooded eyes sunk in a pale and stubbled face. "Nothing," I said. "I see nothing at all."

"I see a good man," she said. "But a man who was formed from childhood to be something he never wanted to be. Something he never knew he was."

I gazed at my own sick, dark eyes. I saw something there I had never seen before. A residing death. "I *am* Robert," I said.

She took my hand, apparently knowing I was nearing the abyss, about to fall. I deserved to fall. She put her other hand gently on my shoulder. I hated the idea of her touching me. How could anyone so pure put her hands on anyone so evil?

"But *I* didn't know." I said. "How could *you* have known?"

"The mirror at Flowers's compound," she said. "That is when I knew. It was a surprise. A shock."

"You saw Robert?" I asked. "You saw me as Robert?"

"No. I simply saw two people in your body. One was you. The other was hooded and dark. But I knew who it was."

"And you didn't tell me?"

"It wasn't time. You had to be prepared for the truth."

"I still can't accept it. It can't be true." I didn't want to think about me. I didn't want to think about *Robert*. "And you?" I asked. "Did you see anything for you?"

Her eyes clouded with a sense of foreboding. "Yes," she said. "But I can't tell you yet."

I looked again at the emaciated figure in the mirror. "How did this happen?" I asked. "How did I become this monster?"

"You were formed from birth. I've found notes in the basement."

"This house has no basement," I corrected her.

"Yes, it does," she said. "One large room. The trapdoor is under the refrigerator."

I was numb with shock. I was someone—a creature—I didn't know, and the house of my childhood held secrets. Terrible, dark secrets.

"The notes show you were schooled from birth to become the ultimate warrior. The physical training was only a small part of it. The main problem was destroying your conscience."

Her words sounded hollow, like driftwood on a murky sea. Nothing mattered now. I was more evil than I could have ever imagined. It was too late for me.

"Your personality was purposely split," Deborah continued. "You were Daniel and Robert. Daniel was trained to do the right thing. Robert was trained to do as he was told and have no second thoughts, no remorse. No sense of good or evil."

"I'm a killer," I said. "A beast." I slowly raised my hands to my face to see if I really had skin. My face felt scaly, like snakeskin. "How many people have I killed?"

"There's no way of knowing," she said. "Robert was mostly a myth. The chances are you were given credit for murders you never committed."

"But I have killed," I said, thinking of the six Cannibals in the sinking canoe.

"You mean the Cannibals in the river," she said. "But that was not Robert. That was Daniel. Maybe it was Daniel influenced by Robert, some sort of personality spillover."

"You know?" I said. "How?"

"Quito told me about the raiding party and how only Quarro survived. Quarro said it was Robert who attacked them. But you and I know that Robert would have been more efficient."

"That night on the way to the mountains. That night you slept against my chest, you knew I was Robert then?"

"Yes."

"And you laid in my arms?"

"I loved *Daniel*," she said. "I still love *Daniel*."

"I have to see the room," I demanded. "I have to see it for myself."

She took me by the hand and led me down the stairs, through the living room to the sunlit kitchen. The refrigerator had been pushed aside, and the small trapdoor stood open. Deborah grabbed a flashlight from the kitchen counter. Descending the stairs, we stood before a massive steel door. Deborah reached into her pocket for a key and unlocked the door. I pulled it open. She stepped inside with the flashlight, spraying a cold beam of revelation, and I followed close behind.

Against one wall hung a small row of weapons. A Bushmaster Bullpup, an Armalite AR-10, a Keltec Sub-9—cases and cases of NATO ammunition. The weapons were civilian, and even the ammo had once been commercially available. I followed the beam to a wall bearing a detailed map of the Interior. Little red pins marked various locations.

Not caches, I thought. *Kills.*

My kills.

The beam moved on. Another weapons wall. A compound bow, a recurve bow, a crossbow. Quivers filled with arrows. An assortment of knives. Then various survival tools. Scuba gear. Rubber rafts. Even a parachute.

None of it seemed familiar.

All of it seemed familiar.

"Everything in here is civilian," I said. "There's nothing here to link any of this to the military." A part of me was still refusing to accept that Robert lived in my body. Perhaps it was Robert himself who was covering his tracks.

The beam continued on to shelves lined with dehydrated foodstuffs.

"I've investigated many rooms like this," I said, "when I was first collecting for my caches. Mormons. Survival nuts. Many average people had tucked-away rooms filled with weapons and food."

The beam scanned a final wall and fell with a cold and sterile cruelty on a single displayed photograph.

Flares went off in my mind. "Oh, no," I groaned. "Oh, no, oh, no."

The person in the photograph was Robert's most recent target. The imprint was grainy and unclear—a fax of a covert photo—but my mind was already filled with the image. It had been imprinted there earlier.

"It's me," Deborah said. "I was Robert's next target, Daniel."

There was nothing I could say. I knew she was right. The photo lived within me. With one exception. This photo was black and white.

The photo inside me had color.

Everything else was the same, except the color in the eyes. Deborah's eyes were the difference. The fax could not capture the beauty and life within her.

Something dark and sinister began stirring in me as the beam lingered on her image. I was becoming Robert again, the killing force of duty. I had studied the image exactly like this, standing in the dark with a flashlight trained on the grainy, smiling face. The tiny, sick thing inside me still commanded me to turn and complete my mission. *Kill her!* it said.

The voice was too small to be listened to. But it was too strong to be ignored.

"Deborah," I rasped weakly. "I have to get out of here. I'm becoming Robert."

"No, you're not," she said. "You will never be him again."

"But I feel the evil."

"The evil is real, but it's small. What else do you feel, Daniel?"

I choked on the words. "I'm sorry," I said. "I'm so sorry."

She turned off the flashlight. We stood in total darkness. I felt relieved not to be staring at her targeted image.

"Listen to me, Daniel." Her gentle voice came through the blackness like warm oil. "My mission was similar to Robert's."

"What? What do you mean?"

"I'm not just a scout, a forerunner for those who follow behind me. I'm more than that. I'm a warrior, a spiritual assassin. I came to the Interior for one main reason: to find Robert and destroy him."

"But how did you know that I existed?"

"Daniel, there are many Roberts. You were all formed within one elite unit but trained separately. I left the cities with two friends. They were martyred by the Robert assigned to the Dakotas. Monotheists are the target, Daniel."

"How did you escape?"

"I don't have an answer for that. It was as if this other Robert never saw me even though I was right in front of his eyes. I can only guess that somehow my identity had not been projected into his subconscious. I had to keep silent as my friends died. The last thing I remember was this Robert turning and staring at Dunamis. It was as if he could see the dog and was trying to decide what to do. Then he turned and walked away."

"And you continued alone, knowing another Robert waited ahead of you?"

"Yes. And I purposed in my heart to see that Robert destroyed."

"But why didn't you just stay?" I asked. "Why come looking for me when you already had a Robert there?"

"Somehow I knew that the Robert in the Dakotas was too far gone for me. I wasn't ready for the challenge yet."

"So you spent weeks preparing for me?"

"Yes."

Suddenly I heard motion in the dark, then the sound of tearing paper. When she switched on the flashlight again, her picture had been removed from the wall. "It's over," she said. "We are not one another's targets anymore."

The room was small and dark and seemed perfectly fitted to me. "Lock me in here," I said. "Lock me in here and let me die."

"No, Daniel." She gently turned me and pushed me from the room. The massive steel door closed. She locked it. "I am throwing away the key," she said. "No one will ever go in that room again. Not in our lifetimes."

My past was locked and stored behind me.

"Come," she said. "We must go back upstairs."

I followed obediently, numb to everything but the authority in her voice. She led me back to the loft, and we stood by the small bunk bed.

Suddenly physical awareness returned. I felt sweaty, clammy, cold, and hot. My lungs ached and my stomach was twisting in pain. "I'm sick," I said.

"Lie down," she urged, pressing me onto the bed. "You are very ill. You have to rest. You need sleep."

Sleep? How could I sleep when I faced the horror of waking and knowing who and what I was? I was, however, too weak to resist.

"I've disconnected the radio," she said. "Whoever commanded you is silenced."

"Maybe I have a chip," I said, feeling feebly at the base of my skull. "Maybe I have a computer chip in my head."

She took my hand away. "Don't speculate, Daniel. I have more work to do. You just lie and rest."

"Work?"

"Cleansing," she said. "I am going to clean this house. I've done much, but there is more to do." She covered me with a blanket then turned and started for the stairway. Stopping, she looked back with one hand on the railing. "You are going to burn with fever," she warned. "I will bring you water and wet washcloths. And more blankets. You will get very chilled."

"Deborah," I said weakly. "Please, just let me die."

She shook her head. "No, Daniel. I am not going to let you die." She took one step down the staircase, then stopped again. "I will let Robert die," she added. Then she was gone.

The moment she left, a bubble of heat exploded within me, and my lungs felt like billows of fire. Sweat beaded on my brow. Ripples of ice burst from my bones, and I shook with cold. The sickness seemed to take advantage of her absence.

"I'm sick," I remember saying. "Oh, God, I am so, so sick."

CHAPTER 19

I had returned to the abyss.

There are no pedantic ways to describe where I was or what I was experiencing.

I was propelled there by sickness, but the destination itself was more than a location of bodily distress. Both body and soul were licked by flame, and sweat rolled off me like liquid fire, leaving a scorched trail across my flesh, burning like acid into the recesses of my soul.

Sickness not only had me. It had become me. Or I had become it.

At first I was alone and then I was crowded upon. The tormented faces of strangers hovered around me. Their searing eyes and tongues branded me as the source of their pain. The focus of their fear. The instrument of their death.

My essence was a cruel nothingness, a wisp of vapor. A toxic smoke that caused death wherever it drifted. But ultimately it amounted to nothing in itself. I regretted the day of my conception.

I had killed them all. I had condemned them to this place of deathless death.

"Those whom you've killed are not where you are."

I heard the voice but I did not understand it. I knew the faces were an illusion. They were not there. I was alone again.

But not alone. A living, breathing darkness wrapped its claws around me, entangled me in a choking grip, and forced me to stare into its fiery red eyes. The eyes claimed me. Then the darkness swallowed me. I was in the belly of the beast.

"Daniel," a voice called to me from far away.

It was good to hear the sound of my own name. Daniel.

"Daniel. Die to yourself."

The beast in whose belly I resided lashed at the words with its tail.

"Daniel. Die to yourself."

This was the real abyss. Lady LeClair's had only been a cheap imitation.

There was no deliverance in the form of woman or man. Deborah could not be my rescuer. Her intercessions had prevailed against Lady LeClair, but only the *source* of her strength could save me now.

Suddenly I experienced a profound regret for all the times she had ministered and I had snuck away. With the Patriots I had gone fishing while she had spoken words of life. With the 'Postates I had looked for new clothing while she taught and performed miracles. Having sought her, I was now impoverished for not having sought the power that worked through her.

I writhed in the beast's belly like a child turning in a womb. "I want Robert to die," I screamed. I felt the darkness contract like muscles around me. Squeezing me. Contractions like a woman in labor.

"I want Robert to die," I screamed again.

"*No,*" the voice spoke. "*Robert is already dead. Die to yourself. Die to Daniel.*"

A bloodline of death, bearing the weight of innumerable tombstones, fell on my chest. How could I die to myself when I was all I had?

"*You are too proud.*"

"You're right," I agreed.

It was as simple as that.

My confession opened a place in my soul for habitation, and deliverance arrived as a small light burning with the purity of life itself. It entered and resided. It claimed me as surely as Deborah's prayers had cleansed and claimed the houses she had prayed in.

My inner house was no longer empty. The Light dwelled there.

I awakened to her face above mine, her hand cooling my forehead with a wet cloth. "You're back," she said.

I was too weak to do anything but nod.

"You must be hungry." She brought me a bowl of weak soup that I sucked through a straw. "Did you see your deliverance?" she asked.

"Yes." I tapped my chest. "Something came inside."

"Something?" she challenged.

"A light."

"A light?"

"His Light," I admitted.

She smiled. "The changes may seem slow to you, Daniel. But you will never be the same."

"I want fast change."

"Don't we all." She smoothed my eyes closed. "Go to sleep, Daniel."

I slept the deepest sleep of my life. It seemed like only an instant when I awakened. I wanted to ask where I was, but I knew. I was in my parents' house. My house. I wanted to ask who I was, but I knew. I was Daniel.

She saw me stir and came to me. "You've had a long sleep," she said.

"How long?"

"A full day and a full night. Twenty-four hours."

I could not comprehend that. She brought me broth again and I sucked it down.

"Feeling better?" she asked.

"I'm hungry.

"I can bake a fish," she said. "I'm not a very good cook, Daniel. But Catfish gave me a setline, and I have learned how to use it."

I weakly pushed myself to a sitting position. "How much of this has been a dream?" I asked.

Her look was clear and cool. "None of it," she said.

I noticed I was wearing clean clothes. She saw my surprise. "I burned your others," she said. "I found these downstairs and washed them in rainwater."

Deborah was still wearing my mother's dress. She saw me looking at it and smiled. "You don't mind, do you?" she asked.

"No," I said, shaking my head. I struggled to look around the room.

"What are you looking for?" she asked.

"Dunamis."

Warm light lit her eyes. "You have grown to like the dog?"

"Yeah."

"Dunamis is downstairs. Asleep by the door. It seems your dog is very tired too."

"*Your* dog," I said. "Not mine."

"No," she corrected me. "Your dog now. I have given Dunamis to you. You'll need Dunamis."

"Help me to my feet," I said. "I'm tired of lying down."

"No," she said, restraining me. "Go back to sleep."

I slept for several more hours and finally awakened with incredible hunger. Deborah heard me struggling to get out of bed and came to me.

"I'm hungry," I said. "Very hungry."

"I'm broiling catfish outside," she told me. "And I found a garden. Not a very well-tended one, but I did find a vegetable or two hidden in the weeds."

She assisted me downstairs to the kitchen. I washed my face and shaved, using a bowl of warm water she had heated on a wood cookstove. "I'm beginning to remember this place," I said. "I remember living here as a kid. I had a dog."

She combed my hair for me then seated me at the table. "Yes, you did have a dog," she said. "His name was Barney."

"You found pictures?"

"No, Daniel. There are no pictures anywhere in the house. I've looked."

"Then God told you."

"No." She laughed. "You were calling him in your sleep. Over and over."

"I was calling my dog? I don't remember that. I don't remember the bad stuff either," I said. "I have no memories of being here as Robert or receiving orders over the radio or putting on the face shield and helmet."

"You hated coming here," she said. "You hated being Robert. That's why you hated all empty houses. But it's over now. Robert's dead."

"But how could I have seen him? I saw Robert following us."

"You were looking within yourself."

"But how did—?"

She brought a finger to my lips. "Don't try to figure everything out. It's all behind you. It's over."

I gripped her by the arm. "But I need purpose," I said. "I need to know there is something for me now."

"There's much for you to do," she said. "There are the others coming. There's a plan for you."

I saw the truth in her eyes, but I saw something else too. A growing distance between her and me. She started to break away but I pulled her back. "Deborah," I said. "What about *us*? What is the plan for us?"

Her radiance was veiled for a moment in sadness, then her eyes again became bright and crisp, like morning light breaking over a mountain lake. "We each have our paths," she said. "If we walk them diligently, we won't be disappointed."

"Separate paths?" I asked. "Are you leaving me?"

She kissed me lightly on the cheek. "Daniel," she whispered. "I love you like I have loved no one else."

Her words soothed me, but her tone gave no comfort. I wanted more. I wanted details. But deep inside, in rooms of my heart just opening to me, I suspected that her love for me had been a hindrance to her. Somehow, that which I had desired the most—Deborah's love—was the beginning of her own undoing. Maybe I really didn't want to know more or hear details. Perhaps the future was charted in a direction I didn't want it to go.

She stepped away. "The fish are probably burning," she said. She turned and went out the back door. The door slammed behind her. Hearing her steps on the redwood deck, I imagined her leaving me forever. I had just found everything—love, light, and life—yet somehow I was losing *her*.

After the meal I relaxed in a living room chair that gave me a view of the outdoors, even to the trees at the bottom of the knoll. In spite of my confusion and concerns, a gentle peacefulness came over me. My physical health was returning, and while one book inside me had been sealed shut, another book was opening. For the first time in my life, I was as relaxed as a well-fed dog.

Where was the white dog? I missed Dunamis. Stretching to look around, I thought I caught a glimpse of motion outside in the trees. Something furtive and tan-colored. There one moment, then gone. *Probably a deer,* I told myself.

Putting my feet up, I settled back for a restful nap. I awakened later to the cool sensation of water and opened my eyes to see Deborah washing my feet. She looked up at me, smiled, and toweled my feet dry.

"Were my feet dirty?" I asked.

She laughed lightly. "No. I did that to honor you," she said. "This is your house. You are the master and priest of your home."

"A priest? Me?"

"Yes. You must establish your authority, your headship."

"I don't have a clue what you're talking about."

"You will." She rose and extended her hand. "Come with me."

I let her lead. It had become evening, and the house was nearly dark except for the dining room where candles lit a table set for two. She escorted me to the table's head.

"*I* should seat *you*," I said.

Deborah shook her head. "You are the head," she insisted.

I sat before a setting of china, crystal, and silverware, while she disappeared into the kitchen. Moments later she reappeared with bowls of baked vegetables and mashed potatoes. She sat beside me, her face apologetic. "I'm not a good cook," she said. "I tried to make gravy, but it didn't turn out. And we have no butter, of course."

"It looks great to me."

She smiled with appreciation, then reached her hand to mine. "Would you bless the food?" she asked.

I hesitated. What should I say? I closed my eyes and bowed my head. If I had prayed honestly, I would have begged God to give her to me. I would have pleaded with him to spare her from his call. But I could not ask that. Instead, I knew I had to give her back to Him.

She waited for me silently.

No words could capture my more turbulent thoughts, so I allowed myself to drift to the surface. "God, I just want to say thank you," I said. "Thank you for everything."

She said amen.

We ate quietly. The meal was wonderful, but I cannot remember how it tasted. I only recall the candlelight dancing on her face and my heart slipping into a world of fantasy. *I will make this house our home,* I vowed to myself. *We will live here and raise children. I will capture horses to breed and train.*

"What are you thinking?" Deborah asked me.

"I was just thinking that the people who are coming are going to need horses. I want to capture and train horses."

"You will," she said. "You will be given the desires of your heart."

Yes, I thought. *But will you be a part of it?*

Moments before, I was willing to release her to God's call, but now I was again fighting selfishly to hold onto her.

I love you, Deborah. I love you more than anyone. I beamed those thoughts toward her as our eyes met, hoping to see agreement shine on her face. She smiled, and in that moment eternity broke across her countenance like a sunrise.

But then her face changed to horror. She was looking past me, over my left shoulder toward the shadowed windows of the living room.

Dunamis barked.

I whirled around. The image hung there for an instant, like a cloud reflected on dark water. Then it was gone. But it had left an imprint that seemed burned onto the windowpane pane. A pale, tattooed face, a gleaming skull. Haunted, hate-filled eyes.

"Quarro!" I jumped up from the table. Dunamis barked again and stood in front of the main door, his tail up, neck hairs bristling, eyes and nose pointing forward. "My gun," I shouted, whirling back to Deborah. "Where did you put the revolver?"

"I threw it away," she said, moving from the table.

"You what?" Then I thought again. "The key to the downstairs room. Give me the key."

She came to me quickly and put a restraining hand on my shoulder. "Never, for any reason, are we reopening that room."

"But—"

"Daniel. This house is a fortress. The windows are shatterproof, and the doors are steel. We're safe in here, and if the Cannibals come back, Dunamis will let us know."

I knew she was right. But just the same I would have felt better if I'd had a gun.

"You're putting your faith in the wrong place," she said. "Do you think God has spared you only to turn you over to the Cannibals?"

"I'm not thinking about me. I'm thinking about you."

"Daniel, I have told you all along that you are not to defend me or worry about me. My fate is not in your hands."

"OK, OK," I said. "But this is all still new for me, Deborah. I'm a trained army officer, a commando. I need to do something."

"What would make you feel better?" she asked.

"A weapon," I said. "Some sort of weapon."

"OK." She went to the kitchen then returned. "How about this?" she said, handing me an axe.

I took it in my hands, hefted it for weight and balance, and ran a finger over the blade's sharp edge. "Yes," I said. "This is better. This is something."

Her gaze was condescending for a second, as if she'd handed a baby a pacifier, then she softened. "It's the only thing resembling a weapon left around here," she explained. "I used it to cut kindling for the fire."

"Thanks," I said, feeling totally foolish. This woman had stared death in the eye time and time again, and here I was, the army commando, crying for some tool or toy with which to defend us. In that moment I realized the separation between Deborah and me was greater than I had feared. It had nothing to do with desire or affection, and everything to do with experience and maturity. Her steely faith and principles made me feel like a diapered baby.

I couldn't even stand beside her, so I excused myself to make an inspection of our "fortress." "You're right," I said when I returned. "This place is almost bomb-proof. I never realized that as a kid. I just thought it was a normal home."

"Brick and cement, Daniel. They can't even burn us out. And I've brought in enough food and water to last us a week."

"We can wait them out," I said.

"That's right. Now you need to get back up to the loft. You're still weak and need rest. Dunamis can come along and sleep at the head of the stairs. Nothing is going to get past him without us knowing."

I followed her up the staircase, the malamute at my heels.

Deborah patted the bunk. "Lie down," she said.

I sat on the bed. "Will you lie beside me?" I asked.

She shook her head. "No."

"But I need you. I want you close to me."

"I'm sorry, Daniel. I can't."

"But you did before."

"Yes. And I was wrong."

"Then stay and tell me stories."

"What? The mighty commando wants bedtime stories?" she teased.

"Explain things to me," I coaxed. "I don't understand any of this. How do you do what you do? Did Lady LeClair really have a horse? Or a bear? How did you stay ahead of me?"

She put her finger to my lips. "Too many questions," she said. "You have much to learn, Daniel. It will take you the rest of your life, and there will still be mysteries."

"You used to ask me if I was ready for answers," I protested. "Now I'm ready for answers."

"But I am not the one to give them to you."

"Yes, you are," I argued. "I want to know everything, and I want to know it now."

"Patience. You won't learn by academics, Daniel. You will learn by experience." She moved away.

I sighed and stretched out on my back with the axe laying on my chest. She sat on the floor and spoke soothingly to the dog. Turning my head, I gazed at her. There was an entire world within her that I knew nothing about. I was like a drowning sailor she had pulled to the banks of a large and wonderful island. But now as I was finding my land legs, she was leaving, off to another rescue.

Our odyssey was coming to some sort of end. Before, I had led and she had followed. Then she had led and I had followed. Now we had briefly come together, in this house, and I wanted us to remain there. But she was hearing another call. She was about to take the lead again, but this time I could not follow.

My eyes lingered on her form. I went to sleep with her image outlined by one candle, the white dog's head reclining in her lap, her hand stroking its brow.

CHAPTER 20

I awakened to a beautiful morning with golden sunlight streaming through the loft windows. I looked down and saw the axe laying on the floor by the bed and remembered why I needed a weapon. I rushed to my feet. Dunamis was not in the room. Nor was Deborah.

"Deborah?" I called out, coming down the stairs with the axe in my hand. "Deborah?"

There was no answer.

I looked around. Deborah was nowhere to be seen. Dunamis was lying near the front door, his face and ears pointed outside.

"No."

I looked at the dining room table. A singular ray of sunlight splashed across the dark wood and illuminated a page of paper. It glowed as if on fire.

I rushed to it, fearing the worst.

Daniel,

The Lord has called me to all peoples. Including Cannibals. Don't try to understand. Rest easy.

In everlasting love, Deborah.

I almost kicked Dunamis aside, getting out the door, then stood breathless on the steps, surveying the situation.

I saw her. She was descending the knoll to the trees.

I saw *them.* They were emerging from the trees like sunburnt ghosts. They held sharpened willow limbs as spears.

"Deborah, no!" I shouted running down the hill. My legs were spinning under me like wheels. My arms pumped as if trying to pull her to me. But no matter how hard I ran, she did not seem to come any closer.

Quarro stepped forward, his crude spear thrust before him. Deborah stopped. She had a book in her hands. She seemed to be reading to him.

The other five Cannibals huddled at the edge of the trees. Their eyes were on me, but somehow I knew their ears were Deborah's.

A terrible, warlike scream burst from my mouth. I thought it would shatter the landscape like glass. The trees would disintegrate. The sky would splinter and fall. The ground would quake and give way. The Cannibals would collapse. Only Deborah and I would remain standing.

But nothing like that happened. My feet continued to spin as if the grass of the knoll were a treadmill and I were running furiously, getting nowhere.

I dropped the axe. It was a burden.

I could hear her voice now. The light, musical voice I loved so greatly. And she was speaking love. The truth of love. The power of forgiveness.

". . . and the greatest gift is love," she said.

"You killed our Queen," Quarro snarled.

"God loves you, Quarro," she told him.

I was running as I had never run before, but I hadn't the speed to make the impossible possible.

Quarro charged.

My shout fell on no one's ears. Deborah spread her arms as if to receive an embrace. Quarro thrust the spear through her chest.

She stood for a moment, arms out, transfixed as a living symbol of everything she believed in.

The Cannibal emitted a vicious growl and pulled the spear out, poised to strike again.

"No," I shouted. "Enough."

The wicked, hideous face of the eunuch looked past Deborah to me. He sneered and almost laughed. Then his face blanched. Apparently he beheld something in me more terrifying than the face of a thousand Roberts, and he backed away quickly. The Cannibals melted into the trees. As I reached Deborah, she dropped gently into my arms. I lowered her to the grass. Her blue eyes gazed up at me. "Daniel," she said.

"Deborah," I sobbed. "Why, why?"

She struggled to take my hand. "To . . . all . . . peoples," she said.

"Don't leave me," I cried.

"All . . . peoples."

"Deborah, what do I do? How do I save you?"

She shook her head slowly.

"No! Tell me what to do. You saved the Slinger. Tell me how to save you."

Her lips parted as if she were trying to speak.

"Tell me, Deborah!" I cried. "Give me what I have to have."

Her eyes met mine and a flash of light passed from hers to mine, binding us. "I'm sorry," she said.

"Sorry! No, no. You have nothing to be sorry for."

"Yes," she said.

The mirror? I thought. *Is this what she had seen in the mirror at the 'Postate compound?* "I need you," I told her. "I can't go on without you."

Her voice became strong and peaceful. "Read . . . my . . . journal . . . ." Then she smiled and looked past me. Toward the sky.

"Deborah, don't leave me."

Her face glowed golden. "Behold," she said, "the Son of Man stands at the right hand of the Father."

And she was gone. As simply and as easily as that. She had left. Her face pulsed once with a golden aura, then slowly paled.

I smoothed her lovely eyes closed. And I cried. I cried until there were no more tears. Then I wailed in terrible bursts of pain. I howled. The white dog came quietly down the hill. He lay his muzzle on Deborah's breast and whimpered softly.

It was hours before I could rise. Hours before I picked up her still form and carried her to a green and shaded spot. I laid her where wildflowers were beginning to grow. Then I lay beside her.

It was hours more before I remembered her command and stood above her with her journal in my hand.

Her entries began with the day she met me.

I read. Then I read it again. I turned to the next page. And the next. Every entry, down to the very last, written the previous night, was the same:

Lord, I have found a man like none I have ever known. A challenge. I would almost dare to have him, but I am betrothed only to you and your purpose. Protect me. Preserve me from my own desires. Keep me from being unequally yoked. Be jealous, my God, and hold me in your everlasting arms. Protect him, too, Lord. Do not let him confuse my love with yours, or your love for him with mine. Forgive me, God, if I have muddied the waters. Bind what needs to be bound. Loosen what needs to be loosened.

I buried my beloved in a meadow where flowers would grow.

I erected a cross, carved from cedar, and set it firmly to stand against the ravages of time and weather.

I left that dark, empty house where Robert had been formed and set out again northward, a wanderer. Weaponless and uncaring.

Dunamis trailed behind me faithfully. At first I did not want the white dog. I even cursed him and threw stones his way. He only looked at me confused, waited patiently until I tired, then resumed following me.

Finally I embraced him and held him close to me as if he were her.

The first day after leaving the Tongue River, I set out for vengeance. I picked up the trail of the Cannibals and followed them down the Tongue and back toward the Yellowstone. My rage blazed such that I didn't want a weapon. I wanted to kill each of them with my bare hands and linger over the extinguishing of Quarro. But my anger soon spent itself. Vengeance was the last thing Deborah would want. It would defile the sacrifice of her life. And vengeance invoked memories of a creature I no longer was. I put the eunuchs out of my mind. They no longer existed.

I crossed the Yellowstone and made my way to Catfish's camp. I needed to see someone. I wanted to look into another person's eyes and know that the world had not ended, that I was not the only man left on the planet. But Catfish wasn't there. His camp was in order, but the old man was gone. Probably off trading hemp, I decided. I ate from his garden and setlines, then headed north.

I was going nowhere in particular.

I was going somewhere.

Sometimes I slept. Sometimes I didn't. Sometimes I lay on the sod and let the sun burn me. Other times I lay on the brittle gumbo and let the night air chill me.

I talked to her as if she were there. I said, "Deborah, I'm sorry I didn't listen to you more. I'm sorry I wasn't around when you taught the Patriots and the 'Postates. I need that teaching now. I know it was your prayers that delivered me from the temptations of the Queen. I need those prayers now."

But only the sky seemed to listen, and while the prairie glowed with life and silver clouds spotted the sky, the heavens were leaden. The heavens listened but didn't respond.

I found food. Or it was provided for me. Mostly for Dunamis, probably, not for me. I didn't care if I ate or not.

One day I encountered the bear. Dunamis and I were sitting beside a small creek when the willows nearby rustled and the big bear ambled out, gaunt and appearing lost. I knew it was the witch's bear immediately. The head scar had reopened. As the bear rose on her haunches and swatted at a bird's nest beyond reach, I saw the wound on her underside. It had not healed either. It dripped with infection.

The bear moved away without seeing us.

"That bear is going to die," I told Dunamis. Strangely, I felt sorry for the beast. The bear was not evil. She was a victim of evil. I wished Deborah were there to heal the animal. *Would she have?* I wondered.

Probably.

Seeing the bear made me feel better. It made my experiences seem solid. But I needed something even more tangible.

All along I had been retracing my steps, going back to where all of this had started. I wanted to touch the sod where I first learned of her. I needed to revisit the place where I'd encountered the dying man.

It was slow going. Half the time I was lost in a land I knew, yet one in which none of the landmarks seemed the same. Sometimes thirst drove me nearly mad, but it wasn't merely a thirst for water. I thirsted for life. I needed direction and instuction. I didn't know how to shape and define myself or make myself grow.

What was I supposed to do?

This questioning and wandering went on for days. How many days? I don't know.

One morning I looked down a long, grassy valley and saw three people coming my direction. I was tempted to flee like a deer escaping hunters. But I had seen no one since Deborah's death, and I needed human touch to center and stabilize me.

A man and two women looked at me warily as I approached. "Are you safe?" the man called out to me.

"Yes," I said, but they still stared at me fearfully. I stood wordlessly for several minutes. My tongue was wrapped around words relative only to my own existence.

"Can we help you?" the man asked.

I shook my head but smiled at the irony. Pilgrims were now asking to help me.

My smile brought fear and suspicion to the man's face. "What do you want?" he asked.

I shrugged. I knew I appeared pathetic to them. They probably thought I was a Babbler.

They looked at one another as if deciding whether or not I was sane. Finally one of the women asked, "Have we seen you before?"

"Maybe," I said. "I don't know."

The other woman whispered in the man's ear and pointed at Dunamis.

"Is that your dog?" the man asked.

"Yes."

"We are looking for a woman," he said. "She travels with a dog like yours."

"What do you want with her?"

"The Pilgrims on the coast have heard stories that this woman with the white dog does miracles. She can even raise the dead."

I was tempted not to say anything. I wanted to keep Deborah's legend to myself. But I knew she would have rebuked me for my selfishness. "The story is true," I said.

"Do you know where we can find her?" he asked.

"Keep going east. You will not find her, but you will find others like her." I did not know that, but Deborah had said it was so, so I spoke it in faith.

A rising excitement lit their faces. "Then the story really is true," the man said. "She raises the dead."

"I saw it with my own eyes."

The woman who had yet to talk looked at me curiously. "You have seen her raise people from the dead," she said, "but you are not with her?"

"No," I said. "Not at this moment."

"Then she isn't near?" she asked.

"No. But keep going east. You won't be disappointed."

"I think we've seen you before," the man said. "Many weeks ago on our way west. You talked to us not far from here. You gave us jerky to eat."

"No," I said, raising my hand to bid them goodbye. "That wasn't me."

"Come with us," one of the women coaxed. "You and the dog can travel with us."

"No," I said. "You know where you are going. I don't. I have to find my own way."

On I traveled. Sometimes I crossed creeks I had crossed before and knew I was traveling in circles. Some days I moved slowly and studied grasses and flowers and beheld the beauty of the sun setting in the west. Dunamis liked those times. Other days I rushed in a mad pursuit that only left me weary at day's end.

But slowly I neared my destination of the sandstone cairn of the man named Storch. It was late in the afternoon when I beheld the rocks silhouetted against a cloud-dappled sky. The prairie had changed from dead brown to green and the creeks bubbled with water, but the sandstone mausoleum was still there. My pain lessened as I approached the grave. I still hurt deeply, but I was no longer numb.

I searched in the grass below the rocks for proof that this was the spot. There I found the empty shell casing from my .223. It had blown off the ledge and been swept downhill by the rains.

I stood where I had buried Storch, expecting the body to be there, though probably half uncovered by the prairie winds. But there was no body. The ground was level, the grave empty.

"Maybe the wolves dragged him off," I said quietly to the dog.

Dunamis didn't seem to be paying any attention to me.

"Then again," I added, "maybe none of this happened. Maybe I am only an insane person who imagines things and thinks they're real."

At that moment, had I had a gun, I might have put myself out of my own misery.

Then Dunamis woofed softly. I looked at the white dog. He was wagging his tail and staring downhill.

"Are you looking for me?" a voice called out.

I looked up, no longer surprised by anything, and saw a man ascending the hill. I walked down and met him.

The man looked tired and weathered, and he needed a shave and bath, but he was human and alive. "My name is Storch," he said, extending his hand.

I took his hand in mine. He felt real. But what was *real*? "How long have you been waiting for me?" I asked.

"I don't know," he said. "Days. Maybe a couple weeks."

"She passed this way, didn't she? On her way to the house on the Tongue."

"Yes," he said. "I guess so. I just remember awakening from a long sleep."

"From a long sleep?"

"Yes. She shouted my name and I woke up. Then she told me to stay and wait for you. You are the right one, aren't you? I think we met once."

"Yes. I saw you die," I said. "Eaten by wolves."

"Is that right?" He seemed neither perplexed nor amazed.

"What else did she tell you?" I asked.

"She said she had to leave but others were coming. I would join them, but first I was to wait for you."

"Are you supposed to follow me?" I asked. "Or am I supposed to follow you."

He shrugged. "I don't know. Neither, I think."

"Am I to go on alone?"

"Yes," he said. "That's it. You're to go on alone."

"Which way?"

"East," he said. "And north."

"Northeast?"

"Yes," he agreed. "That's it."

"And you will be OK here?" I asked. "Do you have food?"

"Yes, I think so. I'll be all right."

"Then I'll be going," I said.

"Yes, you should be going," he agreed. "I will stay."

I continued walking. To the north and to the east. A part of me doubted I'd actually seen Storch. Maybe I was delirious. Or dreaming. Or insane.

But I put nothing past Deborah. And nothing beyond her faith. She might have raised Storch from the dead. She very easily could have told him to stay there and wait for me.

It would be just like her.

By why hadn't she been helped in the manner that she'd helped others? Why did she have to die at the hands of someone as despicable as a flesh-eating eunuch?

Six days and six nights passed. I did not know where I was. I only knew that each step was taking me farther into a strange land.

One day I saw horses but I hardly paid them any attention. They were so curious they followed me for a ways.

Sometimes I forgot all about Dunamis. But the white dog was always there.

On the seventh day after leaving Storch I saw a single form walking a high ridge in front of me. He was like a watchman walking his post.

Maybe there is an army nearby, I thought. I had seen guards like this before. I had slipped past their perimeters and performed my duties without them ever knowing I'd been there.

I could do it again. But I wouldn't. I wasn't a soldier anymore, and there were no duties to perform.

Dunamis and I climbed the ridge.

The man shouted down to us. "Who goes there?"

He is a soldier, I guessed. Perhaps he would shoot me. "My name is Daniel," I called back.

"Who?"

"Daniel," I yelled louder.

He approached. He was a young, handsome man with strawberry blond hair and clear eyes. He carried no weapon, only a walking stick.

"Don't I know you?" he asked.

"I don't know," I said. "It seems I hardly know myself."

"You're him," he said. "The Ranger. I have been waiting for you." He seemed delighted and relieved.

"Who are you?" I asked. "Are you someone else back from the dead?"

He laughed. "Yes, but not as recently as you might think. You were there, Lieutenant. Remember?"

I imagined him in a dirty felt hat and a grimy duster. "The Slinger?" I said.

"Yes. Malachi Watts."

"Oh." I shook his hand. "Good to see you again."

"You don't know what this is all about, do you?"

I shook my head. "Malachi, I don't have a clue."

"I've been back east," he said. "I found the people the woman told me about. The first ones anyway. A man named Jones is with the second party."

Jones? That was familiar.

"Anyway," he continued. "We're camped not far from here. I was told to come walk this ridge and wait for you."

"Who? Who told you that?"

"You know," he said.

"Deborah?" I asked hopefully. "The woman?"

"No, no. We haven't seen her. The Spirit. The Spirit told me."

"Oh," I said, disappointed.

"You shot me, remember?" Malachi asked.

"Yes, yes, that's true. I certainly did that. Sorry."

"Don't be sorry. My scars are a wonderful story. They have done a lot of good."

"Oh, OK," I said numbly. "If you say so."

"Lieutenant, you seem to be in a daze."

"Yes. Yes, I am," I said. "Deborah is dead. The woman who raised you is dead."

"She is? She's gone to glory?"

"Yes," I said vacantly. "Glory."

"How did it happen?"

"She was killed."

"Martyred?"

"Yes," I said. "I guess so."

He fumbled in a jacket pocket and brought out a piece of paper and handed it to me. "Do you remember this?" he asked.

I took the paper and began unfolding it. "No, I can't say I do."

"When you and she left me, she gave me water, food, and a piece of paper that held a password."

"Yes, I recall something like that."

"Read it, Lieutenant."

I held the paper before me and read instructions printed plain and legibly. *Go east.*

And another word. *Dunamis.*

"Dunamis?" I asked, looking at my faithful companion.

"Yes," said Malachi. "*Dunamis* was the password. But read on."

Below, written in a flowing script, was a message that looked hastily added. It was addressed to me.

Daniel, if you are reading this, it means you are with Malachi and I am gone. Don't be sad. It wasn't meant to be. There is another for you. You will live a full life and do good works. You will marry, have children, and raise horses. Enjoy your life.

Deborah

My eyes welled with tears. "She wrote this?" I said.

Malachi nodded. "Yes."

"How did she know?"

He didn't say anything. He knew I wasn't asking him. He just stood respectfully for several minutes until my eyes cleared.

"We hardly knew each other then," I reflected. "Yet she saw things that hadn't happened and things in me I didn't know existed."

"She must have been a remarkable woman," Malachi said. "Actually, I hardly remember her myself. Except for her voice and eyes."

"The people with you," I said, "they must have known her."

"No. None of them ever met her."

"None of them?" I said. "But she knew they were coming."

"Yes, but she's just one of the unnamed, Daniel."

"No, she had a name. Her name was—"

"No," he interrupted. "I mean she was without reputation. She was anonymous."

"Oh," I said. "Maybe she was, but not to me."

"Anonymity was her strength," he said.

"Then I must have been her weakness."

"Maybe," he said. "But now it's time."

"Time? Time for what?"

"Time to be going," he explained. "Our camp isn't far from here. The people are expecting you."

"They're expecting me?"

"Yes. Several of them have had dreams about you."

"About me? Why? What am I supposed to do with them?"

"Two things," he said. "One is to lead them west. There is a land to reclaim, and you must lead them to safe housing."

"But you can guide them," I said. "You have made it this far."

"No, I have to go back. I have others to bring."

So I was to be a guide. A scout. That was one of my roles. "You said two things," I said. "What's the other?"

"Tell them Deborah's story," he said. "Tell them everything you saw her do and all the words you heard her say."

"But you said she was to be nameless. Maybe she wouldn't want her story told."

"That responsibility falls on you as the storyteller," he said. "Don't tell her story to glorify her. Tell it to inspire the people."

Again I regretted not being with her more. "I didn't hear her preach much," I said. "I don't know most of the things that were said."

"But you saw what she did. Tell them the things you saw."

I turned and looked to the west, to that vast, seemingly limitless expanse of prairie, badlands, and mountains. I knew it all so well, yet I didn't know it at all.

An entire kingdom lay before me.

Something inside of me shifted. It was as if another man were inside my skin. I felt him straighten, align himself, and stiffen. Strength surged through my legs. My eyes sharpened.

"If you want, you can tell her story and never mention her name," Malachi added.

I looked again toward the west. It glittered with promise. It was a land where myths could give way to earthy, substantial truths. It wasn't a land of savagery and death, of disease, shame, and humiliation. It was a land of potential and promise.

"No, she had a name," I said. "She was a person. Her name was Deborah."

He looked at me expectantly. "Then can we go now?"

"Yes," I said. Reaching down, touched Dunamis. I needed to know the white dog was near. "We can go now," I said. "You lead and we will follow."

And that is her story. It is more than I ever told the people. More than I ever told my own family. But it is my best recollection.

And the Interior changed. It was peopled. And the people lived in houses. And at nighttime, the houses glowed with light.

EPILOGUE

This was my father's story. He was a quiet and humble man who seldom talked about his life. He raised horses, and a family, on the banks of the Tongue River. Some people still say he was a legend in his time, but he never thought so. When he did talk about the resettlement of the west, he only mentioned her: the woman whose grave lies at the river's edge, in the meadow where flowers grow.

In the months after finding this manuscript I searched everywhere for some record of this woman named Deborah.

I found nothing.

The few times he had mentioned her I had imagined her as a wise older woman. A "mother in the faith." Someone gray-haired, wrinkled, and past her prime in passion and vitality.

I'm sure my mother always knew the truth. Deborah was my father's first love. The one who taught him how to love.

More could be said, but that is all that needs to be known. Her life, even in mystery, speaks for itself in all those who came after her.